SAOIRSE KENNEDY
Old Ghosts

Janina Franck

Crimson Fox
PUBLISHING

OLD GHOSTS (SAOIRSE KENNEDY #1)

First Edition

For those who forget to eat.

Janina Franck

**4 April,
3:00 a.m.
Saoirse**

Sex on the beach had always been one of Saoirse's favorites, and, lying in bed next to Natalia, she contemplated which kind she liked better. Probably the drink. The sand tended to make things uncomfortable and messy. Then again, why choose when you could have both?

She glanced at the slender woman with sun-kissed skin in her bed, some grains of sand still clinging to her face and long, black hair as she slept soundly. Her chest rose and fell slowly, calmly. How peaceful she looked. How defenseless.

Saoirse leaned over to brush the sand from Natalia's cheek before getting up. No need to bother covering up. Naked and unconcerned, she only took the gun from her bedside table.

Downstairs, a man was waiting for her.

She glided down the stairs to her living room, where a shadowy figure sat in her favorite armchair. The man made a choked sound when he saw her, completely exposed.

"Thanks for waiting," Saoirse said, smiling

lightly, hand on her hip.

He'd already been here, waiting for her when she and Natalia had stumbled in, kissing and tearing off each other's clothes for the third time that evening.

He could have stopped them from having such a lovely time together.

He could have stepped out of his hiding place and pointed his gun at them, forcing them apart.

But he hadn't.

Instead, he'd kept quiet, waiting patiently for Saoirse to come back down. Natalia had never even realized he was there. No wonder she could sleep so serenely. There was such innocence in her nature, despite the dark, crooked world she'd grown up in—a quality Saoirse found utterly irresistible and endearing.

Saoirse paced across the wooden floor to the couch across from the intruder, every footfall making a soft, padding sound. There, she gracefully sat down, placing the gun in front of her on the small glass table between them and crossed her legs. Paying close attention to the subtle little movements and breathing patterns of the man sitting across from her in the darkness, she reaffirmed to herself that he was indeed the same individual who'd been here earlier. The notes of sandalwood and mint lingering in the air certainly matched. As did his build and size.

The man cleared his throat. "You're not going

to call for help?"

Even though it was dark, the small movements of his profile made it obvious that he was torn between wanting to look at her body and forcing himself to look anywhere but.

Saoirse smirked, more to herself than him. "If I was going to do that, I'd have done it earlier. Thanks for giving us some privacy, by the way. I appreciate it."

A moment of silence ensued. Saoirse could almost hear the gears turning in his head. It was adorable.

"You *did* notice me then," he eventually said, a hint of disbelief coloring his tone.

"Of course," Saoirse replied. "But since you were considerate enough not to interfere, I figured it was worth taking the time to have a nice chat with you."

"And if I hadn't?"

"You'd be dead."

Saoirse gave him a moment to let that sink in. Judging by the sound of his voice, he was young. Perhaps in his early or mid-twenties. Either way, it was painfully clear that he was new at this. The fact that he'd used aftershave was the biggest indicator of it. Still, there was something to be said for his ability to get past her security. It wasn't an easy feat. So far, only one other person had managed without them noticing. And then she'd hired him. After all, skills like that were far too valuable to waste.

"So why don't we start by you telling me why it is you're here." Saoirse smiled at him and tapped the lamp on the table beside her. A warm glow immediately filled the room, illuminating the curves of her body as well as the intruder facing her.

She'd been right on the money. He *was* young. His beard was barely more than a few fluffy plumes and sprinkled between the freckles on his face were plenty of zits desperately crying out for some skincare. Never mind that he was badly in need of a haircut and a comb. Whoever had sent a young man—though Saoirse considered calling him a boy—like this into her headquarters clearly had no issues feeding a newborn fawn to a den of lions. Now in the light, his discomfort at her nakedness became even more apparent. Briefly, Saoirse wondered if it might be his first time seeing a woman's bare body. Poor kid.

"Would you..." His voice cracked, and he began anew, glancing at her breasts and nether regions a few times. "Would you mind putting something on?"

Saoirse raised an amused eyebrow.

"You break into my home and then ask me to dress? My, the audacity!" She rose to her feet and crossed over to the bathroom. "But fine."

Even as she had her back turned to him to grab a bathrobe, she listened to every one of his movements. Lucky for him, he didn't move from his spot.

She wrapped the silken garment around herself, returned to her seat to face him anew, and found him looking visibly relieved.

"Well?" Cocking her head to one side, Saoirse took note of the young man's ruffled clothing. Black jeans with a black turtleneck. The most Hollywood of outfits for an intruder. She inwardly shook her head at all the mistakes he'd made. Colors that wouldn't blend in, basically announcing exactly what he was with his outfit, not striking when he had the chance, his cologne… The list went on.

And yet. He'd made it this far.

Despite all the obvious flaws, he'd made it here, without triggering any alarms or catching the notice of any of her people. That was certainly something that deserved her respect. Any of the other things could be drilled into him with decent mentorship and experience, but natural talent for this sort of thing was rare.

"I was sent with an offer," he said. "Well, a request."

"By whom?"

"Does it matter?" He seemed genuinely bemused by her reaction.

Saoirse shrugged. "Of course. After all, what if it's from someone I don't want to work with? Besides, I want to know who to thank for demonstrating gaps in my security to me."

He hesitated for a moment, his gaze

wandering through the room as if he were weighing up his options. For just a moment, it lingered on the gun still sitting on the table, untouched, before returning to Saoirse.

"His name is Timothy Carlton, but I doubt you'll have heard of him," he said.

Saoirse was careful to guard her expression. Not even a muscle twitched. "What makes you say that?"

"He's the kind of man who likes to stay hidden. And, as I understand, he only recently began pulling at threads."

A snort almost escaped Saoirse. A man in power who liked to stay hidden? What a joke. That only meant that he was biding his time, perhaps that he was the kind of person who wanted to appear mysterious, but have his name known in the right circles. Either way, vanity was still at the core.

She took a few deep breaths to collect herself before smiling at the intruder once more. "And what's your name?"

"Jean."

"Is that a code name or your real name?"

Jean hesitated, his eyes narrowing as he undoubtedly tried to understand why she was asking him about his own name instead of his purpose here.

"It's a code name," he eventually settled.

He might have been telling the truth. He might have planned out a whole backstory for the character he portrayed. His real name might have been Richard, or Marvin, or anything else. But Saoirse had a feeling that based on Jean's other level of preparation, the chances of having thought up a code name before she asked for his name were slim.

"Smart. If you want to protect anything or anyone, you should always keep your name a secret in this world," she said.

"Does that mean Saoirse Kennedy is a code name?"

Her lips quirked into a smirk. "No. What I'm protecting is no secret. It never has been."

"And what's that?"

If he was trying to get a read on her, he was doing a terrible job. She sighed. "Goodness gracious, do your research. Has your boss taught you *anything* before sending you into the field?"

Her instincts had been correct. He was a newbie. Which either made his skills all the more impressive, or her security that lacking. She'd have to give her men a good talking to when this was over and make some adjustments. She couldn't have people barging into her suite unannounced all the time. Once in a while was fine—it made things interesting—but too often would spoil all her fun.

Jean's lips hardened at her words, and a defiant look entered his eyes as he jutted his chin forward like a bratty child.

"My employer's request," he said firmly, "is

for you to arrange the elimination of a certain individual that poses a threat to his interests."

Now it was Saoirse's turn to narrow her eyes at him. "I need a little more information than that before I make my choice."

Jean nodded, as though he had expected this, and pulled a flash drive from his pocket which he set on the glass table with a firm *clang*. "You'll find all the info on the target on here. Now then."

He stood up, but he barely made it two steps before Saoirse stopped him.

"This is not the information I was asking for," she said, coolly.

He turned back to her. "It's all the information you need."

She had to give it to him… for all his youthful inexperience, the kid had guts. Not many foot soldiers in the underworld dared to talk to her like that. Though, to be fair, there weren't many in the underworld who knew as little about her as he seemed to, which was not exactly inspiring a lot of confidence in his employer in Saoirse.

"As far as the actual hit is concerned, maybe," she admitted. "But not so much for my decision whether I'll accept your Mr. Carlton's request."

"Well, what else do you need?"

Saoirse contemplated him for a moment. How long had he been working for his employer? And more importantly, why?

"What I need," she said, getting to her feet

and strolled past him to her personal bar, "is for you to have a drink with me."

He trailed behind her, watching as she opened the fridge and pulled out two beers. With ease, he caught the one she tossed him.

"You *are* legal, aren't you?"

"Yes!"

His response had come just an instant faster and more vehement than it ought to have. He fished a penknife from his pocket and opened the bottle, while Saoirse did the same with a regular bottle opener.

Though he'd answered so quickly, he hesitated again now that the open drink was in his hand, glancing at Saoirse uncertainly until he saw her take a drink from her own bottle. Then, he lifted the beer to his lips. The smallest twitch in his facial muscles betrayed that he wasn't used to the bitterness, but he had it under control almost immediately. Someone else might have missed the little sign, but not Saoirse.

As she took a seat on one of the barstools and gestured for Jean to do the same, Saoirse brushed a curl of her strawberry blonde hair behind her ear.

"Where're you from, Jean?" she asked, smiling.

"Michigan." Once again, he'd answered without thinking about it first. "You?"

"Ireland." She paused to observe him for another moment. What would make an inexperienced kid like this move from Michigan to this part of the country? Perhaps the direct approach would work best for now. Chances were, he wouldn't answer either way and this would take significantly less time so she could go back to Natalia. "How do you know this Mr. Carlton?"

His nostrils visibly flared at the question and his brows furrowed. "How does that matter? It doesn't impact your job in any way."

As expected, he was being defensive. Saoirse almost chuckled to herself. *So predictable.*

"It doesn't," she agreed. "I was just curious. What I do need to know are his motives, however. You said the target poses a threat to Mr. Carlton's interests. I need to know what those interests are."

Intensifying her gaze at Jean, she changed her pose, so the bathrobe fell to reveal more of her legs. His eyes immediately traveled.

It took him a moment longer to bring his eyes back to meet hers and respond this time. "Why?"

Someone needed to get this kid laid. If Timothy Carlton had known exactly who he was dealing with, he'd have sent someone more experienced with women. Or gay. Or asexual. But newcomers rarely did their homework properly. They all had too much bravado, too much confidence in being bigger and better than anyone else. Sooner or later, they all discovered how this city worked. Those who learned sooner tended to live longer.

"In case his interests clash with my own."

"Your interests?" Jean echoed, bemused. "Is this about money?"

This time Saoirse really couldn't hold back a chuckle. This kid really hadn't been briefed on her at all. Which made her wonder what his employer knew about her, and who had told him about her in the first place. She made a mental note to send one of her people to find out. Paul, perhaps. He was good at that sort of thing.

"Tell me, Jean, who do you think I am?"

"An assassin," he responded, though he sounded significantly less confident and certain than he had earlier. "Supposedly the best in the city."

Sighing, she rubbed the bridge of her nose. "Your information is outdated by about a decade. I'm not an assassin."

"You don't look like one," he admitted.

"Anymore."

She shot him a sharp glance and noticed with satisfaction the twitch in one of the veins at his neck as he tensed.

Calmly, she continued. "What is it your employer wants? Depending on your answer, I may decide to take on the request and make the target disappear."

"And if you don't agree?"

She smiled pleasantly at him. "No need to worry about that just yet. Well?"

He gulped and stood up. "I don't think I'm qualified to give you the information you're looking for. Everything I can give you is on that hard drive."

He was avoiding eye contact now, his searching gaze lingering on all potential escape routes — the windows, the door, even the secret panel. He might not be good with people, but getting around buildings was clearly his element. In the right hands, he could be a great asset.

"All right." Saoirse grabbed a sticky note and a pen from the counter, scribbling a number on it. "Give this to your boss. Have him call me."

Jean took the note readily and glanced at it for a moment before nodding. "I'll be leaving, then."

"Next time, use the front door," Saoirse advised. "And let your boss know that I don't appreciate having people barge into my suite. The next one might not come back entirely whole."

He gave a curt nod to show he understood, though whether he took her threat seriously or not, Saoirse couldn't tell. Truthfully, it didn't really matter. She had no qualms about following through. One didn't survive in this world by holding back and being scrupulous.

She whisked past him before he had a chance

to move and peeked out the front door of her apartment.

As expected, her guard stationed there was in his spot. Though the tall, broad-shouldered man was playing on his phone, he was nevertheless alert and perked up as soon as she opened the door.

"Dillan," she said to him, "I've got someone here who needs to be escorted out. Mind taking care of it?"

He nodded readily. "Sure thing, boss."

"Thanks." She smiled at him and pushed Jean out to be received by him. "This is Jean. Make sure you remember his face." She turned to Jean, who had alarm written all across his face. No doubt he was expecting something horrendous. "Do you need taxi fare, or do you have your own transportation?"

"Uh," his voice cracked, "I'm good."

"In that case, make sure to give Mr. Carlton my best. Dillan, see him out, won't you?"

They both nodded, and she shut the door on them. *Now then. Back to bed.*

**4 April,
11:17 a.m.
Lily**

"And what did he look like?"

Lily listened to the old biddy drone on about the young man who'd mugged her. He sounded like one of hundreds of identical young men found in every city across the country. They all dressed the same, spoke the same, acted the same. This particular young man had been Caucasian, which was the case significantly more often than most men in power cared to admit. The chief of police was no exception.

Chances were that even if she caught the guy, there would be four more to take his place, and he'd be back out in the streets within six months, continuing along his same old patterns. Still. It was her job to make sure he'd be caught, not her job to ensure he'd stay away.

Despite her boredom with her current task, Lily took careful notes. It was her responsibility to clean up the streets, and she was going to do it as best as she could, even if it seemed like she'd gotten to do nothing *significant* since she'd transferred to this city. Then again, even though it had only been a little over six months, she *had* worked her way up. She'd started with a demotion to a beat cop who handed out parking tickets. At least she had returned to detective status now, even if she was only put on petty theft cases.

"Thank you, that's very helpful." She gave the elderly woman her warmest smile as she helped her to her feet. "We'll get in touch with you as soon as we know anything. Just make sure to verify your contact info once more with Officer McCarthy, alright?"

The biddy nodded, and Lily sighed to herself as she watched the lady shuffle away. Because of the recent increase of petty crime in the city, the captain had decided to change the processing of new cases—beat cops brought people in and, depending on availability and degree of crime, passed them to available detectives or more senior cops, after noting down contact info. In some incidences, as was the case here, the people coming in were somewhat unreliable of memory or hearing, and that data needed to be verified and double and triple checked. The whole process was, in Lily's opinion, a big old waste of valuable police time. Never mind that it was also more prone to errors and resulted in overall chaos.

Meanwhile, the sergeant and the more senior detectives got to work The Big Cases. The kind that Lily had joined the force to work. The kind she was *good* at. Or would be, once she got the chance to prove herself in this place. One of them was the whole reason she'd transferred to this city. She'd been leading a taskforce against a drug baron on the West Coast when she'd found ties to this city. She'd expected them to be from a place like L.A. or Seattle, but not... here. A city internationally so insignificant, that no one outside of the country had ever even heard its name.

Even Lily had been surprised at the city's size. Sure, she'd heard the name before, it even came up in the news on occasion, but she still hadn't expected to find a place that rivaled the nation's larger cities in size. It almost felt like the government was intentionally keeping it secret, or something of the sort. And if Lily was the sort of person to be affected by large-scale paranoia, she might have believed it. There was something weird about this city. Something that didn't quite fit together, but so far, she hadn't been able to put a finger on what exactly that was. It was something about the crimes that happened and, more importantly, about the crimes that *didn't* happen. If only she were given access to The Big Cases, she could look into it and figure out why things felt off to her. And maybe finally get some leads that connected back to her last case before she had transferred.

More than anything, right now she needed to

find a way to prove her worth to the captain. So, she was pulling out all the stops for these small-time crimes. She hammered away at her computer to file the old lady's case while researching where in the area she might be able to gain access to security footage, when Detective Benson walked up to her desk in long strides that, despite their speed, looked remarkably slow to the length of his legs. Lily secretly thought he resembled a giraffe—long legs and a long, elegant neck as well.

"You know, I don't think I've ever seen a detective who threw himself into these little things the way you do," he said, leaning at her desk while sipping at his cup of coffee. He pushed a second cup toward her, which she accepted gratefully. "It's honestly impressive how much focus you have."

Lily shot him a disapproving look. "These *little things* matter to people, you know. They worry about them. It's the stuff they see in their day to day, the stuff that affects their lives directly."

He contemplated her for a moment as she sipped at her coffee. "I know, I know, but don't tell me this is why you became a detective. Come on, Tulip."

"Rose," Lily growled. The entire precinct had made the unanimous decision to call her just about any flower, except the two that were actually in her name. This was nothing new, of course. With a name like hers, it was only a matter of time before children started to make fun. But that's what you got when your grandparents ran a flower shop and carried the surname Rose.

"Whatever." Benson shrugged. "Just make sure you ask for help if you need it and that you don't run yourself dry. All work and all that. What applies to Jack goes for you, too. Speaking of which... The boys are all going for a drink after work today. Gonna join us this time?"

Benson had probably been the only one of the other detectives who had extended a hand to Lily at any point of her working here, so he could probably be considered the closest thing to a work-friend she had. He brought her coffee sometimes and offered his help, which was more than could be said about the rest of the boys' club that was the detectives of this precinct.

"Yeah, I'll join. Just need to finish up a few things first. Feel free to go ahead without me if I'm not done. It's the usual place, yeah?"

"Sure is. See you there, Daisy."

He stalked off, and Lily had to do her utmost to stop herself from sighing while he remained within earshot.

While Lily dreaded nothing more than having to socialize with a bunch of men who typically made lewd jokes or belittled her, intentionally or otherwise, being around was the only way she could gain their acceptance, if not respect.

Additionally, it was the fastest way to get her into the sergeant's—and therefore the captain's—good books, which in turn meant the best chance she had at landing a spot on The Big Cases sooner, rather than later.

The other option was, of course, hoping for a dumb stroke of luck where one of her "small time" cases ended up involved with one of the larger ones. But looking at her endless list of drunk drivers and muggers, coupled with a handful of home invasions and family disputes, her chances of that were slim, if not non-existent.

Likely she was going to chat with Benson over a single drink while he egged her on to put herself out there and ignore the other guys. She'd say something about wanting her work to speak for herself and then go home like usual, she admitted to herself with an inward sigh.

Resigned to a predetermined outcome, Lily turned her attention back to her request for security footage for the elderly lady's robbery when seemingly out of nowhere, all phone lines appeared to ring at once and the general bustle in the bullpen increased tenfold. When Lily perked up to catch a glimpse of what was going on, she saw Benson rush toward her.

"Come on, we gotta go. I need you to drive!" He waved in front of his eyes.

He must've forgotten his contacts today, and Benson's partner, Rutch, was out with the flu.

Lily wasn't one to argue when things looked

intense.

She jumped up, grabbing her jacket, and ran out after him, only stopping briefly to take one of the bullet-proof vests on her way out.

Barely twenty seconds later, Benson and she were in her car, speeding under blue lights as he directed her to their destination. Lily's heart pounded. This was her chance to prove herself. It might have been dumb luck that she'd been dragged into this, but if this was one of Benson's cases, it was going to be a big one.

"Fill me in, then," she said curtly between radioed messages he responded to.

"It's a raid. I've been dealing with a group of smugglers, who've been bringing in contraband cosmetics from China and Korea, and we finally got the lead we needed."

He sounded excited, Lily noticed, though she never took her eyes off the road. She'd expected something like drugs, or trafficking of people, based on how much chaos had broken out in the precinct so suddenly, not cosmetics, but it didn't feel out of character for this city. It was a weird place.

4 April,
11:17 a.m.
Saoirse

Saoirse's relaxed, calm, late breakfast with Natalia was interrupted by Mike, a dark-skinned man in his late thirties who'd been with her for about three years, throwing open the doors to her deck. "The Garrison Group has started an assault on one of our warehouses!"

Saoirse put down the slice of melon on its way to her mouth and gave Natalia a gentle kiss on the forehead. "I'll be back in a short while, my love."

"Be careful," Natalia said, her warm smile a ray of sunshine in the otherwise relatively grey day.

Saoirse smirked. "You know me."

"Exactly."

Without wasting another moment, Saoirse whisked inside past Mike and grabbed her favorite boots and jacket, along with the hip holster holding her usual berretta. On the way downstairs to the garage, she listened to his hurried explanation of the assault.

"They've just taken out the front guards, but

Johnny was able to radio it in. Harry and Dick are holding them off right now, but I have no clue how long they'll be able to keep it up."

"How many?" Saoirse asked.

"About fifteen. But I'm sure they've got backup nearby."

Saoirse nodded, pensively. "I'll go ahead. Make sure to cover the perimeter with the other guys and stop anyone else from going inside. I'll back up Harry and Dick myself. I expect that Garrison will give the cops an 'anonymous' tip once he realizes that his little plan failed, so get ready to move the stuff at my signal." She slipped on her boots and strapped on her holster before swinging a leg over her bike. "See you soon."

Starting forward without waiting for a response, she pressed a button on her bike that would remote-control open the gates for the garage. A moment later, she was speeding through little-used alleyways and backstreets toward the warehouse in question.

For the moment, the city was still quiet. Nothing unusual. At least the cops weren't on the scent yet, then. Oliver had done a great job of keeping them away for the moment.

Zipping through the city's streets like a rat on ecstasy, she took corners so sharp her knees almost scraped the floor. Within four minutes, she was at the warehouse in question. The outer perimeter looked normal, except that the gate was opened, and no one seemed to be manning the guard's hut. Saoirse didn't even slow down as she directed her bike into the compound. A single glance into the hut as she sped past showed one of her guys leaning against a wall, his shoulder bleeding. She'd have to get someone to look after him later. For now, she needed to focus her attention elsewhere. Two more guys lay dead on the ground in front of the building. Not Her People, though.

Shots echoed through the warehouse when Saoirse raced inside, her bike's engine roaring. A few bullets barely missed her as they impacted the boxes she passed.

Idiots.

Pinpointing from where the shots had come, Saoirse weaved her bike through the rows and stacks of shelves and boxes, taking care to keep cover as much as she could. They'd hear her approach, of course—a motorbike's roar wasn't exactly the kind of sound one could hide—but it wouldn't matter. She'd already spotted Harry's unmistakable ginger curls along one of the railings farther up, which was a very useful vantage point in this situation, and she had a feeling about where Dick had taken cover. Drawing the fire of the intruders meant that she could reveal the enemies' positions to her own guys. In fact, Harry was already engaging in firing back at the first enemies.

Saoirse had counted shots from about seven

different spots, so either those were the only guys left, or some were smart enough to keep their cover for the moment or had abandoned their mission altogether. Saoirse didn't care whether they ran. If they did, good for them, they'd live another day. If they didn't... well, that was on them.

Leaving one hand on the bike's handle, Saoirse pulled her gun with the other, though it meant slowing down just a little. The moment she saw the person with the rifle peek out from his hiding spot, she shot. She aimed for his hands, but at the speeds she was going, it might hit any other exposed body part. He was flung backward, out of commission, one way or another.

The warning shots and stray bullets were concentrated on her now, accuracy ever increasing. The only reason she was still evading them was because she took active measures to not present a predictable target by weaving and making sudden turns, along with taking cover behind shelves and mounts of boxes. Even though the number of bullets were increasing, the shooters were falling away, one by one, as Harry and Dick took the leads she was serving them on a silver platter.

It was over in less than a minute. When the shots ceased, Saoirse let her revving engine die down and got off her bike to assess the damage.

Harry and Dick joined her just a moment

later—Dick clutching his bleeding shoulder, and Harry visibly limping. It wasn't surprising they hadn't come away without a scratch. Two against fifteen wasn't exactly even numbers.

Three of the assailants were dead, a further four had made off, while two were moaning, clutching various bleeding body parts, and the remaining four were unconscious and injured, but based on a quick pulse check, not in immediate danger of passing away. Those and the two out front accounted for the fifteen Johnny had called in.

"We'll probably be getting some visitors soon," Saoirse told her two men. "Bring these guys with you back to HQ and get yourselves checked out. Johnny too."

"We can help," Harry protested. "We can—"

"You are helping," Saoirse interrupted with a smile. "Mike and Dillan should be arriving any moment now, so they can help me with the cargo. If you can deal with these guys, that's more than enough."

Dick nodded. "Got it, boss."

"Good." Saoirse took one more glance at the group of men who'd been sent to take over the warehouse and frowned. *The Garrison Group, hm? Something to look into.*

She turned on her heel and marched back outside while pulling her phone out of her pocket, dialing Mike's number. He picked up immediately.

"All clear," she said. "Let's try to be out in fifteen. Don't think we've got much more than that."

"Roger that," he replied and hung up.

As Saoirse reached the little guard hut in front, Johnny had just about managed to pull himself to the door, holding himself upright by the doorframe.

He was swaying dangerously, and most of his clothing and open skin were splattered with blood, almost covering the tattoos along his arms, but his crooked grin was the same as usual. "Hey, boss. Nice to see you."

He coughed, the sudden movement jerking his body almost back to his knees.

Saoirse was beside him in an instant, propping him up using her own body. "Let's get you back, shall we? Maybe I'll even come visit you while you're recovering."

"That'd be… mighty nice," Johnny mumbled, his eyes almost closing as he leaned on Saoirse with more than half his weight.

Somehow, she managed to help him walk all the way to and through the warehouse, right up to the van waiting in the back. By the time they reached it, Harry and Dick were finishing up piling the other men into the back, so once Johnny was seated, they could drive off.

The moment she handed Johnny over to Dick, Saoirse headed back to the warehouse where Mike and his faction had arrived and were working at swapping out the boxes. The place was like an anthill in motion. Sometimes Saoirse forgot how many people she had working for her, though she never forgot the individuals. Looking around, she knew each one of them by name and personal history. She'd spoken to all of them and knew what they were like, but seeing them all in one heap, or most of them anyway, was always a sight she couldn't get used to, not even after almost a decade of it.

Mike paused beside her for a second as he carried out one of the boxes. "We should be done in about two minutes, but we might not have time to deal with the mess." He nodded to the spilled blood.

Sirens in the distance reached Saoirse's ears. *Showtime.*

"Make it one and a half. And leave the blood to me."

4 April,
1:22 p.m.
Lily

Benson directed Lily to the docks, and straight to one of the large, privately owned warehouses. The kind that had their own grounds and high stone walls and porter house. If the walls were any higher, it'd look like a very small prison masquerading as a cement block.

Other police vehicles joined them along the way, all speeding toward the warehouse. Whoever or whatever was in there wasn't going to get past the police, at least not without some insane, megalomaniac superweapon from a comic book or superhero film.

Cops were rushing to surround the building, their guns raised as Lily and Benson left the car, both with a hand on their holsters. Lily wasn't sure what exactly was awaiting her, but this looked like a significantly bigger deal than some contraband cosmetics warranted, in her opinion. How much resistance were they expecting, exactly?

Still, the tension was high. She doubted the beat cops knew much more about what was going on than she did, so she stuck by Benson who glared at the building, as though he were trying to convince it to spill its secret by virtue of intimidation.

After a long minute in which no one moved, Benson broke the silence. "I'm going in."

"What?" Lily almost shouted. That was insane. If the situation was dangerous enough to justify this much back-up, there was no way it could be safe to just barge in through the front door—even if it was open!

Benson glanced at her. "They won't shoot if I come for a chat. S'not Kennedy's style. Feel free to come. Might be good to have you along."

Trying to figure out just what he meant by that almost threw Lily into a fit of rage. It was probably lucky for them both that Benson simply started marching toward the open warehouse, so all that was left for Lily to do was to follow him, quietly brooding while trying to remember if the name Kennedy struck any chord.

It did.

Just as they entered the building, Lily finally remembered the connections. While she hadn't exactly been briefed on the names, she'd overhead the sergeant talk about "The Big Five" to one of the other detectives at one point. Kennedy had been one of the names in connection to those. At the time, she'd assumed that this was simply a matter of having singled out five of the most difficult of The Big Cases, but now, looking at the entourage they'd brought with them, she was beginning to think that this Kennedy might be a bigger deal than just a single case. Just what kind of criminal was he to warrant so much security and yet leave Benson feeling safe enough to just walk inside?

"Kennedy? I'm guessing you're still here. This is Detective Benson. I'm coming in with my associate, Detective Rose." He walked inside without waiting for a reply.

Lily hesitated for only moment in favor of throwing a glance to the sides of the compound. The whole thing was surrounded. No one could be stupid enough to shoot. Right? Of course, there *was* still the option of going for a hostage situation, something Benson clearly wasn't worried about. No matter what was waiting for them inside, Lily wasn't going to let him face it alone.

It took a moment for her eyes to adjust to the dim fluorescent lighting inside. The air was laden with dust, and she'd barely gone two steps in before it made her sneeze which gained her a *look* from Benson. She shrugged by way of apology and followed him through the rows of shelves packed with boxes. It was a large warehouse. Much larger than the amount of produce warranted. The shelves were stacked haphazardly, not really keeping in mind good order or note of stock. A lot of empty slots informed Lily that either this Kennedy had been expecting more shipments to come in, or that a decent amount of it had been moved recently. She hoped it was the former. It would be easier to handle.

A familiar smell hung in the air, but it was mixed with other, flowery scents, so pinpointing it took Lily until she noticed a distinctive indentation in one of the metal shelves to realize what it was: The lingering fragrance of gunfire. A quick glance around at the boxes in her vicinity confirmed that none of them had any visible bullet holes.

Frowning, she passed Benson who had taken up stance just beyond the row of shelves, where a large, open space opened up a decent view of the whole area and headed on toward the far wall near the southern corner of the building. Were those… carpets and space heaters?

She didn't make it all the way over when she suddenly heard the footfalls of heels on metal above her. Whirling around, Lily caught sight of the someone—a Caucasian woman dressed in tight jeans, black, calf-high, heeled boots, and a plain, figure-hugging grey T-shirt. Her strawberry blonde curls hung loose, framing her freckled face as the woman smirked down from the metal bannisters above them.

"Detective Benson," she called out, her melodic voice carrying a mild lilt Lily couldn't immediately place. "It's been a while, hasn't it?"

Benson's shoulders tensed at the sight of the woman, and Lily noticed his hand twitching toward his gun.

"Kennedy," Benson growled. "We've got you now. You're busted. You're under arrest. Anything you say can and will be used—"

"Oh, Benny," the woman pouted. "You're no fun. Besides, what exactly are you accusing me of? And stop fidgeting with that thing... I'm unarmed and alone, what am I gonna do? Please."

She strolled, no, *sauntered* to the stairs leading down under the watchful eyes of Benson and Lily. *This* was the person they were here for? This Kennedy person? Judging by Benson's behavior she had to be dangerous, but, as much as Lily tried to figure out why, Kennedy seemed harmless. She appeared to be about the same age as Lily herself, and, as she had stated, was unarmed. The woman looked like she was the kind who enjoyed her spring break in Malibu or Miami with her impeccably painted face—an eyeliner with a wing so sharp it could slice a mango in half, and lipstick so red it might as well have been blood. Her green eyes wandered from Benson to Lily, and her smirk broadened to a genuine smile as her eyes lit up.

"And who is this? Detective Rose, I presume?" she trilled.

Lily was left to glare at the woman as she nodded.

"It's a pleasure," Kennedy chirped. "Allow me to introduce myself. Saoirse Kennedy, at your service." She turned to Benson, an eyebrow raised. "I'm surprised you guys let a woman into that boys' club of yours. I approve."

Her upbeat demeanor did little except elicit a growl from Benson. Lily decided it might be time for her to play a part in this. Whatever *this* actually was.

"What happened here?" she asked, gesturing at the hall at large.

"Whatever do you mean?" Kennedy replied, innocently batting her long eyelashes. Significantly *too* innocently. It was like she wasn't even trying to hide the fact she was toying with them.

Lily narrowed her eyes at the other woman. Kennedy appeared to actually find enjoyment in the situation, and Lily could for the life of her not comprehend how or why. Unless, of course, Kennedy had already ensured that Benson would find nothing incriminating here.

Or perhaps this wasn't an act at all, and she really was as clueless as she pretended to be... Except no. Kennedy's sparkling eyes and the way she thrust her hip out along with that cocky smile of hers said more than any confession could. Unfortunately, those were not indictments that would hold up in a court of law.

The urge to point out the bullet holes, and the

lack thereof in the boxes was strong, but Lily knew better than to talk about that now. This wasn't the place to pull a confession from Kennedy. Only the place to take her in. And it seemed at least like she wasn't going to resist arrest. She almost seemed to be looking forward to it.

"What's in the boxes, Kennedy?" Benson nudged his head to the nearest shelf.

"Artisanal soaps," Kenned responded brightly.

A snort escaped before Lily could contain it, which earned her a glare from Benson. "Let's take a look," she suggested, marching over to the shelves. "Miss Kennedy, mind doing us the honors?"

Kennedy smirked and nonchalantly strolled over to her. "Call me Saoirse."

"I'd really rather not."

She almost looked disappointed. "Oh, very well. Which of the boxes do you want me to open?"

Lily glanced along the row of inconsistent cardboard structures and picked one at random. It looked a little older than the others, the carboard faded and the corners more crooked. Determined, she marched over, picked it off the shelf, and brought it over to Kennedy. "This one."

Kennedy frowned at the packing tape holding the package together, then she peeked back up at

Lily. From this angle, her smile looked dangerous, reminding Lily of a lioness calculating the situation before preparing to jump at her prey.

"Got a knife?" Kennedy asked quietly. "It might be a little difficult to open without cutting the tape first."

Every instinct inside of Lily screamed to get distance between herself and this woman, ideally while keeping her at the other end of a barrel. The calculation in her cold green eyes… If Lily had begun to doubt whether Kennedy could be dangerous enough to warrant the large number of cops outside, it was gone now. She still didn't know how or why, but there was more to this woman than met the eye.

Benson stepped forward and handed Kennedy a pocketknife, which she accepted with a bright smile but not without another assessing look at Lily.

Involuntarily, Lily took a step back, suppressing a shiver. This was fine. Kennedy might have a knife now, but she and Benson had guns. A knife couldn't hold its own against a gun.

Right?

Despite her little rationalizations, Lily watched with extreme unease as Kennedy carved up the packing tape to open the box. Inside, there was paper wrapping, and from it, Kennedy lifted… a bar of soap. It sparkled purple in the light and its sudden spurt of flowery scent almost accosted Lily's nose into another sneeze.

"Soap," Kennedy repeated, holding it up with a winning smile. "Artisanal. Very popular with the older ladies."

**4 April,
1:35 p.m.
Saoirse**

Handcuffed and flanked by the two detectives, Saoirse left the warehouse just as it was beginning to rain, heading toward the welcoming committee of flashing blue lights and raised guns.

"Aw, you shouldn't have, Benny," she chirped at Detective Benson. "A lightshow just for me?"

All she gained was a sour look from the middle-aged man. Winding detectives up this way wasn't the most advisable, of course, but she couldn't help it... it was just so much fun! Besides, they could do with a little loosening up. She could only hope that this new detective on her other side wasn't going to end up like this joyless lot of grumpy men. Detective Rose being the first female detective this city had seen in almost five years, Saoirse had high hopes for her. According to her contacts in the police department, Rose was a straight shooter, determined to catch every perp and do her best for every citizen. From the stories alone, Saoirse had already taken a liking to the woman, but now, after meeting her in person, her feelings on the matter had solidified. Rose and she were going to be great friends, even if the detective didn't see it that way.

Saoirse allowed herself to be pushed into the backseat of a car, never for a moment losing her smile. Forensics and the technicians were already hurrying into the warehouse, hoping to find any trace of her guilt, any shred of evidence that could be used against her. Saoirse almost felt bad for them and their wasted effort.

The car drove off, leaving the blue lights behind them, and Saoirse instead studied the cops in whose custody she found herself. Her hopes of being accompanied back to the station by the detectives had been sorely disappointed. Instead, she found herself with two beat cops, one of which was glaring at her, practically begging her to make one false move, and the other was gripping the wheel significantly more tightly than a person at ease with the situation should have done. She didn't recognize either of them.

"New to the city?" she suggested to the one on the passenger seat. Since that earned her nothing more than the intensifying of the glare, she shrugged and looked out the window instead. The city flitted past them so quickly it became a blur, though the downpour might have had something to do with that as well.

Hopefully Natalia wasn't going to be waiting up for her. Saoirse had a feeling it was going to be a long twenty-four hours. Perhaps less, but she never could be sure. Besides, this had been overdue. At least she was wearing comfortable clothing this time.

They parked directly in front of the precinct, and a moment later, Saoirse was led inside, accompanied by the two cops. Detectives Rose and Benson were already coming up behind her by the time she reached the front doors.

"Interrogation Room Three," Benson muttered to the cop on Saoirse's left, though not quietly enough to keep it secret.

Ah. Three. Her favorite. That was the one with the slightly more comfortable seats. And the air there wasn't as dry either. Benson must've missed her if he was going to put her into the *good* interrogation room.

They'd been playing cat and mouse for years now, all with him desperately trying to find something on her, bringing her in periodically. But, as he was always left without evidence, and only hearsay, time and time again, he had to let her go. As far as the files were concerned, she had never committed a crime in her life. Reality was a different matter entirely, of course.

As she was being paraded past the bullpen to the interrogation rooms, Saoirse threw her brightest smile at the officers gathered there. Most of them had halted everything they'd been doing to watch.

"Stint, did you get a new haircut?" she asked one of them in passing. "And, Milton, I heard about little Clarice, congrats! Heathbrooke, I gotta say, those early morning jogs are paying off! Oh, Pashtu, I heard about Enrique... I'm so sorry."

She could sense Benson behind her growing a little more enraged with each cop she addressed by name. Well, if he insisted on bringing her in, this was the price he'd have to pay. Just because she was being accused of something illegal didn't mean she had to be rude.

"What are you smiling at?" Benson snapped at the cops. "Get back to work and stop fraternizing with known criminals!"

Delighted by the opening, Saoirse glanced back at him, batting her eyelashes. "What criminal? I've never been convicted of anything!"

The blood drained from his face, his trembling body beginning to twitch. Detective Rose stepped closer to Benson and agitatedly whispered something to him which, while it didn't exactly relax him, made him unclench his fists and simmer down. He no longer looked like he would wring Saoirse's neck, given the opportunity. Rose followed this by glaring daggers at Saoirse.

"Eyes up front," she ordered, her petite stature taking away none of the authority in her demeanor.

Obediently, Saoirse complied. This was going to be a much more interesting day than she'd expected when she'd awoken this morning, she could tell.

The interrogation room looked just as grey and dreary as she remembered it. She was quickly sat down at the table, uncuffed, and left alone, facing the grand mirror behind which, she assumed, Rose and Benson were discussing their next move. In all likelihood, Rose was only brought up to speed on who exactly Saoirse was now. Based on what her contact had told her, the detective had been kept out of anything above small fry robberies and abuse. In other words, Rose, unlike most of the detectives here, had been focusing on the important things. The things ambitious detectives quickly lost sight of in the face of praise and promotions.

It would be interesting to see how much attention Rose would continue to give those cases now that she'd been given an entry into the big leagues. Incidentally, that would also determine how highly Saoirse thought of her. For now, at least, she was inclined to think the best.

Goosebumps slowly rose on Saoirse's bare arms. The room's chill was getting to her. She'd passed her jacket and the keys to her bike to Mike before he'd left, knowing he'd take good care of her baby. She couldn't have the cops sniffing at it and taking it apart on some ridiculous notion that she might have hidden something inside.

She was already surprised enough Benson hadn't bothered to pat her down to check for weapons. Or that he had actually handed her that knife. Detective Rose had been more hesitant of handing her a weapon, despite not knowing what Saoirse could do. Benson, on the other hand... While he'd never seen Saoirse in action, he must have heard the stories. Well, gibbering tales were probably more like it.

After a few minutes, the door opened, and Benson entered alone, his face a grim mask, his eyes fiercely glaring daggers.

"Aww, is Detective Rose not joining us?" Saoirse asked, pouting.

Benson heavily dropped in the chair across from her. "She's got other stuff to attend to. You'll just have to talk to me instead."

"I guess you'll do... But she's a real cutie." Saoirse winked at the looking glass, betting on Rose standing just behind it.

Benson cleared his throat. "I'll just come right out. What happened to the stuff?"

"What stuff?"

"The cosmetics. The ones you imported and distributed illegally."

"If you're talking about the soaps, I can assure you there is nothing in them that would be considered—"

"For heaven's sake, you know I'm not talking about those!" Benson slammed his hands on the table.

Saoirse only smiled. "What are you expecting me to say, Benny? You know I'll be walking out again in a few hours just like I came in. And you *know* it'll be for the best. Without me, this city will go down faster than the Titanic. The iceberg's already been hit, you know. I'm the one managing the damage in the hull before the water can widen the gash." Saoirse paused for a moment, to let her words sink in, her smile never fading. "You take me out of commission, you're covering the captain's eyes, letting him steer straight to the bottom of the ocean."

"You," Benson growled, "are a menace."

"I'm not denying that."

Benson abruptly got to his feet and began pacing up and down the interrogation room — his steps short and agitated, his demeanor hectic and frazzled. While he always showed her animosity, he wasn't usually like this. Not this... desperate. Not this concerned. They did their little dance, she provoked him a little to get his ears to turn red, and then she walked out. It was like a delicately choreographed routine. But not this time.

Suddenly, he stopped and turned back to Saoirse. "What's with the carpets drenched in hydrogen peroxide?"

They'd gotten the results of those tests

quicker this time than before. Saoirse could only assume that they had already known what to look for. Always nice to see that they were learning.

"Got some blood on them." She grinned. "I figured airing them out in the warehouse was safer than at home, gasses and all."

Benson's pensive nod quickly gave way to a frown. "Gasses? What... Wait, whose blood?"

"Some animal," Saoirse said lightly. "The butcher made a house call."

"What butcher?" Benson leaned across the table. He was playing the game, and he wanted names.

This time, however, Saoirse only smiled.

"I said, what butcher? Who was it? Damn it, Kennedy!" He banged his fist on the table again.

Instead of responding, Saoirse leaned back in her chair, getting comfortable, and swung one leg across the other.

**5 April,
3:49 a.m.
<u>Lily</u>**

Lily watched as Kennedy strolled out of the precinct in the early morning. Benson had grilled her for hours, but after that cryptic comment about the "butcher" she hadn't uttered another word until Benson had given in and she'd given her goodbyes.

Truthfully, Lily was impressed with how calmly the woman had reacted to the entire situation. Watching the whole thing go down from the other side of the two-way mirror, even Lily had flinched when Benson had punched the table the first time. And the second. But Kennedy hadn't moved a muscle. She'd just sat there, cheekily cheerful without even a moment's lapse. If it weren't for that constant twinkle in Kennedy's eye, Lily would have said it was nothing more than an act, like a stage performer's smile.

After Kennedy had left, calling out to several of the night shift's cops on her way out, similar to her arrival, Lily entered the interrogation room where Benson sat slumped over a chair, face resting on his arm which was cradled across the backrest.

She'd wanted to ask a million questions, since nothing had actually been explained yet, but seeing him there so miserable... Something else had to come first.

"You look like you need a coffee," Lily suggested. "And possibly a ride home."

He raised his head, his eyes blearily focusing on her. "I'll take that coffee."

Lily glanced over at the two-way mirror, her own, tired reflection staring back at her. "What happened today? Why go for a raid and take her in if we had nothing to catch her out with? And exactly how often does she get brought in?"

Benson coughed, hiding a chuckle. "You noticed the greetings, huh?"

"Hard not to."

"Fair." He sighed. "I keep... almost getting her. I keep being in the position that I know she did it. And she knows I know, but... somehow, she manages to never leave a trace of evidence that actually condemns her."

Lily watched him for a moment, his nostrils twitching in frustration as his hands balled into fists once more. She didn't fully understand why he was acting the way he did. After all, how could she? She had no idea of Benson's history with Kennedy. But she recognized the frustrated expression on his face. It was the look of someone chasing a perp they just couldn't grasp.

Like a person trying to catch a fish with their bare hands.

A fish was so much easier trapped and cornered by four hands instead of two.

"I think it's about time someone filled me in on who exactly Saoirse Kennedy is. And I think you're just the guy," Lily said, appraising Benson.

The chair creaking with the shift in weight, Benson got to his feet, towering over her by a good foot and a half now. Sometimes Lily forgot just how tall he was. Or how short she was in comparison.

"Let's talk over coffee," he agreed. "And bagels. I would murder for some cream cheese right now."

Lily pretended to speak into her coms. "Sir, we've got a motive. I repeat, we've got a motive."

Cracking a grin, Benson clapped her shoulder jovially. "Let's go."

Instead of heading out to a Starbucks, Benson ordered two take-away coffees and three cream cheese bagels from a café near the station and headed back to the precinct with their haul. Benson commandeered one of the empty offices for the night and locked the door before he even voiced Kennedy's name again.

"Can't be too careful," he said. "I'm sure Kennedy's got ears everywhere."

They sat across from each other at the desk, clasping their coffee cups, until Benson caved and grabbed one of the bagels. "Two for me, one for you."

"Thanks."

While Lily nibbled at her bagel in silence, Benson devoured his first in two large bites. Then he sighed. "Where to begin with Saoirse Kennedy... No. Where to begin with this city?"

"The city?" Lily frowned.

"Yeah. The city. It's a mess of a place, but... different to what you might expect from somewhere like New York or L.A. to be. You've got the ear low to the ground; I'm sure you've noticed."

She didn't have to respond. They both knew her answer.

"Drugs," she said anyway.

"Drugs," he confirmed.

The lack of drug-related problems in this city was astonishing. Sure, there were small things like weed and ecstasy, but none of the big ones. None of the really dangerous ones. On occasion, it looked like a trail was opening up, like some of the drugs washed into the city from the rest of the country, but before the police even had a chance to intervene, they disappeared again. Vanished, as though swallowed by the earth. It just didn't make any sense.

"It's Kennedy we've got to thank for that," Benson said.

"What?"

"I'm serious. See, this city… it has a kind of strange eco-system. Imagine it like a pond. We're dealing with everything that's above the water—birds, insects, sometimes frogs. Anything that comes there to drink. But the stuff underneath the surface… well, we try to deal with it, but it's like reaching in with one arm without really seeing what's going on. Like what we see is distorted by the refraction and it's dark and…" He paused, noticing Lily's bemused expression. "Look, I never said it was a perfect metaphor," he grumbled. "But it works. Anyway. Look. You've got this pond, right? And then you've got people like Kennedy. It's like she's an octopus down there. Got her tentacles in everything, ruling the pond like a mastermind, and if we reach for her, she spurts out ink and makes it impossible to see anything."

"You said people like her. Got names to go with that?"

"Five names. Kennedy is one of them. Then we've got Garrison, Piarelli, Johnson, and Yamaguchi. Each and every one is a criminal that needs to be taken of the streets. They're menaces to society. But, as much as I hate to admit it, they also keep the city, and each other, in check."

All those names sounded vaguely familiar. Some were names she'd heard in passing, floating around the precinct in whispered conversations she hadn't been meant to overhear. Others had come up in connection with other cases—suspected links that couldn't be proven. Lily didn't like where this was going. She didn't like it one bit. "What do you mean?"

"They run the pond. And it seems that they don't like drugs floating around in it, so they make sure to fish 'em out as soon as they fall in. There's other stuff too, I'm sure, but this is just the obvious one. Octopodes, the lot of 'em." Unhappily, Benson bit into his second bagel.

Kennedy's words were beginning to make sense to Lily. Comparing the city to the Titanic... She'd been saying that without her around, drugs would flood the city and things were going to take a turn for the worse. Still, it was difficult to believe that the handsome woman could really influence that much. Then again, considering how confidently she'd held herself, how calm she had remained... Perhaps Lily could believe it. *What an interesting person.*

"You know an octopus doesn't belong in a pond, right?" she noted.

Benson only gave her a *look.* Of the disapproving, somewhat annoyed variety.

"So, you're after Kennedy. I'm assuming some of the other guys are dealing with the other four names. But if she's that influential for the city, surely she's done something other than import and sell banned cosmetics. Right?" Lily was tapping the lid of her coffee, trying to figure out how all this really tied together. So far, it just sounded like a clichéd premise for a crime movie. "Got any files on what else she's done?"

"I wish," Benson growled. "If I did, I'd have been able to get her in. When it comes to Kennedy, we barely get anything more than hearsay. She's good at covering her tracks. Like that stunt with the hydrogen peroxide? I guarantee you there was a fight this morning. And there must've been blood, but the techs couldn't get any valid samples. We found some gun residue, but that's about it. And it's really not enough to do anything more. It's always been the same way. I think we've got her in a corner, we're finally ahead, but as soon as we get there, she's waiting for us, alone, playing all innocent. So we take her in, try to question her, but she just waits it out until we *have* to release her. She never even bothers to ask for a lawyer. Which really just means that any files we got are… vague. She's slippery. Like an octopus. And cunning."

More like a fox, Lily thought, remembering the green eyes framed by strawberry blonde curls.

"So, what do you *think* she's been involved in, then?" she pushed.

"I'm pretty sure she's connected to a number of deaths in and around the city, but again, there's nothing tying her to them. It's just a gut feeling. That look she gives me when I ask her about it. Like she's laughing at me. She knows I know. But she also knows there's nothing I can do." He slammed his fists on the table again, brows knit together to form a single dark line above his eyes. "There was some kidnapping, too. The fiancée of a city diplomat vanished after the guy had a run in with some thugs in a bar she's been known to frequent. Some thefts, also. Cars, mostly. Bikes. Even phones." His fists were clenched so tightly, his knuckles were white.

Lily watched him contemplatively. "I'm assuming you've tried to have her followed or have someone go undercover and infiltrate her network."

Benson only grunted and took a sip of his coffee, his expression dark as night.

"Well?" Lily raised an eyebrow, though she had a feeling she knew his answer.

"It's like a bloody syndicate," he grumbled into his cup. "Nigh impossible to get anyone in there. It's like she can sniff out who's loyal to her and who isn't. We tried to get some of her guys to fess up before, too. Couldn't get a word out of 'em. The other four's guys, they squeal like there's no tomorrow, as soon as it looks like there'll be consequences, but not hers. I heard that one of the others, Piarelli, I think, tried to get a double agent in there once. Apparently, he never saw the guy again." Benson shuddered. "I don't even want to think about what she's done to him. That woman is evil incarnate. Just wish she wasn't so hot." He glanced at Lily, realization dawning on his face. "Sorry."

Lily shrugged. Being a woman in a male dominated profession, she was used to things like that slipping out sometimes. She didn't like it, of course, but with guys like Benson, who acknowledged their missteps, she figured she could let it slide, even if it was unprofessional.

Saoirse Kennedy. The woman became more and more of an enigma. What Benson had just told her didn't seem to reflect the woman she'd observed that evening, and yet... It certainly wasn't a mismatch, either. And by the sound of it, this city's underworld was just as much of a boys' club as its protectors. So if someone like Kennedy could rise to the top there, then Lily could do the same on this side of the pond.

Lily's decision was made in an instant, its force almost toppling her over.

"Let me be your partner," she said, pinning Benson with her gaze.

He narrowed his eyes at her. "I already got one of those. Rutch, remember?"

Lily cocked her head to the side. "And how often has Rutch been sick in the last six months?" She thought of the boisterous man who seemed to prefer a drink over real police work any day and didn't make a secret of it. "And how much good has he really done to your investigation?"

Benson granted her a mirthless chuckle. "All right, Poppy. And what makes you think you'll do any better?"

"Kennedy seemed curious about me. We're similar, she and I."

Though merely stating facts, Lily had mixed feelings about her words. The way Benson squinted at her certainly didn't help that.

"And how is that?"

She shrugged. "I don't expect you'd understand, to be honest."

"Try me."

"I'll let you see for yourself," Lily promised. "Just as long as you give me a shot. Even if it's only as long as Rutch is out sick."

Benson contemplated her for a moment, studying her expression, her determined gaze. Finally, he gave her a slight nod. "You've got yourself a deal. First order of business, *partner*, gimme a ride home."

**5 April,
3:50 a.m.
Saoirse**

Good old Benny hadn't sent anyone to follow her out of the precinct on her way home this time. Saoirse almost felt disappointed. She'd already planned out a route in her head to lose her tail on foot. Pity. She'd have to save that game for another day.

Determined not to let it spoil her fun, she decided to take a roundabout route anyway. It wasn't like she had anything useful like money or her phone on her in any case. She'd been very careful to hand it all over to Mike, who, in turn, would give it to Natalia.

It was only about three a.m. when Saoirse strolled across the street and into the side lane beside the public library. Despite the time of night on a Wednesday, or rather, Thursday by now, the city was far from silent. Plenty of traffic whizzed through the streets, and howling singing and laughter could be heard from many directions as the first drunks began to spill from the clubs into the streets. Saoirse made sure to avoid them. She knew these streets like her backyard, and she systematically crossed from one dark alleyway into the next, never emerging into the light of the street lanterns for longer than a few seconds. Taking paths law-abiding women walking alone at night would avoid was normal for her. After all, the worst thing that could be waiting for anyone in one of those shadows was… well, her.

Before long, a figure peeled itself from one of the deeper shadows she passed. The sound of footfalls in barely worn sneakers on the loose gravel covering the asphalt rang out like a music to her ears, and she intentionally slowed down just a little. It wasn't fair, really, taking out her penned-up energy on some downtrodden guy who saw an opportunity. Then again, he couldn't be that poor wearing those sneakers. Unless, of course, he'd stolen them, too.

The click of a switchblade being opened was enough to spur Saoirse into action. Mid-step, she spun around, ducking low with one outstretched leg sweeping her would-be-attacker off his feet. Taken by surprise, he didn't stand a chance. Falling flat on his back suddenly enough to knock the wind out of him, he even dropped his blade. Saoirse picked it up to inspect it. In the well-worn wooden handle, the golden engraving reflected the dim lights. *Cody 08/02/2011.*

It looked like a reminder. A grim reminder, if Saoirse guessed right. Sighing, she took a look at the young man who'd thought she'd be easy prey. His sneakers, blindingly white with thick soles, were of the upper price range. The kind a successful rapper might wear. The rest of his clothing didn't show any obvious signs of wear and tear either, but plenty of logos indicating pricey brands. So he'd fallen from grace only recently. That explained his clumsy approach.

"I suggest you think twice about attacking a random person minding their own business in the future," Saoirse said as he groaned. He must've hit his head on the way down, but there was no blood. He'd be fine. And maybe the bruising would remind him for a few days to reevaluate his choices before repeating something stupid like this. "Next time we meet, I might not be so favorably inclined." Closing the switchblade, she leaned down and pressed it into his hand. "And take better care of this. The blade is starting to rust."

She left him there to gather himself and continued on her way. There would always be people like him. Some because they didn't know another way out, others because it was all they'd ever known. And then, very, very few did it because they wanted to. Because they enjoyed it. Got a thrill from it.

Saoirse wasn't interrupted again on her way to her usual haunt, *Gonzalo's Place*, where she swung the doors open with gusto, mostly because they were heavy, and the momentum made it easier. The place was emptier than usual. Though, admittedly, Saoirse wasn't in the habit of rocking up on her own at close to four a.m. Scattered among the tables in the dimly lit, cigar smoke-heavy room were a few familiar faces, and Saoirse nodded in acknowledgement to them as she made her way over to the bar where the tan man with a vine tattoo she called Gonzalo was already in the process of preparing her a drink with quick, long fingers. He always knew what she needed, the moment he saw her face.

"Cold out?" he asked, his cleft lip pulling up in a smirk, as he placed a scotch on the rocks in front of her.

"You wouldn't believe."

She swirled the golden liquid in her glass for a moment, watching it cling to the ice, before she took a sip that burned her throat and awakened a prickling warmth along her throat, and, after a moment, her stomach.

Gonzalo placed a pager on the bar in front of her and leaned in. "One of your boys left this for ya. Said he'd be here in a jiffy."

"Mike?"

"One and the same. Reliable, ain't he? Like a well-trained dog."

Saoirse nodded absentmindedly. Since the moment she'd met him, Mike had been thorough. It didn't take long for him to join her and become her right-hand man. It was all the more laughable that Piarelli had sent him her way, hoping Mike would create a weakness. But Piarelli had a twisted understanding of compassion and family at best. Else he never would've held Mike's sister hostage to get him to do his bidding. He only knew how to apply pressure, not how to weave a bond. Not even with his own family.

Saoirse's glass was empty before she'd realized, but Gonzalo was quick to replace it with another.

Instead of using the pager, she was spinning it around in her hand, thinking.

"He ain't gonna come if you don't call him," Gonzalo advised her after he replaced the second scotch as well.

"I know, I'm just thinking."

And she was. That was one of the nice things about Gonzalo. He never asked questions. He stuck to his own business and let her keep hers as well. Though, grateful for her continued patronage and dealing with some unruly customers on occasion, he did generally let her know if anyone had been asking around for her which was unnecessary but appreciated.

But the moment she let Mike pick her up, there'd be questions. No doubt there'd be questions about her visitor the night before. And about how she intended to retaliate to the rat of a man that was Garrison. She didn't have an answer to either one just yet, not having had the chance to look at the contents of Jean's flash drive, hidden inside of her bedside lamp, or to follow up on the name of his employer, Timothy Carlton. As for Garrison… she'd deal with him after she'd talked a spell to the men he'd sent.

She glanced at the clock. Already closing in on five a.m. and she'd just finished her third scotch. Perhaps it was time to call Mike. He'd be up worried sick all night otherwise. Saoirse had to keep herself from rolling her eyes at the motherly behavior of her right-hand man. At least she didn't have to worry about Natalia staying up for her sake.

As she punched the numbers into the pager, a familiar smell wafted into her nose—the acute mix of cigar, cedarwood, and a hint of ocean. She heard steps of a familiar weight. Steps she'd heard a million times before.

Steps that belonged to a dead man.

She didn't turn around, not even as the steps went past her and then, with a creak of the door, disappeared. Graham O'Shea was long gone. He'd been around for a long time, guiding her, molding her into shape, showing her the path to the person she was today. But, despite the nostalgia she felt, he wasn't here now. Not anymore. Even though she almost wished he were. This was just his spirit haunting her, or rather, her brain tricking her into sensing him. She'd turned around often enough to know he was never there.

O'Shea was dead.

She'd killed him herself.

Saoirse only remained in the bedroom for long enough to pull the drive from its hiding place, doing her best not to disturb Natalia. Mike was still anxiously waiting for her when she returned to the living room, drive in one hand, laptop in the other.

"Planning on sticking around?" she asked him, raising one eyebrow.

"I figured maybe I could help."

"Honestly? I doubt it." Saoirse sighed. "Actually, no, you're right. Can you make me coffee?"

Mike grinned and saluted jokingly. "On its way, boss."

While he busied himself in the kitchen, Saoirse got set up in one of the lounge chairs and pushed the flash drive into the laptop's port. Opening readily, it showed her a few files with names that, at first glance, appeared to be senseless jumbles of numbers. Saoirse had been working in this business for long enough to recognize a simple alpha-numerical code when she saw one. Translating the numbers in her head into words revealed a text document labelled *Target Details*, and another document labelled *Timetable* along with a picture file labelled *Target*. Saoirse sighed to herself. It looked like the work of an insidiously-minded third grader.

She opened *Target Details* first, skimming it quickly, the frown on her face deepening with every word she read. Frantically, she clicked on the image file, verifying that she hadn't misunderstood. She read over the target file again, her eyes lingering on the familiar name. *Jeremy Benson*. The person Carlton wanted her to kill was Detective Benson. Benny.

5 April,
8:00 a.m.
<u>Lily</u>

Lily was back in the office right on time for eight o'clock, taking no more than a two-hour power nap to gather her strength for the day. Arriving at her desk, she had a good view over the office, already busy in motion like every morning. Benson's desk looked the same as it had the night before, proving he hadn't come in yet, or else it would have held remnants of his breakfast, or his distinctive purple takeaway coffee cup at the very least. It didn't surprise her. If he came in at all today it would be a miracle.

Deciding not to linger on the previous day's events for too long, Lily got to work on the case of the elderly lady who'd been robbed, putting in the requests for the CCTV footage she'd meant to get yesterday, while filing a request for tips that the web team should add to the website within the next half hour, complete with a rough sketch of the miscreant. While waiting for it to go up, she passed through the internal systems, comparing the sketch with the perpetrators of similar cases within the last six months.

The bullpen filled up with the other detectives and Sergeant Whitman, all going about their business, which appeared to be mostly chatting over some sports game that had aired the previous night. Lily wasn't even sure if it was football, baseball, or something completely different they were discussing. It could have been minigolf for all she knew.

When she took a breather from staring at criminals' faces, she briefly wondered if she should inform the sergeant or captain that she was going to be helping Benson with the Kennedy cases from now on, but she elected to wait. While Benson had agreed, there was no reason to believe the sergeant would take her word for it, especially considering that Benson did technically already have a partner in Rutch. And while the captain typically stayed out of the detectives' business—effectively shirking his duty, as far as Lily was concerned—the sarge wasn't exactly Lily's biggest fan.

He didn't seem to mind female beat cops, but apparently, he drew the line at detectives. He'd been the one who had pushed for her to be put on traffic duty when she'd transferred, after all. No, without Benson's backup, she didn't dare bring up the issue. However, there was nothing that ought to stop her from combing through the files allegedly connected to Kennedy.

But first things first. Kennedy wasn't urgent, not as long as Benson wasn't here. Not while there was nothing to go on. On the other hand, the old lady was missing her wallet, including various insurance cards and, apparently, a handmade keychain from her eight-year-old grandson along with a photo of her late husband.

By the time noon came around, Lily finally had three names and faces which she could follow up on with the victim, and she'd filed three more cases—one domestic abuse, one further theft, and one cyber fraud. Unfortunately, she could already tell there wasn't much she could do for the fraud victim, other than take note of the case and send it on to the cybercrime department to investigate. The victim, a young man barely twenty-one, was understanding. He'd already expected to hear a response like it, which didn't do much to make Lily feel better about telling him.

During the sergeant's extended lunch break, Lily finally found the time to check out the cases in which Kennedy's involvement was suspected. If he wasn't around, he couldn't question Lily as to why she wasn't at her desk. Not that she expected him to notice.

What she had intended to be merely an hour turned into the rest of the day of her laboring over various case files Benson had mentioned, trying to draw connections and get a good overview over the situation. The range of cases stretched from tax fraud across the import of illegal goods and kidnapping all the way to murder. Kennedy's name kept coming up in the collection of evidence, but never directly, never distinctive enough to pin her down. The only times there was something concrete was when an anonymous tip came in. And yet, it seemed like exactly what Benson had told her before. Whenever he got there, Kennedy was waiting for him, innocent as a lamb, and yet expecting him. There were transcripts of the interrogations he held with her, all of them amounting to more or less the same as the one Lily had witnessed.

Even though Lily didn't uncover much, she did gain a clearer picture of the position Saoirse Kennedy held in this city. Based on these records, each one of the other four big names had been in serious trouble before, serious enough to warrant a court date and in some cases even time in prison. But not Kennedy. She was like a dancer in the night—involved everywhere, the world her stage, and yet moving with the rhythm, sidestepping every obstacle with graceful ease. Several perps Benson had interviewed had referred to Kennedy as the "Queen of the Underworld." By the looks of it, they hadn't exaggerated. Even Lily could connect the dots after reading the files.

Kennedy had been somehow involved in every single major operation in the city within the last ten years, all of it beginning with the death of one of the city's leaders and a bunch of systematic fires set around the city's outskirts. The connection to Kennedy in those was loose, to say the least. However, there was a photograph that had her chatting with the dead man shortly before his demise. Kennedy's choice of clothing hadn't changed much since then, though at the time, she'd worn her hair shorter, and the difference in years was just about noticeable in one or two lines less around her eyes. Perhaps a little in her stance as well. Another man with grey hair stood behind her, though his face was hidden in shadows. It was a candid shot someone had taken just outside of a function, it seemed, judging by the other fancily dressed people in the background. The date scribbled on the photograph's back confirmed that it had been taken the day before the man in question had been found dead, and, according to the photos attached to the coroner's report, still wearing the same clothes. Cause of death: Poison, in his bloodstream. No injection wound had been found, but traces of it had been detected on the lower half of his face and his hands. The police hadn't been able to track it further. They'd questioned everyone who'd been in contact with the man within the previous twenty-four hours, and everyone who'd had access to his suite for the previous week, including Saoirse Kennedy, because of this photo, but it had all come to nothing. Kennedy had only arrived in the city that day, having proof in her passport of her journey from Ireland. She also had no motive.

But then the report of the fires. They'd all been warehouses, and the fire brigade had confirmed that there had been intentional kindling—there was even the suggestion of a Molotov cocktail used to create an explosion in at least one of them. They'd all had different addresses, held different cargo, and had been rented on different dates by different people. The one thing connecting them all, aside from going up in flames within twenty-four hours of one another, was that they'd all been signed over to Saoirse Kennedy a few hours before lighting up.

Again, no motive or means had been found on Kennedy. If anything, she'd come out as the victim. But it had turned her into a person of interest. Benson had been the secondary in both of those cases, with different primaries, but unlike his partners, he'd clearly made it his mission to figure Kennedy out. And he'd been working hard at it, by the looks of it. On the surface, it looked like some form of crazy conspiracy theory, at least in the beginning, but once there were whispers and mutters from other criminals… it became something more.

An octopus, Benson had called her. No. Perhaps the other four were octopodes, but Kennedy, she was more than that. She was the

Kraken.

**5 April,
6:02 a.m.
Saoirse**

Saoirse had never been one to procrastinate when things could be sorted out right away.

"Mike, get Talitha to find out who Timothy Carlton is, and to check in with Bailee and Oliver. Tell them to look into Benson's recent cases. I want to know everything they've got on them."

He nodded and pulled out his phone to follow her order immediately, while she whisked out past him. There had to be a reason Benson had gotten on Carlton's bad side, and, him being a detective, it was more than likely work related. Before she could really gauge the situation, she needed more info on the new man in town. She should have more to go on by nightfall. That gave her… the entire day, judging by the slow brightening of dawn outside. And there was still Garrison to deal with as well. But first, she needed to check on her own men.

Marching down the hall, she soon made it to the section she'd dedicated for medical purposes where Johnny, Harry, and Dick were resting after having had their wounds treated. All three were sound asleep, Johnny with an IV drip stuck in his arm. While Harry and Dick had come away with minor injuries—minor enough that there certainly hadn't been a need to keep them here overnight—Johnny was looking a lot worse for wear. His shoulder was heavily bandaged, as was his head, and blue and purple bruising was beginning to discolor his skin across vast stretches. His calm breathing assured Saoirse that he'd be alright, however. It might take some time to heal, but given a few weeks or months, he'd be good as new.

Time to tick off more things on her mental checklist.

She left the ward and headed toward what she liked to refer to as "the good guest rooms"… which, in reality, were little better than a holding cell at the police station. There were extra blankets and mats in there now, to allow for Garrison's injured henchmen to lay down. Her doc had looked after them almost as well as Johnny. Their injuries had been treated and were all wrapped up. Unlike her own guys upstairs, these men were having a rough night. Likely, they hadn't been given any pain-relieving medication. Plus, the uncertainty of being stuck in enemy territory—*her* territory—was enough to keep any man awake.

Saoirse casually leaned against the bars of the

holding cell door. "Morning, boys."

Those who'd had their eyes closed flashed them open with a spark of fear which quickly turned into anger but then gave way to defeat.

"You," growled one of the braver ones, a burly, white, bald guy with animosity glittering in his small eyes.

He looks a little like a large baby on steroids, Saoirse thought.

"Me," she confirmed, smiling brightly and batting her eyelashes at them. "So why don't we have a chat? Willing to talk to me?"

The bald guy let his gaze pass across his compatriots. Then, reconfirming their situation to himself, he sagged, the fight leaving him. "You already know everything. You always know. So what would you wanna know from us?"

Saoirse shrugged. "There is one thing I don't know. *Why* did Garrison send you this time? I haven't trespassed on his territory. Nor have I corrected any of his deals. Additionally, he must know that even if you *had* succeeded, it wouldn't have been a huge loss for me. So why bother provoking me?"

He mimicked her gesture, a little twitch of his nose accompanying it. "Look, we don't know nothin'. We get told what to do, and we do it. We don't ask *questions*."

He spit out the word as though it was leaving a disgusting taste on his tongue.

Typical.

This was nothing new. For some reason, men had a tendency to want their underlings to just act like cogs in a machine, never thinking for themselves. It was such a waste of their potential. If *her* guys were to only ever do what they were told, Mike wouldn't have left a pager for her at Gonzalo's and these guys' wounds would have been left as they were. And yet, it didn't seem like this particular guy of Garrison's men wanted autonomy. What a pity. He had the makings of a leader. By the positioning of the group, it was clear that the rest of them had relied on his presence to hold them together.

"What's your name?" Saoirse asked, but the bald guy only spit on the floor at her feet. "Fine. Well, go home to your master and tell him you failed." She tossed him the key to their cell. "And let him know I'll be paying him a visit soon to ask him about this nonsense personally. I suggest he tell his hounds to stand down when I get there."

Opting to not wait for another reply, she left the room, nodding to Paulette and Yao guarding the area. "Do me a favor and escort them out. Any of them lash out, you have my full support for any action you deem necessary."

She said it loud enough for the guys in the cell to hear, and then suppressed a yawn. Going on no sleep had left her wired and impatient, it seemed. Perhaps cuddling up to Natalia in bed for a few hours was just what she needed now. Everything that needed to be dealt with immediately had been done. She could allow herself a few moments of rest.

Golden light was painting the walls and ceiling of her bedroom when Saoirse came to once more. Sighing, she stared at the ceiling. The fact she'd been left to sleep this long meant that either nothing else had blown up, or that her guys had handled it without needing her. Both were always nice to know.

She stretched as much as she could, using the entire length and width of the bed.

"Morning, sleepyhead," Natalia smirked at her from the doorway, her long, black hair tied into a messy bun where one particular unruly strand of hair had come loose, now teasing Saoirse by caressing Natalia's bare neck.

"Good evening, darling," Saoirse purred as she got to her feet and quickly crossed over to her lover, only to draw her into a tight embrace and deep kiss. "Got time to join me in the shower?" she asked with a cheeky smile when they came up for breath.

Natalia smiled. "I thought you'd never ask."

To both of their disappointment, however, Saoirse's phone rang before they could move even a step. Unknown number.

At glance at Natalia, a nod confirmed everything she needed to know. Saoirse kissed the top of her head and lifted the phone to her ear.

"Speak."

**5 April,
8:41 p.m.
Lily**

Lost in her research, Lily barely noticed time pass. The sun had set by the time she left the precinct, Benson never having come in, as she'd expected. At least he'd called in sick to the sergeant, as she'd overheard one of the other detectives mention.

She'd planned on going home and having frozen, store-bought lasagna for dinner, but as she stepped into the rainy streets, she changed her mind. Pulling out her phone, she headed toward Benson's favorite café.

Where do you live? She wrote. **I'll bring cream-cheese bagels.**

Benson's response was almost instant, encompassing no more than his address and the instruction to buy him at least four bagels.

Within thirty minutes, she entered his apartment in a run-down looking building in a lower middle-class area.

"Evening, Gardenia." Benson was dressed in jeans and an old T-shirt with the faded print of some rock band branding on the front, tour dates on the back.

"And this is really how you usually dress?" Lily asked by way of greeting, one eyebrow raised.

He grimaced. "Laundry day."

Lily took a quick look around his apartment. While it wasn't exactly dirty, it certainly was messy. Though, she supposed, one could call it a contained mess. Things were generally in the right areas, just not entirely put away. Her own place, she had to admit, was significantly more chaotic.

Thrusting the bag of bagels into Benson's hand, Lily passed him, making her way to what passed as the living room in this place and sat down on the couch.

"I looked into Kennedy's old cases," she said, no mind for beating around the bush with politeness after a long day of work.

"I figured you might. And?"

"I can see why you're frustrated enough to miss work over this. Even though it's still highly unprofessional."

He flopped down on the other length of the L-shaped couch. "And I'm guessing you're here to tell me you still want in, huh?"

"Got it in one, buster."

He yawned. "I won't argue. You're in if you want it that badly. But you're my secondary, got it?"

"Sure." She pulled out the notes she'd taken.

"Let's get down to it. Have you checked these out yet?"

"Jesus, woman, do you ever take a break from working?"

Lily responded to his incredulous expression with a smirk. "Not really."

Accepting his fate, Benson sighed and leaned over her notes, inspecting the addresses written there. "Don't think I've seen these before. What are they?"

"They're all owned by the same estate agency. Vulpes Limited."

He frowned at her. "And this relates to us how exactly?"

Lily had expected this. The case lay a decade in the past, Benson had only been starting out as a detective at the time and he hadn't been the primary on the case. It wasn't surprising that he'd never gotten obsessed with the details like she did, coming at the whole scene with fresh eyes.

"Do you remember the random fires ten years ago? It was one of your early cases. All the buildings that burned were in Kennedy's name, and uninsured."

"Yeah? But all the places had different owners until the day before."

"Yep. They did. But the agency facilitating the sales was Vulpes. They were done by different agents, and some of the previous owners drew up their own sales contracts, but I did some digging. And Vulpes was involved in all of them. Without exception." Lily paused for a moment to see how Benson would react, but all he did was sit there, waiting for her to go on. "The CEO of the company is a person called Sinead Norsekey. And these are the addresses of buildings they have owned for at least a year, but don't have on any listings."

"That does seem strange," he admitted. "But if they haven't had any ties with Kennedy since that incident ten years ago, I really don't see how that can be useful. And," he added with a meaningful glance at her, "why it couldn't have waited until tomorrow when I'm back at work."

Lily was beginning to question how Benson had ever made it as a detective. He certainly wasn't doing a lot of thinking. "There's a mole," she explained. "I guarantee it. Someone who tips off Kennedy every time you're about to move in."

He shook his head vehemently. "You think I haven't thought of that? There was a full investigation three years ago. We checked everyone—daily routines, phones, computers, past, personal connections. Guess what? We came up empty. In fact, we got reprimanded for wasting police time and resources." He leaned back on the couch, his gaze going up the ceiling. "But all that means is that Kennedy's good at covering her tracks. Not exactly news…" He returned his gaze to her. "Alright, you might have a point. Go on. Why is Vulpes still important? What makes you think they're connected, other than that one incident?"

Wordlessly, Lily wrote down the name of the company's CEO and passed it over to him.

He stared at it for a few moments, his lips moving but no sound coming out as he worked it out. When he finally came to the right conclusion, a pallor replaced the color in his cheeks.

"It's *Kennedy*!" Jumping up, he threw the notepad on the table and paced the room, hands running through his messy, short hair. "How did I not see that before? *Kennedy*! It's a kindergarten trick! I..." He dropped on the couch again. "I feel so stupid."

Lily didn't disagree with him. It was a simple trick, no doubt. But it was easy to miss when you weren't looking for it. When you didn't understand that Kennedy liked to play in plain sight, keeping the veil thin enough to feel the thrill without actually putting herself in any danger of being found. The really impressive part was that she was doing it so well. Someone less intelligent would have slipped up by now.

Watching Benson fight with himself, Lily was reminded of the last case she'd taken before transferring here. When she'd made a careless mistake, allowing the criminals to get away without leaving a trace.

"We need to keep this on the down low, so

Kennedy doesn't have a way of finding out what we know," she reminded him. "So not a word of this at the precinct, not even the sarge."

"But the sarge—"

"Could be the mole for all we know," Lily cut Benson off. "All we need to do now is to talk to a judge directly—ideally without a paper trail—and get them to give us a warrant for these places." She tapped on the addresses in the notebook. "Any judge familiar with the city's past should want her behind bars, right?"

Benson seemed less certain about that than she felt. "Yeah..."

**5 April,
8:53 p.m.
Saoirse**

Timothy Carlton was a businessman who had most recently been active in NYC, mostly dealing on the stock market with heavy shares in prominent IT and pharmaceutical companies. The man knew where the money came in, that was certain. He himself had founded a company about ten years prior, providing all-rounded security: Physical, Technological and Cybersecurity. While his clients' data was unattainable, there were suggestions of very prominent, paranoid, sometimes even royal customers. Despite his head offices being in the United States, his work was done all across the globe, it seemed.

Saoirse didn't like the smell of it all. Why would such an influential man have a problem with a detective like Benson? A detective who, by all accounts, didn't exactly put in more effort than he needed to, except when it came to herself.

Talitha's quick report didn't shed any light on that, either. According to the files Bailee and

Oliver skimmed at the precinct, Benson had never come into contact with Carlton, one of his associates, or one of the companies in which he had shares. There was absolutely no connection whatsoever. Benson had never even been to New York, apart from, perhaps, a field trip in high school. So why?

Until she was contacted by Carlton again to get more information, she wasn't going to move a muscle to harm Benson. The detective, while lazy, was a good man. There would have to be a damned good reason for her to kill him.

However, while she was waiting for Carlton to make his move, she could focus her attention on her own business... and on Garrison's interest in it. As per usual, she'd have to get right to the source and scare a little sense into the man. It was odd though. Garrison had so far been one of the more timid of the Five, usually not seeking conflict with her. Unlike men like Johnson and Piarelli, he actually used his brain. Most of the time.

She'd decided to spend the evening lingering with her own thoughts in *Gonzalo's Place*, the familiar surroundings with its typical susurrus and quiet jazz music soothing her. Gonzalo had made her a gin tonic this time, which sat barely touched on the tissue in front of her.

"Looks like you're having a rough few days," Gonzalo noted as he wiped down the bar near her.

Saoirse sighed. "Not rough. Just busy. And some people are terribly inconsiderate when it comes to other people's schedules."

She granted him an unwilling smirk, and he chuckled to himself.

"At least you have Miss Natalia waiting for you."

"Yeah." A flash of guilt washed over Saoirse. She and Natalia had actually met in this bar years ago, and after some trouble with Natalia's fiancé and father, she'd moved into Saoirse's private suite. Since then, the woman had taken on the running of several of Saoirse's operations, helping out wherever she could using her IT skills—something Saoirse herself had little to no knowledge of.

While this week was busy, it wasn't far from the norm. Due to the nature of Saoirse's operations, there wasn't such a thing as regular office hours, and every action invited a reaction coupled with danger of injury and death. In a perfect world, Saoirse would be treating Natalia like the queen she deserved to be. But reality didn't allow for that. Not without Saoirse sacrificing something else, and that wasn't something she could do. Natalia understood, even without conversation, but it didn't change the fact that Saoirse was painfully aware that she was neglecting her. This couldn't be kept up for long. Chances were that sooner or later, she'd have to let Natalia go and watch her build a new life for herself. A normal one. The kind where she didn't constantly have to check who walked behind her.

"How is she doing?" Gonzalo's question caught Saoirse in the middle of her troubled thoughts, and it took her a moment to realize what he was talking about.

"Hm? Oh, she's fine. Mike should be bringing her by in about an hour, actually. Miss her, do ya?" She winked at him, and he snorted his laughter.

"She is a breath of fresh air," he relented. "Plus, I find that orders go up whenever she's around."

"Oh, so it's business you're after?" Saoirse smirked at Gonzalo, but his expression grew more somber.

"Speaking of business, someone's been asking about you." Her silence but alert gaze was enough to keep him talking. "An older gentleman. A suit, all neat and tidy. Silver hair and strikin' blue eyes. White. Honestly, if I were on the lookout for a man, he'd be the one I'd go for. Never seen him 'round before, though. Was asking about how you were doin', if anyone was givin' you grief."

Someone asking about Saoirse wasn't too unusual, but the questions this particular individual had elected to ask were. The description didn't ring any bells for her, either. It certainly didn't match the other four of the Five.

"What did you tell him?"

Gonzalo shrugged. "Told him I never saw no one who could handle their problems better than you. Also reminded him that I'm a barkeep and not exactly part of the scene. He seemed pleased enough when he left. Generous tipper, too."

"Did he give you his name?"

"Naw, he just came in, nursed his drink for an hour or two, asked his questions, and left. Paid in cash. Didn't talk to anyone, just watched the room from what I could see. Anyone you know?"

"Not sure, but I have a suspicion."

There was only one well-off person she could think of who might be asking about her at the moment, though the timing was unusual. Who would go out and ask about her in the middle of the day? That didn't make much sense. After all, the majority of her work was done in twilight hours. She was also struggling to understand why Carlton might ask about her *after* trying to hire her. And why these were the questions he asked. It wouldn't have affected the job in any way. Unless...

Saoirse sat up straighter, wiping her mental whiteboard clean and scribbling on it from scratch.

Carlton was interested in who gave her grief. The one detective who was always after Saoirse, leading all investigative cases against her was on his blacklist, the prime candidate for anyone qualifying for the title of "giving her grief."

What was he playing at? What was he hoping to achieve? And why hire her to remove the threat to her own person?

She really needed to meet this man if she was to make sense of any of this.

**6 April,
10:00 a.m.
Lily**

Technically, it was Lily's day off. However, the thought of the elderly lady fretting and worrying about her belongings — including the safety of her home — brought her into the precinct anyway in an attempt to identify the perpetrator with the lady's help. Once they had an identification, they could search his apartment, and, with any luck, a small-time perp like him wouldn't be smart enough to dispose of the evidence and perhaps some of the old lady's possessions could still be located and returned to her.

It was a straightforward enough task — the three potential perps had been picked off the streets by beat cops and brought in for the line-up while Lily had phoned the victim and asked her to come in for an identification. Once she saw the three men in the interrogation room lined up against the wall, she didn't fail to point out her robber almost immediately.

"That one," she muttered excitedly, doing her best to keep her voice down. "I recognize that tattoo. I forgot, but I saw it on his wrist before!"

Though she was inwardly groaning once again at the unreliability of witness reports, Lily smiled. "Wonderful. Thank you, Mrs. Pinsickle. We'll be sending one of our best people to look for your belongings right away."

"Oh." Mrs. Pinsickle trembled, glancing back at the men nervously. "Aren't you speaking awfully loudly, hon? I wouldn't want them to come after you next!"

"Don't worry, they can't hear a word unless I press this button." Lily pointed at the push to talk button just below the microphone. "But thank you for worrying about me. And thank you for coming in on such short notice."

"Oh, that's all right, hon. You are doing this for my sake, after all. My Dennis, he said there was no way going to the police would do a damned thing, but I said to him; I said: 'Dennis Pinsickle, you mark my words. The police arc here to serve and protect, and I am certain that is what they will do.'" She patted Lily's arm gratefully. "I'm glad to see I was right. I would love to give you a review on the Yelp, could you send me a link?"

Startled, Lily stared at Mrs. Pinsickle for a moment before she caught herself. "I'm afraid that as a government institution, we don't have a Yelp page, but I'll be glad to pass on any feedback you have."

"Oh, that would be mighty sweet of you, hon."

Lily wasn't entirely certain to whom exactly she was going to pass on said feedback, because the sergeant sure as hell wouldn't care, and the captain was... *absent*, but perhaps the cops helping her with this case might appreciate having Mrs. Pinsickle's words repeated to them.

After miming for the officer standing in the room with them, Pashtu, to take charge, Lily escorted Mrs. Pinsickle out, made her sign the papers for the identification, and sent her on her merry way with the promise of contact within the next forty-eight hours.

Then she pulled out the address of the perp and set the steps for getting a warrant to search his home in motion.

Within thirty minutes, it was in her hands, and, accompanied by a small team of officers, she broke down the doors to the small flat and searched it. It didn't take long for them to find the bag and its contents. And along the way, they also found that the young man was illegally downloading movies, burning them to DVD, and then selling them. Enough evidence was scattered around the rooms to procure him a quick conviction by a judge.

Lily ensured that all necessary evidence was photographed and then taken, leaving no room for anything to be left to chance. While she would be among the first to admit that the legal system was perhaps a little flawed, she was equally certain that there could be no excuse for stealing from innocent old ladies. Luckily, justice had a way of coming around. At least if she had anything to say about it.

She sent the officers back to the precinct alone, deciding to leave the paperwork for a day when she actually was meant to be working. It was a bad habit, working when she ought to be spending her time relaxing. But kicking back and doing nothing while she knew someone else was fretting about hearing from her just felt wrong, and that stressed her out more than going to work ever could.

On her way home, she picked up the ingredients for her mother's empanadas recipe, telling herself to call her abuela once she got there. She always called her abuela when she made empanadas. After all, she was the person who'd taught Lily's mother how to make them. But when Lily saw the small, white envelope that had been pushed through the gap underneath the door to her flat, she forgot all about the food or the call.

The letter was addressed to her. *Detective Rose.*

The handwriting was long and cursive, probably written with a fancy fountainpen. The ink wasn't very old yet.

She had just about enough mindfulness to shut the door and stow away her shopping in the fridge, before putting on gloves and opening the letter, her analytical brain already taking notes on the feel, on any little smudge, on the smell. So far, the clues were very non-confirmative: it was plain printer paper, there were no ink-stained fingertips, and the smell was, as one might expect, that of paper, mixed with just a hint of lavender. Not exactly something that gave her much to go on. The contents were cryptic as well... and concerning.

Detective Benson is in danger. It falls to you.

Nothing more.

Frowning, her eyes not leaving the page, Lily pulled out her phone and dialed Benson's number.

**6 April,
2:11 p.m.
Saoirse**

Removing her helmet, Saoirse looked toward the golden gates of the luxurious mansion belonging to Garrison. Two burly men dressed in black suits and wearing sunglasses were stationed out front, the curly wires of earpieces clearly visible. Beyond them, a tidy, graveled driveway went up all the way to the building's front steps, past a row of hedges cut to resemble a variety of animals. The lawn was neat English, and Saoirse almost expected to find signs telling her to keep off the grass. It wasn't her first time here, but the sight never failed to make her roll her eyes. She dreaded heading inside, knowing that the interior of the building was no less unnecessarily extravagant than the outside. She recalled marble floors and a split, open staircase leading up to the second level, the walls of which were decorated by oil portraits of Garrison's ancestors, or so he claimed. Hailing from impoverished English nobility, he had in time lost his title, but gained plenty of material goods and riches, now flaunting his heritage at every possible opportunity, his home providing a case study of a man desperate to prove himself.

Saoirse was not looking forward to the encounter. The Earl Grey tea he tended to serve always tasted weak, with a hint of dish soap. Then again, she wasn't calling to share his crumpets today.

Leaving her motorbike just out of sight behind some bushes in the surrounding woods, she ignored the two security guards, and watched the cameras up on the walls surrounding the property instead. She waited for the sequence of rotation to begin anew and then made a quick calculation at which point in time the fewest of cameras could catch her movements. There was no blind corner or moment; Garrison had been in the game for too long to make a mistake like that again. In hindsight, Saoirse might be to blame for that. After all, she had broken into his mansion a few times before.

When the time was right, she ran up to the wall, pulled herself up, and hauled across it. She nailed the landing and continued racing across the lawn. She was well aware she might already have been spotted; it was only a matter of time until—

And the sirens went off. The guards at the gate hurriedly checked their surroundings and comms, before turning toward her, as the gates were slowly moving open. By the time they could squeeze through the gap, Saoirse was already at the building.

Getting in through a window wasn't an option—Garrison had learned from past incidences and installed an expensive security system which lowered metal plates in front of each one. But, racing around the corner to escape the view of the security guards, Saoirse found what she'd been looking for.

Just like nobility of old, Garrison hadn't thought of blocking the servant's entrance with the same measures, relying instead on a heavy door and plain locks alone, probably expecting anyone attacking to stick with the front door, and, before even getting the chance to think of looking around, being caught by the guards out front. It was also likely that he had more security precautions inside.

Knowing very well that she had neither the time, nor the need, to pick the door's lock, Saoirse instead took note of the cameras. Yes. Just as she'd suspected. The camera that ought to have been checking the door had been moved and disengaged from movement, likely because Garrison's employees liked to have a smoke while on the clock every once in a while.

Saoirse used this gap in his security to dive into a hedge of sweetbriar, making herself small and keeping low by the main stem to attract less attention.

A moment later, the security men came around the corner. Saoirse watched their polished black shoes halt in front of the door, then turn on the spot uncertainly.

"Where'd she go? Tom, you got a visual?"

They must be talking to whoever was observing the camera screen.

"Makes sense. No... wait, it's still locked." A pause. "You really think... Yeah, okay. Roger that."

"I'll scout the perimeter," the other one said, and one set of shoes disappeared around the far corner.

The man who'd spoken to "Tom" rummaged in his pockets and produced a key card to swipe through the card reader, but before he had the chance, Saoirse jumped out of her hiding spot, incapacitating him with a swift chop to the neck while simultaneously kneeing him in the groin. While the jab to his neck didn't have the desired effect, the knee jab did its job splendidly, making him keel over with a low groan. Saoirse used his momentary disorientation to snatch the key card from where he had dropped it on the ground and used it to enter the building. Until the guard called in the incident on his radio, no one should realize what had happened, which meant that she had at least a few seconds to make it past the second level of security using his card.

She dashed inside once the door swished to the sides in the same fashion as mall doors. A quick glance around informed her that she was in some form of storage area, seemingly used to keep the gardening equipment alongside cleaning apparel. Among them was a barrel used as a table, currently only housing a recently used ashtray, between two wooden stools. The room only had one other door, and Saoirse wasted no time in getting to it. This one was also opened with the key card, allowing her to enter what appeared to be the kitchen. There were two farther doors, but as only one of them was secured by key card lock, Saoirse surmised the other to be a walk-in pantry.

She just about made it through this door before she heard yelling behind her. Two more men were already waiting for her in the large entry hall, dressed the same as the guards outside, pointing their guns at her.

Saoirse smiled her best cheerful smile, raising her hands in resignation and slowly advancing toward them with carefree steps. "Now, boys, that's no way to ask a lady to have tea."

As expected, they barely responded with more than a low growl.

"All I want to do is talk to Garrison. Look, I didn't even bring a gun." She gestured to her hips, clad in tight black jeans, wearing an equally tight leather jacket over her olive-green T-shirt.

Her having come unarmed obviously came as a surprise to the guards, because for just a moment, they glanced at one another in an attempt at wordless communication. That rookie mistake was all Saoirse needed. She dashed forward, keeping her body low, and ducked underneath the gun one of them was holding, ramming her head into his ribs. He not only stumbled backward, but he fell, his gun clattering onto the floor. By the time it was in Saoirse's hands, the other man's gun was pointed at her again, while hers was aimed at him. However, after a moment's reflection, she moved it from him to the unarmed man on the floor.

Still smiling, she tilted her head to one side. "I'm sure your boss wouldn't care if I killed him. But would you? Willing to risk it?" She paused to let her words sink in. Then she repeated her earlier statement. "All I want to do is talk to Garrison. Are you gonna let me go up those stairs, or does he need to die first?"

Her eyes were on his, unblinking and firm. Now it all depended on whether he knew who she was. Though, judging by his glance from her to his partner on the ground, he had a fair idea. Excruciatingly slowly, he lowered both his gun and head.

"There's a good boy." Saoirse beamed at him and pranced past him and up the stairs. Except for the guy manning the computers, Garrison wouldn't have any more security in the building. He didn't like having too many people around.

It made things too confusing, and it lost a significant amount of class.

She had barely made it to the first landing, when she heard the click of a gun's safety. Dropping her body to the ground immediately, she twisted and fired. The guard's shot missed her by several meters as her own hitting his arm threw off his aim. Instead of retaliating further, Saoirse sprinted up the last steps of the stairs, and determinedly kicked down the door to what she knew to be Garrison's office. He wouldn't change it. Not when it had the perfect view across his grounds and ideal lighting from its positioning.

She was right.

He sat at his desk, facing the door, looking very grave.

"Saoirse," he said, his tone level. He wore a navy suit today, and a light grey, almost silver tie. His brown hair was brushed and perfectly parted at the side, and his beard neatly trimmed. His hands were clasped together, his elbows stemmed on the table.

"Hello, Luis, old chap," Saoirse responded. "Mind if we have an uninterrupted chat?"

He watched her for a moment, expression unchanging, then gestured to the chair in front of him before pressing the intercom's button on his table.

"Cease your attack on Saoirse. And prepare some tea and biscuits."

**6 April,
2:33 p.m.
Lily**

"What do you want now, Orchid? I was watching a movie, you know."

Benson sounded, while alive and perfectly well, annoyed at the prospect of getting pulled away from what Lily had to assume was a solo movie date. But she had no mind for soothing him or letting him go back to his movie.

"Hi, Rose, nice to hear from you, how are you doing? Hey, Benson, thanks for asking. I was just about to ask you the same thing because someone just sent me a card telling me you were in danger."

Lily stared at the note during the ensuing silence, wondering if they'd be able to find a match for the handwriting in the database somewhere. Or else, if, whoever had sent this, had left prints she couldn't make out right now.

"I'm not going to be able to watch my movie in peace and quiet, will I?" Benson grumbled after reflecting on what Lily had just told him.

"Nope," she confirmed. "Meet me at the station. And please make sure to put on pants first."

"Hey, it's not that kind of movie! It's just—"

Lily hung up before hearing the rest of the sentence. She didn't need him to justify himself. What she *did* need was find out who was warning her about Benson's safety, and why. For a moment she wondered whether she shouldn't pick him up on his way to the precinct instead of letting him go on his own, but she shook off the thought. He was a grown-ass man, and a cop at that. He'd be fine going to work. It was more likely that someone would set a trap for him somewhere. Maybe place a bomb or arrange for a shooting along one of Benson's regularly scheduled habits. Heading out right now and to the precinct shouldn't be among those. None of the detectives in this town seemed keen on doing work if they didn't absolutely have to. And even then, they were lazy and slacked off, especially on paperwork.

Taking a cursory glance around her apartment, to check if anything else was out of place, Lily pulled the door closed again, locking it behind her before she headed back toward the precinct, note in pocket. As she walked the few blocks to the subway station, she kept a close eye on her surroundings, just in case anyone was watching and following her. She did her best to keep her walk jaunty and casual, as though she were merely on a late afternoon stroll, and she even paused to look at some magazines at a street vendor's cart. Though she couldn't be sure, no one watching her jumped out at her. Sure, there were the common passing glances that were the norm in cities like this, especially for a short, curvy Latina in figure-hugging clothes, but nothing more sinister.

Eventually she reached the subway, and then the precinct. Benson was already waiting for her, leaning against her desk with crossed arms and a smirk on his lips with a twinkle in his blue eyes. "You know, Daffodil, if you wanted to see me on our day off this badly, you could've just asked for a date, or better yet, just pop by my flat."

Instead of responding to his ridiculous insinuation—though it had made some of the surrounding officers peek up from their work in curiosity, and, frankly, shock—Lily punched him in the arm and passed him, heading straight for the forensics lab.

With a frown on his face, Benson trotted after her. "So what's all this about, anyway?"

Lily waited until they were through the door to the lab, where two of the forensic scientists were working away—a person named Chuck Swinton with thick, horn-rimmed glasses and short, messy, brown curls, and a full-figured woman named Bailee Rawliss sporting straight, long, brown hair with blonde highlights.

"I received this note," Lily said, slamming the letter on the nearest empty spot on a table... of which there weren't many.

Most of the available spaces were packed with papers and a variety of implements, microscopes, petri dishes, photographs, samples in vials, and other things. The whiteboards near the far wall were both covered in scribbles written in handwriting Lily wasn't sure even the forensic scientists themselves could make out. Another wall was covered by a bookshelf housing a number of reference works and documentation. The third wall of the windowless room was bare, leaving a little space for two desks with computers and a printer, all of which were also covered in stacks of documents.

Benson looked at the note before either Chuck or Bailee could approach, an incredulous frown appearing above his eyes. "*This* is what you're all frantic about?" He started to laugh. "Come on, it's not even a threat!"

Lily only shot him a glance and pushed the paper toward Chuck. "Can you check this for prints? If there's any unusual chemical on this, anything at all, I wanna know. Any chance you guys can analyze the handwriting as well and give me some info on that?"

Bailee shrugged. "Should be able to, I guess. Where'd you get this though? Under which case should we file it?"

"Currently none." Lily bit her lip. She'd been talking to Benson about a potential mole at the precinct just the other day. It could be one of these two, just as well as anyone out there in the bullpen right now. But she had no choice. She needed those leads, and they were the people who could give them to her. "I found this note slipped under my door when I got home."

Bailee gave her a long, contemplative look, then nodded. "We'll do what we can."

"Seriously?" Benson chuckled, shaking his head. "You guys are blowing this way out of proportion. This is probably just some prank."

"And what if it isn't?" Lily whirled around to face him. "What if you really are in danger?"

"Then why would they come to you? Come on... *it falls to you*? They're making you sound like you're some kind of chosen hero. Give me a break." He let himself fall into one of the office chairs.

"I hope you're right," Lily said seriously. "I do. But just on the off chance that you're wrong, I want to be certain. And I want to know that I've covered all angles. So be careful. Keep a look out. Whoever sent this was warning us. If it was some joker with nothing better to do than play a prank, so be it, I'll be happy to laugh along if it comes to that. But just in case it isn't..." She didn't finish.

She didn't need to.

Benson leaned forward, resting his elbows on his knees as he looked up at her. "You're overreacting."

She shrugged.

"But I'll take the warning." He sighed. "Not like I've never gotten any death threats."

Lily wasn't surprised. It came with the job. You put a perp away, others were angry. The perp, too, of course. But few actually ever ended up acting on their vengeful thoughts. Lily hoped this would be no different.

"Start thinking about who might be holding a grudge against you," she suggested. "Kennedy, maybe?"

"Nah. She's not the kind to hold grudges. If she wanted me dead, I'm pretty sure I would already be six feet under."

Based on everything Lily had learned of the woman, that take didn't seem overly farfetched. She turned back to Bailee and Chuck. "You've got my number, right? Can we keep this under the radar for now? Feel free to call or text me as soon as you've got anything, even if it's the middle of the night."

"We usually go home for the night." Bailee grinned. "But gotcha. You'll hear the moment we got anything. Right, Chuck?" She nudged them playfully in the ribs.

Chuck, wearing their usual colorful tie-dye clothes, seemed dubious about the whole situation. "I don't know… Shouldn't we at least tell the captain or sergeant? We're talking about a potential threat here, after all—"

"Or some kid's prank and Chrysanthemum's

overreaction, which, I for one, think is far more likely," Benson cut in.

"Come on, Chuck. It's fine," Bailee agreed cheerfully. "Think of it as some kind of undercover mission. Or, if it makes it better, as a favor to a friend."

"I guess…" Chuck nodded hesitantly, black braids slipping across their shoulders.

Lily let out the breath she'd held. "All right, that's all settled then. Thanks, you two. I seriously owe you one."

"Don't mention it." Bailee winked.

Benson got to his feet again, groaning. "So does that mean I can finally go home and actually watch my movie?"

Lily grabbed him and pushed him out the door toward the records room. "Far from it. We're gonna find out who might have it out for you."

"What? Now?" he moaned. "But my movie!"

"Will still be there tomorrow. But if we don't take this seriously, you might not be, so there's that."

Approaching the door to the record room, Lily was still pushing Benson farther, but was stopped short when he put out his arms against the doorframe and pushed against it, and, by extension, her. Seeing him smirk back at her, Lily was only spurred to clench her teeth and push harder. Her feet started slipping on the ground, despite her stemming all her weight against his back.

"Would you," she pressed between breaths, "stop being a kid… and just… go… in?"

"Okay."

Suddenly all resistance was gone, and Lily stumbled forward, barely able to catch herself before crashing into a filing cabinet. Standing up straight, she glared at Benson, who'd sat on a table, grinning at her.

"I'm trying to protect you here, you realize that, right?"

"And I'm trying to get you to loosen up a little. C'mon, Hyacinth. This can wait until tomorrow. Or the day after that. How about we grab a drink instead and play a round of darts?"

Lily knew she was overreacting. In all likelihood, Benson was right, and this was nothing more than some silly prank. On the other hand, what if it wasn't? She'd seen it all before—an ignored warning that led to dire consequences. No way was she going to let that happen to her new partner. But she supposed she didn't have to pull out all the stops immediately. She could observe and stick beside him for the moment, just ensuring that no one got the drop on him. It wasn't very likely that they'd get a real lead on who the warning was about from his old cases, anyway. It had been a long shot, just a way to cover all her bases.

"Fine," she sighed, forcing herself to let go of her pent-up anxiety, and then smirked up at him. "If you want to lose that badly."

6 April,
2:45 p.m.
Saoirse

By the time the tea arrived, Saoirse had made herself comfortable in the red satin armchair facing Luis Garrison.

Despite feeling that he generally went overboard and out the other side, she appreciated his style when it came to choosing seating. Unlike Piarelli's leather chairs, for example, these satin ones didn't make a sound when she moved just a little, and they were significantly more comfortable as well. The combination of the gold painted wood with the blood red satin only served to make her feel more like a queen than she usually did. They were perfection… though she'd rather be caught dead than get one for her own home.

"Saoirse," Garrison said coolly after the guard serving the tea had left again. "Judging by your presence here and the distinct lack of bullets in my brain or knives in my neck, I am guessing you have something to say."

"Oh, Luis, ever the charmer, aren't you?" Saoirse sighed. "But you're right. I would like to know what the hell possessed you to come for one of my warehouses."

Garrison only stared back at her. "Can you blame me? I retaliated. I didn't make the first move in this war, you know."

Saoirse's eyebrow pulled faster than a gunslinger in the wild, wild west. "We're at war now, are we? Who's fighting?"

"You are." As confident as Garrison's words appeared in the first moment, he lessened their impact significantly by adding, "Aren't you?"

Saoirse watched him carefully. He was serious, there could be no debate. She'd suspected that something had happened to provoke him, but she couldn't imagine what it might have been. If she'd done something, she had done so completely ignorant of the line she was crossing.

"What is it I did again? I'm afraid I'll need a reminder. I live a fairly busy life, you know."

Garrison grabbed a fountain pen from his penholder and began to tap with it on the table in agitation. The sound was hard and loud enough that Saoirse glanced down to see if he was making dents in the polished redwood. Looking back at his face, she found Garrison narrowing his eyes at her, eyelids and lips twitching.

Saoirse waited patiently for him to say what ailed him. It didn't take long before he couldn't hold back his agitation anymore.

"You can't be serious," he exclaimed, slamming the pen down flat on the table.

Saoirse crossed her legs. "Quite serious," she confirmed. "I haven't the faintest idea as to why you would risk my wrath, so please, enlighten me. What is it I did to start this... war, as you call it?"

Garrison gave her a long, hard look, something the English were quite fond of, Saoirse found, before taking a sip of his tea. Meanwhile, Saoirse took a taste of her own, doing her best not to move a muscle in her face at the unpleasant taste of soap mixed with hints of bergamot. The Brits may consider themselves pioneers in the ways of tea, but it never quite did the trick. Though, Saoirse had to admit to herself, the Americans weren't much better. And the Irish perhaps favored one particular type of tea a little too much. The Chinese and Japanese, however, they had the right idea about tea and the ceremony it deserved, something that was, sadly, sorely lacking in the Western world.

One agitated brush over his moustache was Garrison's way of telling Saoirse that he was beginning to change his mind.

"So it wasn't you," he said and his gaze strayed from her to the metal ball knickknack on his desk.

"Why don't you tell me about it?" Saoirse suggested. "Perhaps we can figure out together who's attempting to set us up against one another. We always were friends, after all. Weren't we?" She cocked her head to the side and smiled to enhance the effect she hoped her words would have on him.

Finally, a smile broke on his face as well, though his shoulders remained tensed. "Very well. It can only be to our mutual benefit."

Saoirse agreed. Garrison wanted to know who deserved his payback, and she was more than a little curious to find out who was behind this impeccable impersonation. Whoever had wronged Garrison had known how to make it convincingly seem like it had been her. At least, convincing enough to fool Garrison. Without more information, she couldn't prevent them repeating their little stunt with one of the other Five, and knowing their hot-headedness, there was a good chance she wouldn't be able to talk those down as easily as Garrison.

"I think we'll need something a little... stronger than these." Pointing at the tea, Saoirse also gave a suggestive glance at the large globe standing beside the desk, one which, she knew, could be opened to reveal various types of spirits, alongside a small vial of fast-acting poison and a gun. To Saoirse's knowledge, the gun had never been used.

Taking her not-so-subtle hint, Garrison flipped open the globe and produced two glasses, filling them about a quarter of the way with cognac each.

He pushed one of them across the table, then took his own in hand, lightly toasting to her. Returning the gesture, Saoirse waited just one moment longer to take a drink herself, instead watching the golden liquid stick to the side of the glass as she swished it around.

The first sip burned her throat in a familiar way, almost unpleasantly, before warmth washed down the length of her throat, all the way into her stomach.

Setting the glass back on the table, she refocused her attention on the Englishman in front of her. "So. What happened?"

"It was an attack in three stages," Garrison sighed. "First, one of my warehouses was raided. All of my informants returned with varying intelligence, none of which matched up." He took a sip of his drink, stood up, and walked over to the window overlooking the garden sprinkled with tacky shaped bushes. "Then there was an attempt on my life. My drink was poisoned by someone who had intruded while I was attending to the aftermath of the aforementioned raid."

"Poison?" Saoirse exclaimed, feeling in equal measures surprised and offended. "Poison is your choice of weapon, not mine. I haven't poisoned someone since—" She stopped herself, reminding herself that even while working together, there was no need for Garrison to know anything about her past. A reminder she shouldn't have needed. "You should know perfectly well that I don't reach for poison to get rid of people who annoy me," she settled instead.

"True." Garrison inclined his head. "But it is somewhat like you to turn a person's weapons against them."

He certainly had her there. She couldn't deny that she'd always been a fan of turning the tables for others that way.

Saoirse glanced at the open globe. "They used your own vial? It's what I would have done."

"Yes." Garrison, a grave expression across his face, took his seat once again. "And then, to finish it all off, there was an attack on one of my men involving an explosion that killed him. Another man saw a motorbike just like yours speeding away with a person who matched your typical choice of clothing and stature quite well."

Saoirse leaned back in her chair, shuffling around a little to make herself more comfortable and swung one leg across the other. "I can see why you suspected I was behind it."

Though, personally, she thought it had been too sloppy to be her handiwork. Clearly the dose of poison administered to his drink hadn't been enough to be lethal. She'd have made sure of that. Especially considering that she knew that he had a certain level of resistance to poison. It came with the territory, after all. Particularly in his case.

"Did they leave any other traces?" she asked.

"Only this." He pulled open the drawer of his desk and took out a business card, promptly pushing it across the table for Saoirse to see.

The edges of the card were singed, the cardboard already going yellow with age, especially along the creases created by folding the card time and time again.

The black letters on the card spelled out a word Saoirse knew very well.

Vulpes.

6 April,
4:58 p.m.
Lily

The bar Benson had chosen wasn't the usual detective haunt, probably because he didn't want to risk Lily voicing her concerns about his safety to the sergeant or one of their other colleagues. Or perhaps, because he wanted to make sure that if they spoke about it, it was in private, which suited Lily just fine. But she'd accepted that now that she had made him aware of the potential threat and they had the forensics team working on it, there wasn't much more she could do. So instead, perhaps it was about time to let loose just a little and enjoy her time in this city that, even after six months of living here, was still new to her.

It was a dim, dingy-seeming place Benson picked. The kind where she'd expect the barkeep to know everyone who came in by name, because no one except the regulars would come twice. It was neatly tucked in between two much grander, larger buildings — one antiquity shop that had closed several months ago, judging by the state of the letterings, and a Chinese takeaway that announced its opening hours from 3 p.m. to 3 a.m. in glowing red, digital lines. To get to the front entrance, Lily had to follow Benson several steps down, so it almost seemed basement level, and if it weren't for his decisive lead, she'd have no idea there was anything of interest down here. As she followed him inside, she just about made out some faded letters spelling out *Samson's Crib* above the door.

Lily both loved and disliked the place in the first instance. The low ceiling and dim lighting along with the wooden décor provided a certain level of cozy atmosphere, the many nooks and corners promising ample space and opportunity for privacy. Nothing more than an illusion, Lily knew. The clientele was of the kind that she suspected to be mostly honest people working crappy jobs. The kind that was often profiled by type and suspected of crimes they'd never even imagine committing. Mostly, it was visibly non-whites, like her, though there weren't many people here at the moment. A few bearded men playing pool, a lady in a corner dealing cards to a mixed group, a drunk chick swaying back and forth in a corner with an equally drunk man. And the barkeep—a middle-aged Latina with a tattooed sleeve from the shoulder to her wrist along her left arm and several facial piercings—who wore, as far as Lily was concerned, a little too much make-up.

"What's it gonna be?" she asked, her voice

deceptively deep as she built herself up in front of the two, her shoulders much broader than Lily had realized at first.

"I'll have whatever pilsener you've got," Lily said and glanced at Benson.

"And I'll take a Cosmo."

The barkeep nodded and got to working on their drinks while Benson leaned on the bar, taking a look around the establishment. Lily noticed that his sweeping gaze paused at each of the other guests for just a moment, assessing them, much like she had done when they'd entered.

"Thanks, Mindy," Benson said when the barkeep placed the drinks in front of them. "Mind pulling out the darts for us as well?"

"Anything for you, Benny." Mindy grinned and pulled out a box of darts from under the counter.

So apparently Kennedy wasn't the only one using this particular nickname for Benson. The detective inside of Lily wondered if there was a connection, while the rest of her threw the idea into the wind right away. Turning Benson into Benny wasn't a far throw. For all she knew, he might have suggested it himself.

Lily watched as Mindy poured her pilsener, the technique practiced and refined. "Cheers," she said when Mindy placed it in front of her, the head rounded off with a nice, clean layer of foam without taking away from the drink's volume.

Benson led the way into one of the nooks, where they set down their drinks and took off their jackets, before already turning toward the dartboard a few feet away. Markings had been established with colored tape on the floor, though Lily had to strain her eyes to really see them now, they'd been trodden on by so many feet.

Gesturing at the box of darts, Benson stood to the side to let Lily go first.

"Gotta see what you've got before I decimate you." He grinned.

Lily smirked back at him. "Well, be prepared to have your plans burn like cinder."

Positioning herself on the farthest marking with one of the few blue darts whose top hadn't yet been bent by less skillful players, she squinted at the board, aimed, and threw. Bullseye. Glancing at Benson to gauge his reaction was the only thing she could do to keep herself from doing a little victory bounce. She'd been talking a big game, and she knew she would never miss the board, but she hadn't expected to start off quite this well. Benson watched the board with interest, though no concern was visible just yet. His gaze returned to Lily as she leaned over to take the next dart. Doing the best she could to replicate the exact aim and force used the previous throw, Lily let go of the dart. Bullseye again. A little gasp escaped her, and she grinned widely at Benson.

"Think you can beat me yet?"

Benson's eyes had begun to bulge a little. He gulped. "Are you in a league or somethin'?"

In response, Lily only smirked and took her third dart from the box, giddiness making her arms feel lighter. Double twenty. Dang it! Her aim had been thrown off by her elation. Either that, or her dumb luck had run out, which, if she was honest with herself, was the more likely case. Still, she gave Benson a winning smile and jerked her thumb at the darts as she passed him to take her own darts from the board. "Your turn. Think you can follow this?"

"I'll certainly try."

Watching him position himself, Lily took a drink of her beer, the fizziness prickling on the roof of her mouth. Benson's stance looked expertly certain. His posture as he aimed at the board was impeccable, flawless. His throw, however…

"What was *that*?" Lily asked, staring at the dart that stuck in the wall a foot to the left of the board.

"That," Benson said, without so much as looking back at her, "was my patented 'Benny Smackdown'."

He took his second dart, and, lo and behold, missed the board in its entirety once more.

"I'm starting to think you should need a license for this game," Lily mumbled, shaking her head. She was glad the wall at this point stretched a little farther to both sides than some of the other areas of this bar. She'd hate to think about what might happen if a player like Benson threw a stray dart while someone was walking by...

"Just watch," Benson said, squinting at the board with his third dart in hand. Bullseye.

"*What?! How?*" Lily had jumped to her feet, staring at the board. How could someone who had so spectacularly missed the board entirely suddenly hit right in the center? And after announcing it, no less? Rationalizing the situation quickly, she shot her partner a sour look. "Are you hustling me?"

Snickering, Benson dropped into his seat and took a sip of his cosmopolitan. "Nah. For some reason, I'm just either terrible or awesome. It's like a law of nature, or something. You should see me bowling. It's a real roller coaster. But wouldn't it be neat if I were?"

"Phew. You almost had me there, you know."

"Ha. Your turn, by the way. Let's see if you can keep up against my lucky flukes." He winked at her, and she rolled her eyes.

"So you come here often?" she asked, taking all three of her darts in hand.

He shrugged. "Every now and then. It's where I catch my tittle-tattle."

Taking her first shot, Lily nodded. A lot of cops had specific places where they'd meet up with their sources who told them what went on in the streets, maybe dropped off a useful hint or two about someone specific—like Kennedy—without getting themselves in trouble. None of that would hold up in court, of course, but it was useful for catching the bad guys.

Back on the West Coast, Lily had her own group of tattlers to fall back on, but here... she hadn't gotten the opportunity to build up the same web yet. Partially because of the kind of work she was getting loaded with. But even so, she'd made one or two connections with the streetwise. Come to think of it, she ought to ask them about Kennedy specifically. They'd mentioned the *Five*, in passing, but since it hadn't been relevant to her cases before, she hadn't paid too much attention to it. Time to dig again, perhaps.

"Only thirty-five points this time," she announced, turning away from the board, and back to her drink.

Benson got up in turn to throw his darts, this time missing with all of them. When he took his seat again, he almost downed the remainder of his cocktail.

"Made any friends in town yet?" he asked, peering into her face.

Startled by the sudden change in topic, Lily fumbled. "I, uh... Yeah! I guess. Sort of."

One of Benson's eyebrows shot up so far, Lily was amazed that it hadn't merged with his receding hairline yet.

"Sounding very sure over there, Marguerite."

"I'm working on it," she grumbled. "I'm friendly with one of my neighbors. They let me borrow an egg last week. And you know, thanks to the marvels of the internet, I'm still in regular contact with my friends from back home."

"Back home?" Benson ran his hand through his hair in exasperation. "Jesus, Carnation, you still don't think this is your home now? It's been six months and your only connection with anyone outside of work is asking one of your neighbors for ingredients, which, I bet, you returned promptly the next day."

Lily bit on her tongue to stop herself from asking what kind of monster would *borrow* something and then not return it.

"I've been busy," she argued instead. Busy with work. Throwing herself into the cases no one else felt like doing because they were "boring" and "insignificant." But Benson was right in a way. She hadn't made any effort to get to know anyone in the city. Her life had been on the West Coast. If she put in a transfer again, she could fit right back in there, as if she'd never left. But she'd made this choice for a reason. She wanted to find the drug operator who'd slipped through her fingers. Needed to. She owed this much to Anoush.

"Look, maybe go on the apps for a bit. Meet some new people," Benson suggested, and, when he saw the horrified and disgusted look she gave him, he quickly added, "I'm not telling you to go date anyone. But it's a way of getting to know people these days. Especially when you have nowhere else to begin. What's the harm? You're never going to really arrive here if you don't carve out a niche for yourself."

Lily could think of a gazillion reasons that went against his suggestion, but she kept her mouth shut. Perhaps he was right. Just look at today—she'd been working most the day, despite it being her day off.

"I'll think about it," she promised. "So, on a different note, what's that movie you were gonna watch?"

**6 April,
10:20 p.m.
Saoirse**

Her mind whirling with thoughts and considerations, Saoirse sped home, the business card Garrison had presented her in her pocket.

It was late, the streets empty of people headed home after their daily routines and not yet filled with the party people finishing up their night. All the better. Though admittedly, the routes she traveled didn't usually present any issues with traffic. Largely because any group of people would make space for a roaring motorbike speeding their way, and no driver was crazy enough to steer their car down the narrow lanes in the backstreets.

Vulpes, she thought, racing past trashcans and crates. *Why?*

Reaching the city's outskirts, Saoirse sped along a dirt track and pressed a hidden button on her glove. Moments later, she raced through a narrow opening, the metal gates swinging aside just in time before shutting again behind her. She parked the bike in the squad and bounced up the stairs to the front entrance. The door was opened by one of her people inside, watching through the camera. She briefly signaled to them and smiled.

Who's on duty right now? Oh, right. Ravi. She'd encountered him when he'd tried to pickpocket her at Heathrow Airport in London. A lucky find, as far as she was concerned, since he had a real talent for sleight of hand and was good in the engineering department, something her team had still been lacking at the time. She'd like to think that sticking with her had improved his life somewhat as well.

Once inside, she power-walked through the halls, nodding to her people here and there, but didn't linger for a conversation with any of them. Shortly, she arrived at her apartment, guarded by Dillan once again. As she walked up to him, he stepped into her way for just a moment, leaning in toward her.

"There's that kid from the other day again," he murmured in her ear. "Natalia and Mike are keeping an eye on him. He used the front door this time."

Bollocks. Saoirse had really hoped that she could use the rest of the night digging into the connections between Vulpes and Garrison's set up, as well as preparing counter measures should the culprit try the same with the other members of the Five. But since a potential customer—or enemy—had sent his lapdog to see her, that would have to wait. As would the extensive snuggling session with Natalia she'd been promising herself. She'd have to do something about the time they could spend together soon. Sadly, her job didn't exactly stick to regular office hours. When it rained, it poured. And boy was it coming down.

"Thanks. Stick around for a while, would you?" she asked the burly, bald, white man with tattoos sneaking their way past the collar of his T-shirt.

He nodded curtly, his back immediately straighter, chin jutted forward with purpose and shoulders pushed back. As ex-military, he was probably one of the most reliable security men she had, Saoirse marveled as she pushed open the door to her quarters.

Like Dillan had announced, Jean was perched on the couch's edge, Natalia leaning against one of the pillars by the window, watching him with cold, eagle eyes, beretta in hand, though not trained on Jean, while Mike stood to the other side of him, arms crossed continuously moving his gaze between Jean and the windows behind Natalia, just in case the young man should be nothing more than a decoy for a larger attack.

The gazes of both men flicked to Saoirse as she entered. Only Natalia remained focused on her task.

"Evening, Jean," Saoirse said. "A bit late for a visit, don't you think?"

Jean shrugged. "It wouldn't be if you'd been

around when I got here."

"He's been here since seven," Mike growled, narrowing his eyes at Jean.

"My, you're tenacious, aren't you?" Saoirse asked, eyebrows raised.

"I have my orders," Jean responded.

Saoirse accepted his reasons wordlessly and walked past him to Natalia, slipping her hands gently around her waist and pulled her tightly into a kiss which was readily returned. They ended the embrace by pressing their foreheads together for a long moment with closed eyes.

"Later," Saoirse growled suggestively, deciding that the Vulpes issue could wait until morning while her desire to make Natalia feel loved could not. Perhaps she could delegate part of the research to Mike, giving her more time to spend with her lover without neglecting her work.

"Make sure you keep that promise," Natalia whispered back.

Together, they sat down across from Jean, who was looking more uncomfortable by the second. Mike, unphased, held his position as expected.

"I've been waiting for Carlton's call, you know." Saoirse smiled at Jean, curious to see what exactly he was here to say, though she could imagine. "I was *so* disappointed when it never came. Did he change his mind about hiring me?"

"Not at all. But he felt his safety would be more assured if he didn't allow you to hear his voice or potentially track his location via the call. I'm here as his proxy." Jean's gaze was serious, his voice steady. Whatever he might think about Saoirse's exhibitionism, or choice in partner, he wasn't scared of what she might do to him. A rare occurrence in this city these days, and, as a result, oddly refreshing.

"Very well. So tell me, why does the esteemed Timothy Carlton want Detective Benson dead?"

"Mr. Carlton would like to make it known that he does not intend to disclose his motives for the kill order. In his opinion, an assassin does not need to know the reasons for the assignment of a target. An assassin is a weapon to be directed by a steady hand."

The stiltedness of his rehearsed words was a charming contrast to his usual adolescent disposition. It reminded Saoirse of a schoolboy who'd been forced to learn a poem off by heart.

"Then clearly," she said, smiling with amusement, "your Mr. Carlton has no idea who I am and how I operate. I am *not* an assassin."

Jean cocked his head to one side, his eyes bright. "Do you take contracts to kill people?"

"When the goals match my own, yes."

"Then you're an assassin. A selective one, perhaps, but an assassin nevertheless." There was no glee in Jean's demeanor; it was merely the statement of fact. The kid was sharp, even if he was young.

"Be that as it may," Saoirse said, "without real reason, I will not harm a single hair on that man's head."

Jean nodded. "Mr. Carlton said you might feel that way. That is why he gave me this."

He pulled a photograph from his pocket and placed it one the glass table in front of Saoirse. She made no moves to take it, but Natalia leaned forward and picked it up, inspecting its depiction with careful interest.

"He has a message for you. *An Sionnach Airgid.*" Jean paused, allowing for Saoirse to finally throw a glance at the photograph portraying two people looking at the camera, the backdrop a church-like stone building. Her stomach twisted like it hadn't done in a long time. Those words… This image.

"What does that mean?" she asked, her smile gone, her tone as cold as her gaze.

"Mr. Carlton said if you want to find out more, you'll have to complete his task. Apparently, there is a key to a lockbox that should hold a lot of interest to you." Jean glanced down at the man in the picture. "And him."

Saoirse didn't respond. Illusions of that smell returned to her, the mixture of ocean, cedarwood and cigar. The voice, smooth and expressive, full of charisma. The striking blue eyes stared back at her from the photograph, next to a younger version of herself. A *much* younger version of herself.

Ghosts came back to haunt her. There'd only ever been two kills she'd regretted. But whatever Carlton had, it couldn't be worse than adding a third to that list. She wasn't going to be enticed or blackmailed into servitude to a man who had ties to the *Money Fox*. Not for anything.

Determined, and without breaking eye contact with Jean, she took the image from Natalia and crumpled it in her fist.

"I think we're done here," she said. "You can tell your employer that I decline. And that if he knows what's good for him, to retract his slimy tentacles from my city. There is no place for him here."

**6 April,
10:46 p.m.
Lily**

Several games and drinks later, Lily and Benson had loosened up enough to just sit in a corner swapping tales of funny police stories, from events in their academy days to comparing the most bizarre arrests and finally coming around to the case that had brought Lily to this city in the first place.

"That's the dumbest thing I've ever heard." Benson shook his head after hearing that she'd put in the transfer because she wasn't willing to let that case rest and was determined to find out just how she'd come up empty handed. "You moved away from the city you call home — a city you *love*, where you actually had a social life outside of work, and hobbies and friends — to follow a *case*? Not to mention a case whose trail has gone cold? You've got to be kidding me."

Lily shrugged sheepishly and took a drink. "I couldn't let it go. I worked too hard on it. Four years, I was on his trail. Four years! It's like you and Kennedy... I don't think you could give up if she were to suddenly move her operations to, say, Chicago, or something."

"Yeah, but Chicago is *fun*," Benson argued. "People move to Chicago because they like it there. Here? Not a chance. Anyone who moves here voluntarily is bound to be insane."

Giving up on convincing him of the validity of her choice, Lily decided this might be a good opening to figure out more about how this city worked. "Does that mean the Five are all from here?"

"Nah, I think only Johnson's even got roots in the U.S." Benson waved her suggestion away and drank the last of his newest cocktail, a strawberry daiquiri, before suddenly squeezing his eyes shut and holding his forehead in both hands. "Ow... Brain freeze!"

"You should pace yourself, you know," Lily chided him. "And once you've gotten over your little owie... why do you think Kennedy came to the city? I mean, what attracted her to it to move to another continent? She could've just run her operations in Europe, couldn't she?"

Benson shrugged miserably. "Who knows? Of all the things I've wondered about that woman, *that* has honestly never come up. Random chance. Maybe some connection with one of the crime bosses already in the city. Who knows?"

"Were they the same?"

"Wha?"

"The other bosses," Lily insisted. "Was it also Garrison, Yamaguchi, Johnson, and Piarelli back then?"

"Back when?" Benson seemed honestly puzzled. Watching him struggle to keep his eyes fully open and focused, Lily began to wonder if she'd let him drink a little too much for conversations like this.

"Never mind," she sighed. "Come on, I'll get you home before you fall from your chair."

The alcohol had clearly hit him suddenly and hit him hard. In fairness, he'd been drinking just as many glasses as she had, though filled with stronger alcohol, and mixed different types of spirits while she'd stuck to her beers.

She propped him up as he stumbled to his feet.

"Need me to call you a cab?" Mindy asked, an amused glint in her eye, as Lily dragged Benson past the bar.

"We'll be okay," Lily chuckled. "But thanks."

Hailing a taxi along the way shouldn't be too hard and would involve less waiting time. After deliberating over how to push — or pull — Benson up the stairs, and then failing in several attempts, Mindy left the bar and practically hauled the detective up on her own, leaving Lily with little else to do except follow.

"Thanks." Lily gave the barkeep a crooked grin.

"Don't mention it," Mindy said with an appraising glance. "He's one of the good ones. And if he brings you here, you must be, too."

Having nothing to respond to that, Lily was left to step in, and take Benson's weight off of Mindy, who added, "You're a killer dart player. Wouldn't mind having someone like you on our team."

"Your team?"

"Yeah. We play other bars in the city. Each one has their group of regulars."

Lily reminded herself of what Benson had said about her needing to make an effort to carve out a home for herself. Perhaps this could be the first step.

"I might just join, then," Lily said, watching Mindy's reaction.

Mindy gave her a warm smile and patted her shoulder. "You're welcome anytime. Who knows, maybe you'll even be able to pick up a lead or two for your cases that way."

"Perhaps. But I think maybe it's time I do something outside of work. Something just for myself."

"Like dating!" Benson's head shot up, as if he hadn't already been half passed out and been carried up the stairs out of *Samson's Crib*.

"Go to sleep," Lily grumbled, pinching him. "And stop spouting nonsense. Thanks, Mindy. I'll be by again some time."

"I'll have a drink ready for ya." Mindy waved and headed back inside, leaving Lily to deal with Benson on her own.

"Alright, big guy," Lily huffed as she heaved

Benson toward the street, wishing he would make it just a little easier for them both by participating in the moving and keeping himself upright departments. "Just a little farther. Come on, pull yourself together. It's like you've never had alcohol before in your life."

"It's okay, I can sleep here," Benson mumbled, his knees sagging. His weight was too much for Lily to keep up without a proper grip, so she let him sink to the ground. "It's comfy. The ground is soft..."

Shaking her head, Lily watched the mess curling up on the asphalt in front of her. It was amazing how much like a teenager a grown ass man in his late thirties could act.

"Hey, Benson!" She tapped him lightly with her foot. "We gotta get you home. The street's no place to sleep for a softie like you."

Blearily, he looked up at her. "Alright, alright. I'm coming, Rose." He propped himself up and stumbled to his feet, standing, though shakily, on his own two legs. Then he chuckled. "Your name is so much fun... Rose... Lily. It's all flowers. It's like a name in a story for kids. Like some kinda magical girl, or some shit. A fairy. Y'know, the kind that's all fluttery and sparkly and... yeah. Lily. Rose. Doesn't suit being a cop. It just sounds silly."

He chuckled some more, but Lily just rolled her eyes, linking her arm with his to guide him down the street to one of the corners where she knew taxis often waited for their next fare. It wasn't like she hadn't had the same thoughts herself. Especially as a kid. She'd imagined herself as a superheroine, with absolute power over plants—making them grow and move at will. *That* would have made her name as fitting as could be *and* she'd have been saving people. Being a part of the police force was the next best thing, she supposed.

They made it to the corner, past a group of partygoers who, clad in neon-colors and clothes that Lily felt were too cold for the weather, sang songs from prominent musicals. Badly. Three taxis were waiting where Lily had expected them, and she shoved Benson into the back of the first one, before slipping in herself. She gave the driver Benson's street and looked out the window in silence, watching the nightlights go by. After a few moments, she glanced over to Benson to check on his state and found him watching her.

"Seriously," he said, as though they'd been in the middle of a conversation, "lemme set you up with someone. I know some people you might like…" Slurring his words more with every passing syllable, he paused, his brows knit together as he contemplated something only his intoxicated mind could follow. After moving his lips silently for a few moments, he seemed to figure out the phrasing he wanted to use. "What's your preference?"

Amused by Benson's concern, Lily shrugged. "Neither. Well, actually, all, I guess."

"Huh," he said.

"What?"

"I dunno. Guess I didn't take you for the type. Kinda started to think you might not have any interest that way, y'know?"

"Well," Lily sighed, "now you know. Happy?"

"Yeah, kinda. I've finally gotten you to loosen up a little tonight." He grinned at her. "You even joined a bar's darts team."

**6 April,
10:46 p.m.
Saoirse**

While Mike escorted Jean out of the building, Saoirse wordlessly left Natalia's side to cross over to the bar to fix herself a drink.

"What are you making?" Natalia asked. Her tone of voice suggested that this was only the intro to the questions she was dying to ask, testing the waters before she dared.

"Iced Tea," Saoirse sighed, stirring the brownish liquid in the tall glass.

"Long Island?"

Saoirse glanced back at her lover over her shoulder, trying to determine if she should feel offended or concerned. "Peach. I do drink non-alcoholic beverages, you know."

Natalia cracked a smile, busying herself with checking for any bugs Jean might have left without their noticing. "Make me one, too?"

Saoirse nodded, fixing two more glasses of the same drink in silence before bringing all three over to the table, just in time for Mike's return.

"He's gone. There was a car waiting for him

past the tree line. Already gave the plates and description to Talitha to check with Matt." He dropped onto the couch and reached for one of the three glasses on the table.

"Thanks." Saoirse sighed and repositioned herself in her armchair so she could sit in it cross-legged. "Go on then. I know you're both dying to ask. Get it out before you choke on it."

The other two exchanged a glance, silently battling out who would be the first to ask. After a moment, Natalia placed the photograph Jean had brought on the table again, straightening it carefully.

"This man." She tapped on the blue-eyed, silver-haired, tall white man next to Saoirse on the picture. "He seems familiar, but I don't know why. Who is he?"

Mike took the photo in his hands to take a look as well. "And where was this even taken?" he asked. "And when? You look so young... Wait." His gaze shot up at Saoirse, horrified. "This is you, right? Not your daughter or something."

His expression was enough to make Saoirse laugh, despite the shock she'd received. "Relax. It's pretty tough getting pregnant with other women, y'know. It's me."

She took the picture from him to look at it again. She could barely remember the day it had been taken. It must've been something like fifteen years ago, about a year or so after she'd been recruited by the man standing beside her, one hand on her shoulder. Graham O'Shea.

"You would remember him," she said to Natalia, though her eyes remained fixed on the familiar face of her mentor. "This man was my predecessor. He had plenty of dealings with your father before I came here with him. It's not surprising you might have crossed paths with him once or twice."

Piarelli, Natalia's father, had already been one of the Five back then. As had Yamaguchi. Both Johnson and Garrison had replaced others—by force or succession. In Saoirse's own case, it had been a little bit of both.

"His name was Graham O'Shea," she continued. "This picture was taken back in Ireland, in a ruin of an old abbey in a little place called Cong, in Mayo. It was where I was trained. Those words, *Sionnach Airgid*, Irish for Silver Fox, or Money Fox, I guess." The striking blue eyes, the handsome jawline, and the silver hair, fashioned in style along with a dapper blue-grey suit... He'd always liked his wordplay, O'Shea. And his money. "It was what he was known by in... our circles. Silver Fox. He founded *Vulpes Ltd* and passed it on to me. He's the one who turned me into the person I am."

"Shit!" Mike scratched his temple, astonished and at a complete loss for words. "Is he... like... your dad?"

Saoirse snorted at the suggestion, dropping

the photograph back onto the table. "Him? No way. He forced me into this life, you know. Not that I'm complaining." Though after a moment's thought, she added, "Now."

"But what does he have to do with this Mr. Carlton?" Natalia asked, taking a sip of her drink.

Saoirse shook her head, a frown creeping onto her forehead. "I don't know," she muttered. "But I do know about that lockbox Jean mentioned. It's safely tucked away in Phoenix Park. Or it should be, anyway."

"Phoenix Park?" Natalia shot Mike another look. "I'm guessing that's in Ireland? Why there? And… where? It's a *park*. Isn't it?"

Saoirse gave her a faint smile. "Never been, have you? It's a park all right. First of all, it's huge. Not only does it house several government buildings, like the president's residence and several embassies, there are also some more or less abandoned military facilities. And another few places the public might not be privy to." She glanced between the two of them. "The real question is how Carlton knows about it. They weren't in business together back then. I'd know about that, and that lockbox wasn't something O'Shea would have advertised."

"It could be a fluke," Mike suggested, leaning forward. "A ruse to get you to do what he wants. It's not that farfetched to believe a powerful man might have something stowed away somewhere, and calling it a lockbox leaves it open to interpretation. Could be anything, really. A safe, a buried treasure, a postal box."

Saoirse nodded. "That's what I'm thinking. That's why I'm calling him on his bluff. He can't know about it. And I don't believe he actually knew O'Shea."

"You're going to pay him a visit, then." Mike grinned, and Saoirse joined him.

"You bet I am."

Only Natalia didn't seem to be wholly convinced that Carlton was lying. Her brows still furrowed, she pursed her lips, tapping her finger on her cheek as she considered the possibilities. "But," she began, "couldn't Carlton have made the connection to O'Shea since you took over? I mean, it's been something like a decade, hasn't it? That's a long time."

"It is a long time," Saoirse agreed. "But there's no way he could. Not unless he can talk to the dead."

"So he was taken out, huh?" Mike asked, though he didn't require an answer. Few people survived this world to see a natural end. The powerful least of all. "Who got him?"

Saoirse took a long sip of her drink, reminiscing on that eventful night ten years earlier. The night she stopped being an assassin and became something else. Something more.

When she set down her drink, she blinked up at Mike, her gaze clear and gentle. "I did."

**7 April,
8:02 a.m.**
<u>**Lily**</u>

Lily half expected Benson to miss work the next morning due to a humongous hangover, but he was already in, sitting at his desk by the time she arrived.

"Begonia!" he called as she entered the bullpen, waving her over. "Come 'ere!"

With a theatrical sigh, she made a B-line toward his desk. "What you got?"

He grinned at her, holding up his coffee and bagel. "Only goodness, Magnolia. Only goodness."

Lily raised an amused eyebrow at him, scanning his face for hangover signs, but came up with nothing.

"Talked to the sarge." He nodded to the wizened man heading toward the breakroom. "You're officially on the Kennedy Squad."

"That's great and all, but can we call it something different?" Lily grimaced, forcing herself to stay calm and not give in to the sudden excitement surging through her arms and legs.

"But it's so catchy!" Benson pouted.

Rolling her eyes, Lily turned away and crossed to her desk to drop her bag and turn on her computer before she made her way over to the bathroom. Her face a stony mask, she locked the door behind her before finally letting go. Bouncing on the spot, her hands clenched to fists, all she could do was scrunch her entire face to press her lips shut and prevent them from making herself make excited squeals.

She'd done it! Finally! She was *officially* on one of the Big Cases! She didn't mind doing what the other detectives considered the grunt work, but this was so much bigger! This was going to be a huge step toward ridding the city of underlying evil, no matter what Benson said about his ponds and octopodes.

She allowed herself a full two minutes for her victory dance before taking several deep breaths to calm herself and splash cold water in her face. Although, looking at herself in the mirror, she noticed that her huge grin hadn't moved an inch.

This was only the start. One step closer to finishing up her old case, too. Benson had mentioned that the Five didn't like drugs in their city, which meant that since her lead on her West Coast drug case had disappeared here, they likely had something to do with it. Kennedy was as good a start as any.

Plus, she reminded herself, her smile slowly fading into grim determination, working as

Benson's partner was going to be the easiest way to keep him safe. Unlike him, she still hadn't discounted the warning, whoever it had come from. She'd checked her phone first thing last night and again this morning, but she'd received no word from either Chuck or Bailee. She'd need to check in over the course of the morning, under the guise of another case, preferably.

Finally ready again to face her work with a professional expression, Lily left the bathroom and returned to her desk where her computer waited for her to enter her password. Already, a line of people waiting to speak to an officer or detective had formed. Let them come. She was ready.

Three interviews about petty crimes later, Lily was ready for a break. Whenever she wasn't talking to a distraught citizen, she was filling out and filing paperwork, as well as inducing the first steps toward apprehending the culprits wherever possible. She'd been going non-stop for about four hours, and she really needed to take a break, if only to pee.

Catching the whiff of a free moment, that's exactly what she did, almost running from her desk so no one could stop her. When she returned, Sergeant Whitman was waiting for her.

"Prep Room. Now." He jerked his thumb toward the assembly room, not waiting for Lily to nod before he pushed himself away, carrying his rotund waist through the desks. She followed him quickly, receiving several curious or misgiving glances from other detectives.

In the room, the sarge closed the door behind her, and gestured toward one of the many empty seats, his expression dark and a touch grumpier than Lily usually saw him.

"I see Benson's taken pity on you," the sarge grumbled, looking Lily up and down.

She looked straight back at him, refusing to give him the satisfaction of appearing meek and grateful. Instead, she pushed her shoulders back and held her head high. "He's seen that I am an asset."

He grunted, narrowing his eyes. "I'll allow it. You and Kennedy are both women. Maybe you can bring somethin' useful to the table. I s'pose your instincts aren't too bad considering the number of cases you've closed so far, though they are on a different level than this."

Despite Lily having used the same argument to convince Benson previously, her stomach turned in anger at hearing the sarge say it to her in his demeaning, patronizing manner. Still, she held her tongue, reminding herself that though he was a sexist jerk, he was still her superior.

"Detective Benson needs a partner, and with Rutch being out, I'm the best option. Everyone else has their plates full," she reasoned.

The sarge glanced through the windows at

the bullpen and the other detectives.

"They do," he agreed. "But that doesn't mean you can slack off on your other duties, Rose. Someone needs to deal with those cases."

She saluted. "I won't!"

His nostrils flared as he looked her up and down once more. "See that you don't."

"Will that be all, sir?" Lily asked, coolly, getting up from her seat.

The sarge stepped into her way, his expression mimicking a thundercloud. "Just remember that Benson's the primary. You do nothing without his explicit request, understand? It's *his* case. I know how you lot can get. And you're off once Detective Rutch is back."

"Of course." Lily pushed past him, seething. Treating her like she was an unreliable newbie… a loose cannon, paper pusher! She wanted to vomit in fury. She deserved better than this treatment. She'd been one of the top detectives in her previous precinct. To get treated this way because of her *gender* was unacceptable. When were they? The seventies?

But reporting treatment like this to the captain was going to be no use. With an apathetic captain who preferred to take credit for other people's work without getting involved, the sergeant was the real man in charge. He was left to run the precinct while the captain enjoyed the public functions and the benefits of his role, not greatly concerning himself with what went on within his ranks.

And going above the captain's head could, in turn, get her into serious trouble.

So for now, as long as she could continue working on this case, she'd push down her anger and just keep going. Before long, she'd show them all what a *woman* could do.

Speaking of women in the force, Bailee was waiting for her by her desk, looking cheerful as usual, today wearing a purple beanie on her long, brown hair with blonde highlights.

"I have the feeling that's not standard-issue," Lily noted when she approached.

Bailee grinned. "Sure isn't! But I'm in forensics, so who cares? Speaking of, I got that report you requested, on the prints on the picture frame."

"Really?" Lily asked, surprised, glancing down at her computer. She'd only taken down the report this morning, and the issue to the forensics team had gone out less than thirty minutes ago. "That was fast."

"Yup! Oh, shoot, I forgot the report back in the lab." Bailee playfully bonked herself on the head. "Save me a trip and come pick it up?"

She batted her eyes at Lily in feigned innocence, and Lily snorted. "Sure."

Following the forensic scientist to the lab, Lily threw a look Benson's way, but he was currently busy with something displayed on his screen that looked like the database for known criminals in the city.

The lab was just as chaotically disorganized as it had been the previous day, if not a little worse. Lily made sure to close the door as Bailee skirted around to her desk.

"Chuck's not in till later," Bailee said when she noticed Lily's cursory glance through the room. "But I've checked out your note."

"And?"

Bailee shook her head. "No match. No DNA samples. Virtually nothing. There are a few samples of handwriting we've got that come close, but none are distinctly close enough to rule out the others. Here's the list." She snatched a small, unmarked file from her desk and handed it to Lily. Then she also took another file from the shelf in the back and handed that over as well. "And here are the prints from that picture frame."

While she was disappointed that Bailee hadn't been able to find out more, getting a list of potential matches was more than Lily had had the previous day. She let out a sigh of relief. It was one step closer, if nothing else. "Thanks, Bailee. I seriously owe you one."

"Don't sweat it!" Bailee grinned at her. "You can buy me a drink sometime. Or one of those bagels Benson gets. They look seriously delish!"

"Got it," Lily laughed. "You'll get your bagel *and* your drink."

"Neat." Bailee raised her hand in a fist, and, a little puzzled, Lily bumped it with hers.

**7 April,
10:37 a.m.
Saoirse**

After surprising Natalia with breakfast in bed to make up for their interrupted meal the other day, Saoirse made her way over to one of her newer storage halls on her bike. The two trucks were already parked out front, Mike and Talitha directing Saoirse's other people as they speedily carried the merchandize inside and organized it, along with the decoys. Even Dick and Harry were helping, despite their recent injuries. Overall, it looked like the endeavor was going fast enough. There should be no problems with the first outgoing shipments later today. One to Madison, the other to Dallas, if Saoirse remembered correctly.

Talitha spotted Saoirse first. The tanned woman wearing her dark, straight hair down pushed her clipboard into Mike's hands and hurried over.

"How's it going?" Saoirse asked, her helmet pinned between her arm and hip, nodding to the storage hall.

Talitha shrugged, her almost black eyes

darting back for just a moment. "Pretty well. We're practically done. Shouldn't even be ten minutes left now."

"Good." Saoirse nodded, satisfied. There hadn't really been a need for her to come check it out—Mike and Talitha obviously had it under control—but she liked still seeing how things were going for herself. She liked to have her fingers in every part of her organization, even though she knew her people could handle it without her. It was nice to know that things could continue smoothly even if she were taken out of commission for any reason.

"Oliver sent me some info on your man, by the way," Talitha said. "It's not much, but it's pretty interesting."

"Brief me later, when you're done here," Saoirse suggested. "What about Bailee?"

"Your favorite new detective asked her to do a little private sleuthing on a note." Talitha gave her an odd look, curious, and somewhat knowing, but slight enough to be dismissed.

"Did she now?" Saoirse asked innocently, a small smile creeping onto her lips as she scanned the sky. No aircrafts currently in sight. Excellent. They'd timed it perfectly. And Ravi was ensuring that the satellites had no visual on this spot right now either. They'd ensured the timing so even the ISS was on the other side of the planet, just in case. By working during daytime instead of night like movies and TV shows always suggested, they even looked less suspicious to any person randomly passing by. In other words, all security measures necessary and possible taken.

"You… wouldn't happen to know anything about that?" Talitha probed, though her face still gave away next to nothing.

"Me? Warning a cop of a potential threat to one of her colleagues? I would never! I'm a criminal, remember?" Saoirse winked at Talitha before placing her helmet back on her head and climbing onto her bike.

Everything here was just as it should be. No need for her to stick around. They had this.

"Talk to you later," she said to Talitha before putting the bike in gear and driving off.

Her next stop was checking in on one of her antique stores. After parking her bike in the back, she strolled up to the backdoor and entered unceremoniously. Lysander, the tall, bespectacled Greek immigrant she'd hired to run the shop, was sitting behind the counter, reading one of the books normally kept on view for customers to browse through and buy near the front. It took them a moment to realize Saoirse was there before they carefully placed a bookmark in their spot and closed the book.

Saoirse leaned against the doorway, grinning at them. "Any good?" She nodded toward the book.

Lysander shrugged. "I'm enjoying it."

"Slow day, huh?" Saoirse let her gaze wander through the empty store.

"Afraid so. Though the newest pieces did go quite well. We've only got two of them left, I think." Lysander got to their feet and came out from behind the counter, to lead Saoirse between the rows of antique bookshelves and knickknacks and even a piano and several armchairs to some beautifully ornamented wooden chests. Like any good counterfeit product, it was placed in plain sight, hidden by genuine articles that looked just like it beside it.

Lysander shook their head, puzzled. "I just don't get it. We've got all this real stuff, the stuff people come in here to find, but... they always end up buying the imitations. It's truly befuddling."

Saoirse stroked the chest, the wood smooth, yet not without the texture one would expect from an older piece. The colors matched, too, the aesthetics practically radiating the image one would expect from an antique. But that wasn't all... The smell, though synthetically created, was that of an antique, or rather, what people wanted from an antique, but without the musky muddy fragrances. And yet, created especially for this purpose by Saoirse's team of craftspeople, the cost of making it didn't even come to half of what she'd need to spend to buy actual antiques for the shop. She did buy a few, of course, bargains, designed to cover up the fakes, but since the real ones rarely ended up being bought, she was saved from the expenditure of having to replace them.

"Don't worry about it, Lys. I'll send some more of these your way soon." She glanced back at the gradually emptying bookshelves. "And some more books, too."

The books were the truly surprising part. Saoirse herself had never found pleasure in reading. It was a necessity, something to absorb information, not something to distract her or take her away. And yet, people soaked up the stuff like they were drinking it. And more than that, the books they sold in this shop were the ones that were being more or less given away in other places. Books people were throwing away, would burn, rather than bother with anymore. And yet here, in this shop, every customer ended up taking at least two books with them, by Lysander's estimates. In other words, these books, old and dusty, almost falling apart though they were, could end up bringing in significantly more revenue than a piece of furniture when taking into account costs associated. It made her wonder if she ought to invest in a bookstore.

"Any other news?" Saoirse asked Lysander, who doubled as one of her street team.

"There's been whispers," they said. "Specifically some of the older grunts. They say that a ghost has appeared. And that he's just as ruthless and terrifying as he's always been."

Saoirse surveyed the street in front of the little shop. Not many people passed in front of it, but there were a few, now and then. Several of them ended up entering the hair salon just across the street where one of Lysander's main contacts worked. This part of town was just at the edge between what was considered sketchy and what was still considered safe by the cops. And as such a crossing point, you got all sorts of chatter from both sides of the city. It was ideal for collecting information.

"Who's the ghost?" Saoirse asked, though she wasn't expecting to find out anything interesting. There were always rumors, always some homeless rat who thought he'd seen someone who ought to be dead in their complete drunken delirium. And once the idea was voiced, it spread, and more people saw the same thing. Most of the time, it all proved to be nothing more than that—an illusion. A ghost of someone's mind. Someone's past.

Lysander knew this. They'd been around for long enough to have witnessed this phenomenon plenty of times. More often than even Saoirse. And yet, now, their gaze was serious, their expression dark. "Graham O'Shea."

**7 April,
6:11 p.m.
<u>Lily</u>**

After a disappointingly ordinary workday, Lily was finally on her way home, contemplating what the contents of her fridge and freezer had to offer in terms of nourishment. The answer was not an awful lot. Especially considering that now that she thought about it, she was fairly certain that about half of her fridge's meager contents had passed their best-by date by several weeks, if not more.

Truthfully, she also didn't exactly feel like going shopping and having to cook. That sounded like more effort than she had energy for, even though she had always quite enjoyed doing it back home, at least when it came to her grandmother's dishes.

"Heya, partner!" Benson came up behind her with a wide grin, lightly punching her shoulder. "Excited for our wild goose chase after the most elusive person in the city?"

Lily chuckled. "Just wait and see. Now that you've got me on your team, it'll be done in a flash."

"Oh yeah?" Benson smirked. "I'd like to see that. You show me, and I might actually start using your name, Hydrangea."

"What? That almost sounds like a miracle! You're not going soft on me, are you, Benny?"

"Not a chance. I'm pretty sure I've still got a thing or two to show ya. Well, I gotta run."

Lily raised an amused eyebrow. "Got a date with a movie again?"

"You know it!" He shot finger guns at her and jogged off, down the street.

Watching after him for a moment, Lily suppressed the urge to shout for him to be careful. Even if he'd forgotten and dismissed the warning note, she hadn't, though she hadn't had the time to go through Bailee's list yet. He was going home. He should be fine. And the warning might have been a prank, anyway.

A sudden craving for pizza rushed over her. She'd seen a nice enough pizza place near *Samson's Crib* the other night, just by the taxi ranks. Perhaps she ought to give it a shot. She could drop into Samson's for a drink after and talk to Mindy about their darts team. Benson was right, Lily needed to make connections, and the darts team was as good a place as any to start. It was low key, casual, and would give Lily the opportunity to chat about superficial things with a random assortment of people. Briefly, she wondered if she ought to ask Bailee for a game some time. The woman's upbeat nature made her seem like someone who'd be fun to hang around.

Strolling down the streets toward the pizza place, Lily took her time to observe the city around her. It was busy, people not really looking at each other twice, a place of near-perfect anonymity, similar to any other large city. It was strange. People craved individuality, standing out, and went out of their way to make it happen, whether with colorful haircuts, enough metal in their face to have serious problems around magnets, funky clothing, or expensive, extravagant jewelry, and yet they were drawn to large groups like this city. Places where what you thought you were became irrelevant. Places where individuality counted for nothing because, at the end of the day, you were nothing more than another face in the crowd.

Lily kind of liked it, though. Having grown up in a much smaller place and knowing all too well what villages in Ecuador were like, having that anonymity here felt like a nice break. You weren't judged because no one noticed your differences. Everyone was simply too busy focusing on themselves.

Just as she passed *Samson's Crib*, Lily changed her mind about the pizza and dipped down into the bar instead. Mindy was in the process of wiping down the counter, today wearing a T-shirt that hid her striking, broad collarbones and shoulders better than the tank top from the other day had done. It was only now that she saw the woman in something approximating daylight, Lily noticed the faintest shadow on Mindy's chin.

"You're back," she said, her painted lips curling up just a little. "How's Benny feeling after last night? Alive?"

"Yeah, he's good. I just wanted to drop by to check if that offer to join the darts team still stands?"

As she replied, Mindy poured two shots of tequila and placed them on the bar. "Of course. It'll be nice to have another lady on the team. On the house. Cheers." She took one of the shots in hand, waiting for Lily to take the other before they both chucked them back.

"So you're playing, too?"

Mindy shrugged. "Usually. I'm more of a fill in, really. It depends a little on how busy the bar is."

Lily nodded knowingly and took a look around. Since it was still rather early, the bar was mostly empty. Only one or two people sat in the nested establishment, drinking by themselves, their faces flushed, eyes bloodshot.

An impatient rumble from her stomach reminded Lily that she'd had made plans for dinner.

"Thanks for the tequila. Here's my number." Lily scribbled down her digits on the back of a receipt from this morning's takeaway coffee and slid it over the counter to Mindy. "I'm sure I'll be by again, but just in case you've got a game or a training session before I do."

"Awesome. Looking forward to seeing you on the team, hun. Enjoy your dinner."

Lily tapped her index finger against her temple and turned to the door. Just as she climbed up the steps to the street, she noticed a familiar flash of strawberry blonde hair on the other side of the street, a few doors down, just opposite a hairdresser.

Her instincts to follow the rules shouted at her to call Benson and check in with him, or to stand down, since she had nothing on that woman, but her other instincts overruled them. Kennedy was right in front of her, strolling out of an antique shop and sauntering down the street as though she had all the time in the world. If this wasn't the perfect opportunity to follow her and maybe find out something new, Lily didn't know what was.

Kennedy wasn't rushing, so keeping up was no trouble. The crime boss wasn't even looking around to check if anyone was following. She seemed wholly unconcerned with the world around her, occasionally even stopping to admire things in storefronts.

Lily made sure to be far enough away that her own reflection wouldn't be visible in the windows in case Kennedy was using them as a way of checking behind her. It was an old trick, after all. Any young woman walking around alone had used it at least once; Lily was sure that even criminals—or perhaps especially criminals—were no exception to that.

If she were being honest with herself, what she was curious about more than anything else, was why a person as powerful and shady as Saoirse Kennedy would roam the streets so casually on her own. The small-time crooks, sure, they belonged in the streets, but no one ever expected a boss to be there, the same way Lily wouldn't expect to meet the police force's High Commissioner in the discount grocery store.

Kennedy strolled down the street, and turned at the next larger corner, before dipping into one of the less crowded side alleys. Here, Lily made sure to keep a little more distance without running the risk of losing her target, just in case Kennedy would turn around. Unfortunately, less people also meant less cover, and Lily didn't exactly want to draw the criminal's attention to herself.

Keeping a mental note of the path they took and discovering plenty new passages she hadn't even known existed in the process, Lily eventually still lost track of Kennedy. They'd dipped into a side alley before merging back into a more crowded street, only to then go into another side alley which split into several directions. Due to her caution, Lily hadn't seen which way Kennedy had gone, and when she jogged up to the junction, there was already no sign of her.

**7 April,
7:19 p.m.
Saoirse**

Saoirse had always loved playing cat and mouse. It was probably her favorite part of being a criminal. There was a reason she'd been glued to the TV for Tom & Jerry when growing up. So, when she left her bike behind Lysander's shop and went for a stroll toward *Gonzalo's Place*, she was pleasantly surprised when she noticed Detective Rose tailing her.

The detective was very good at keeping herself hidden on a busy road. Truthfully, noticing her had been a fluke. Saoirse had been admiring a pair of heels in a storefront window when a car had driven by. The reflection of Detective Rose watching Saoirse had then been cast from the car onto the window. Still, Saoirse would have probably dismissed it, if it hadn't happened again just a moment later. From then on, she'd made an active effort to take her time, just to see how Rose would react and what she might do. Flaunting herself as an ignorant target, Saoirse eventually dipped down into one of her back-alley routes, to give Rose the opportunity to call her out without drawing attention.

But sadly, the detective did no such thing, instead opting to drop back farther to avoid detection. Now that Saoirse knew she was being followed, the detective was easy to spot, especially down in these emptier paths. Saoirse kept her casual pace, allowing for plenty of time to let Rose come for her, but when the detective didn't, Saoirse eventually decided that it was time. She was close enough to *Gonzalo's Place* by now, and she really didn't want to have to postpone her info-session with Talitha or give away her favorite bar to the new detective. Benson already knew about it, but he'd also realized that he had nothing to gain from trying to find her there. With Rose, that would be a completely new matter, and would make things rather uncomfortable for a few weeks or potentially even months. Entirely and wholly unnecessary as far as Saoirse was concerned. So, when given the opportunity, she lost her tail, cutting a corner before dashing forward suddenly, disappearing into one of the many alleyways, and speedily scaling an emergency fire escape, where she waited for a few minutes.

Rose didn't appear, probably realizing that there were too many different ways Saoirse might have gone, and since she clearly didn't have a real goal in mind, must have given up.

Before long, Saoirse was back on her way, though remaining careful, and headed straight for *Gonzalo's Place*.

The bar was already half-filled with the usual clientele, including some new faces who didn't pay Saoirse much attention when she pranced inside and went straight for the bar. She'd barely sat down on a stool when Gonzalo set down a whiskey and a cola in front of her.

"You know that's a crime against whiskey, right?" Saoirse asked, frowning up at him.

Gonzalo only smirked and took the whiskey away, leaving only the small glass bottle of cola. Saoirse shrugged and took the bottle, looking around the place properly. Same crowd, another day, none of which were showing any more interest in her than the usual level. A few nods here and there, a few stolen glances, a few people who had no idea who she was, including a group of college students sitting in a booth, playing cards or some such game, laughing away. Saoirse watched them curiously from her place at the bar, observing their interactions and hidden actions alike. It was always so interesting to see what one could infer from body language alone, or even the level of care someone put into their appearance.

Which reminded her, she needed to repaint her nails. A quick check down at her hands confirmed a few chips in the red lacquer. This week had been a little too busy for such things, she supposed. She'd had a hard enough time finding a moment to put on make-up before going out. She didn't need it, but it filled her with confidence. Sure, a gun at her hip did practically the same thing, but it was a different kind of weapon. Saoirse liked to think of it as war paint, perhaps even a form of armor. She put it on when going into battle; she took it off when she stood down.

"Waitin' for someone?" Gonzalo asked after he had served a few orders and Saoirse's cola was half-gone.

"Talitha," Saoirse said. "She's got some info for me."

"Sounds like you wouldn't want anyone to overhear. A bar may not be the best place for that, you know."

Gonzalo needn't have worried with his advice. Saoirse smiled. "Nevertheless, it's safer than home." There was always the chance that Jean had placed a bug while Saoirse and Natalia had been out. Without Natalia there, no one was in the apartment to check, and Saoirse didn't want to waste time on searching the place for bugs before listening to Talitha's intelligence. Few people would suspect her of conducting her business in the backroom of *Gonzalo's Place*. Not even the people who knew her to frequent the bar.

"Well, the back's yours. You know where to go," he said, shrugged, and turned to one of the approaching students to take their order.

Saoirse made no attempt to move yet. She was

enjoying the atmosphere here in the front. In that back she'd just be sitting alone with her thoughts until Talitha arrived, and that wasn't something Saoirse was particularly keen on. Besides, she could contemplate things just as well here, sitting at the bar, a cola in hand.

When Talitha finally poked her head inside, Saoirse slid from her stool, and disappeared behind the bar, heading toward the backrooms. Talitha was quick to follow, closing the door behind her. Back here, there were taps and a fridge as well, so Saoirse grabbed herself another cola, shooting a questioning glance at Talitha.

"I'll take a juice, I think," Talitha said, taking a seat by one of the chairs in a corner.

On occasion, Gonzalo rented out these rooms for private functions, but most of the time, that happened to just be Saoirse, giving her people an opportunity to let loose.

Once they were both seated, beverages in hand, Talitha took her smartphone from her pocket, flicking through it until she'd found a particular photo in her gallery.

"This is Timothy Carlton," she said, turning it over so Saoirse could see.

He was a middle-aged man on the pudgy side, white, and brown eyes with short brown hair, wearing an expensive black suit and briefcase. In looks only, he was completely and utterly unremarkable, standing out on neither end of the aesthetics scale. He didn't even look particularly shrewd or criminal. But if anyone knew how much looks could be deceiving, it was Saoirse. Being underestimated by one's enemies, no matter the reason, was an opportunity, a strength, and not something Saoirse would make herself guilty of. Especially after she'd met one of the people working for Timothy Carlton.

"You got anything else on him?" Saoirse asked. "Your report painted a pretty clear picture. He does look like he loves dealing in shares."

Talitha chuckled for a moment and took her phone back. "He definitely does. There also appears to be a generous amount of daddy's money involved, a certain Mr. Benjamin Carlton who was a successful businessman himself."

"And where's he from?"

"The West Coast, I think. Carlton Junior is a bit more difficult to pinpoint. Because he didn't need to hold a steady job, it looks like he was floating from place to place a little. He's got apartments in several cities there though. Got one in San Fran, L.A., Seattle, Portland, Las Vegas, Chicago... Some in Canada, too. New York as well, of course. And D.C."

"Do you know where he is now?" With so many places to choose from and the world in the digital age, there was next to no need for Carlton to be present in the city himself. But she hoped that he was, if only out of some sense of propriety. None of the other Five took to the front lines quite the way Saoirse did. They liked to sit in their secure offices and delegate all the dangerous tasks. Saoirse had always been more hands-on. She liked to be in the first line of combat, seeing everything with her own eyes and simply trusting that her guys had her back. It was a reckless approach, certainly, and one that left her organization quite vulnerable, but at the same time, Natalia and Mike were both more than capable of taking over behind the scenes without Saoirse. Knowing and trusting in that gave her the freedom to continue doing things the way she liked, even if none of the other bosses would follow her example.

But even they wanted to be nearby. None of them would dream of having operations continuing in the city without being here as well. She could only hope that Carlton felt the same.

"I know that he'll be in town tomorrow. It seems he has a luncheon with the CEO of Verse at the Glitz," Talitha said.

Saoirse almost gave a sigh of relief. He was in town. That made her life so much easier. If he weren't, she'd have to travel, and currently it was an extremely bad time for that, since there was still an impostor on the loose. Potentially two, if Jean's insinuations about O'Shea were to be believed.

If the issue with her impostor harassing Garrison hadn't already been going on for several weeks prior to Carlton's arrival in the city, she would have suspected a connection. Even now Saoirse didn't entirely dismiss the idea. While it wasn't as suspicious as it could've been, the timing still crossed, and she still didn't know what his ultimate goal was.

"Did you look into what local companies he owns shares in?" Saoirse asked, following that trail of thought.

Talitha nodded. "I did. But there are none. At least none that are specific to here. None that have large offices in the city."

So it was unlikely that he might be looking for revenge for her compromising one of his shares.

"Some that compete directly with his?" she prodded, though she was beginning to feel like that line of inquiry might just be a dead end.

Talitha pouted. "I mean, Verse, I guess, but other than that? Not really."

Verse, being one of the more prominent tech companies in recent years, belonged to one of the few industries Saoirse's doings wouldn't have affected, and while Yamaguchi had ties with them, so far it didn't seem like Carlton was particularly interested in anyone except Saoirse. Or Benson, for that matter.

"Any links to the police? Benson, his past, or family?"

Talitha only shook her head apologetically, and Saoirse sighed.

"All right. Thanks, Tal. Well, I guess we're

done for the night then. Cheers." Saoirse raised her glass, and Talitha clanked hers against it.

"Cheers."

The door burst open, and Mike stormed in, his gaze frantic and his eyes searching the room manically until they found Saoirse's.

He gulped. "There's been a development."

**7 April,
8:34 p.m.
Lily**

Lily got the call before she'd even made it home.

By the time she'd reached Benson's apartment, it was already filled with cops and forensics. The sergeant was there, too, examining the window with a thunderous expression. Even at a first glance, Lily noticed the stiffness in his spine, the pronounced shape of his jaw, indicative of clenched teeth.

When Lily had been here last, the carpet had been a dark green. Now, it had even darker patches. Splatters of red painted the white walls. But all of that vanished from Lily's sight when her eyes fell on the white sheet cast across a person's body on the living room floor. The rest of the world simply stopped existing, all sound quieting, the room shifting into monochrome. Her feet pulled her toward the body, her hand reaching out for the figure without her mind ever taking part in the transaction. No one stopped her as she moved the sheet.

She'd known. She'd been told over the phone

already, after all, the news coursing through her body with flashes of heat and frost since the moment her brain had processed the information. But hearing it and seeing it were two entirely different matters.

She was looking straight into Benson's face.

Or rather, what little was left of it.

Lily wasn't squeamish, and she'd seen her fair share of atrocities without batting an eyelid. She'd seen people die. Hell, she'd held one of her colleagues as he'd died in her arms from a gunshot. But seeing this was on a completely different level. She recognized the type of injury; he'd been shot in the back of the head. She'd seen it before, but never had she been impacted as much by the sight as now.

Retching, she dropped the sheet back over his head and stalked away to lean against the wall, her forehead touching the smooth, cold surface. Her pulse pounded in her head, the sounds around her so loud, distinct, almost ear-shattering, and yet blending together into one monotonous mass of noise. Her body felt numb and only the convulsion of her stomach remained. She squeezed her eyes shut; it was too bright, far too bright.

She should have stopped this. She should have prevented this. She'd known he was in danger. There had to have been more that she could have done, maybe tell the captain, or at least the sergeant. They could have put Benson into protective custody or something, and then...

Lily steadied herself against the wall, her knees weak.

No. She could have said something, but it wouldn't have changed a thing. She'd warned Benson and she'd tried to find out who'd sent the warning. Outside of outright shadowing Benson and forcing him to stay beside her at all times, there'd been nothing. Even he hadn't taken the threat seriously. And now he was dead.

"Hey, you okay?" Bailee stood beside her, holding out a bottle of still water.

Lily accepted it gratefully and took a drink from it, before wiping away the beads of sweat that had formed on her forehead.

"Ugh, ignore me. I don't know why I asked." Bailee grimaced, the concerned frown never quite disappearing as she watched Lily.

"I," Lily said, surprised that she could find her voice. "I'm okay. I just needed a moment."

She took a deep breath and got back on her feet. Her head still felt faint, and her stomach was doing summersaults, but she was a detective. Her partner had just been murdered. She had a job to do.

Crossing over to the sergeant, she finally took in the rest of the apartment. Beat cops had sectioned off the area, some standing guard by the door to ensure no one coming in or leaving without permission. Benson's body lay in the center of the living room on his carpet, a spray of blood across his table, TV and wall, which Chuck was inspecting at the moment. Judging by that, Benson had been sitting on the couch when he'd been attacked from behind, possibly watching that movie he'd been talking about wanting to see.

Lily came to a halt beside the sergeant, by the windows. They'd been closed but not locked. Anyone could push them open from the outside with ease. And with Benson sitting with his back to the window, the deed could have been done quickly and effortlessly.

She cleared her throat, hoping her voice would continue to follow her command. "Think we can find some security footage for the street outside?"

She'd glimpsed a camera mounted on the wall of the opposite building guarding the back entrance of a questionable establishment in the alleyway.

"You get on that, Detective. Make this your highest priority. You can pass your open cases to Clifford. I want to know who did this," he growled, anger blazing in his eyes. "Don't hesitate to pull the others in if you need. Detective Benson spoke highly of you, *vouched* for you, even. Don't disappoint him."

This was the highest level of trust in her abilities the sarge had shown since she'd arrived in the city, but she couldn't bring herself to be happy about it. Not under these circumstances. Not when her friend was lying dead on the floor only a few meters away. When she'd already failed him.

"Of course," she said, doing her best to keep the shake out of her voice. Then she grew silent. She didn't know what else to say. It was as though the words had left her.

The sergeant nodded and brushed past her, leaving the room, only stopping briefly by the door to say a few words to Chuck and one of the beat cops, judging by the brief glances her way, telling them that they were to report to Lily on this matter.

Turning back to the window, Lily closed her eyes for two moments, calmed her breathing, forcing herself to inhale and exhale slowly. Another person might have cried and wanted to be alone. But Lily's eyes were dry, and when she opened them again after her exercise, they were full of fire and determination. She had a case to solve and bring her friend justice.

**7 April,
8:37 p.m.
Saoirse**

It was easy enough to find a vantage point from which Saoirse could look directly into Benny's apartment on the roof of the opposite building. Watching the sergeant and Detective Rose inspect the window, it seemed they assumed that the culprit had entered the apartment through there, but if it had been Saoirse, she knew she'd have had a sharpshooter aim from here. If Benny had left the window open to air out his place, it would've been easy. Forensics would be able to tell soon enough, but Saoirse wanted to get a start on investigating the incident.

Talitha and Mike were watching the building's front entrance to keep a log of the police comings and goings for her. Unfortunately, by the time Mike had come to tell them of Benson's death, they'd already been busy at work, so Saoirse hadn't had the chance to take a look in the apartment herself. The view from here allowed for a few small deductions, but nothing definitive. If there'd been a shooter on this roof, they hadn't left any evidence of their presence. All Saoirse had found on her small round up here had been a sun-bleached snack bar wrapper and a used condom, not exactly items assassins would typically leave behind at a scene.

Saoirse watched Rose collect herself while facing the window, taking a few deep breaths, her eyes closed, her skin a pallor that almost matched Saoirse's own easily burnt complexion.

There's a good chance she's blaming herself, Saoirse thought. After all, she'd received Saoirse's note with the warning, and she'd been taking it as seriously as Saoirse had hoped she would. But it evidently hadn't been enough.

Saoirse had been hoping that the note had been overly cautious of her. That Carlton didn't want Benson dead quite enough to order another hit. But clearly, she'd underestimated him.

She bit her lip, her nostrils flaring in anger. She'd refused the contract for a reason. And Carlton had no idea what he'd unleashed. He hadn't even bothered to make it look like an accident. He *wanted* her to know he'd taken matters into his own hands.

But why?

To tell her that he would no longer be requiring her services? To inform her that his grand offer of O'Shea's legacy had run its course and wouldn't be renewed?

No.

He needn't have bothered with either one. There were different reasons at play here.

Saoirse watched the goings on of the apartment for a while longer, but as nothing worth knowing seemed to come to light there, she eventually left, jumping across to the roof of the adjacent building and climbing down its fire escape hurriedly. Heading back to grab her bike from Lysander's backyard, she phoned Mike to let him and Talitha know they could clear out as well.

It looked like she was going to crash a certain someone's lunch meeting tomorrow and demand some answers. And, depending on whether she liked those answers, get some retribution. When good people like Benny were killed, people took notice. *Saoirse took notice*. And affront.

Torn between feeling angry and full of regrets, Saoirse took to the night on her motorbike, racing through the streets and out into the darkness, leaving the city lights behind until she made it to the open road where she needed to pay attention to nothing other than the wind tearing at her clothing and the wisps of her hair peeking out from under her helmet.

She drove straight to her favorite spot — one of the overgrown, grassy hills bordering the coastline north of the city. Out here with the diminished light pollution, the night sky sparkled with all its might as myriads of stars watched over the city.

Her city.

She might not have been born there, or even lived there for as much as half her life, but it was her city all the same. And Carlton was going to poison it, she could feel it. His way of doing things, the underhandedness, the business-like attitude… she didn't like it. Sure, it was typical of the powerful men in the underworld, and the other Five were no exception to that rule, but they'd adapted to Saoirse's rules to create balance in the city, allowing each of them to prosper without suffocating the city with ideals of grandeur and megalomania. Each of them *cared* for the city in their own way, for their own reasons. Carlton didn't. If he did, he wouldn't have had Benson killed. Though, Saoirse had to admit to herself as she let herself plop into the meadow covered in blooming flowers—all appearing grey in the dark of night—she didn't actually know for certain that Carlton was behind it. So far, it was no more than a gut feeling, as though the whispers of the breeze brushing through the grass and the murmur of the waves crashing on the shore were telling her.

Well, gut feeling and circumstantial evidence, she supposed. She was glad she'd listened to her instincts before and sent Rose that message, but she regretted not taking action herself. She'd liked him. He'd been so much fun to tease. She'd respected him, too, and she had no doubt that he'd respected her as well. Something that was hard to come by in the detective department these days. They had a knack for keeping the decent cops at the bottom. Something Saoirse's co-workers encouraged, she knew. They all had moles in the police, and she had a pretty good idea who those moles were. Benson hadn't been one of them. In fact, aside from Rose, he might have been the only detective entirely unconnected to the underworld.

Reminiscing, Saoirse remained in her spot on the meadow looking out at the sea where silver crests of seafoam glittered in the starlight until the first hints of changing light appeared in purple and pink streaks across the horizon in the east.

With a sigh, she stretched her stiff joints and brushed the dirt of her clothes before swinging herself back onto her bike.

Time to teach a man about the rules of her city.

8 April,
8:05 a.m.
<u>**Lily**</u>

With no rest and a lot of emotions pushed down into deep, dark abyss of her mind, with a shiny new lock on the lid, Lily headed into work.

She'd stayed in Benson's apartment for a long time the previous night, imprinting every detail of the layout in her mind, taking notes of anything that stood out to her and giving instructions to everyone still working. She'd been the last to leave, after the clean-up crew, before leaving two cops on guard duty who were to ensure that no one disturbed the flat for the next twenty-four hours in case she wanted to come back to check something else.

Bailee was supposed to end her shift and leave things to Chuck, who was apparently in charge of the night shift this week, but from what Lily understood, Bailee had insisted on staying in the lab overnight as well to help with the evidence. Appreciative of both their efforts, Lily had brought in coffee for them. The fancy kind.

She'd intended on heading straight for their

lab but was stopped short as soon as she'd entered through the front door of the bullpen. Unlike normally when she was one of the first to arrive, the detectives were already gathered, any conversation stopping when she walked in as every head turned her way.

Word spread fast.

Undoubtedly, they'd all received a call from the sergeant the previous night, informing them of Benson's passing, and, judging by the way they were watching her, that she'd been assigned the task of uncovering the culprit. Even Rutch was there, his bony features and hollow eyes pinning Lily in place.

The sergeant stepped out of the captain's office, looking straight past all the other detectives at Lily. "Rose. Good, you're here. Captain wants to speak with you."

Obediently, Lily walked up to the door he held open for her and went inside ahead of him. Captain Miller, a rather portly older man who, Lily was half certain, wore a toupee made from wet dog, considering the smell, watched her sit down with his small, blue eyes.

"Detective Rose," he said, his voice squeakier than one would imagine for a man looking like him, "Sergeant Whitman has informed me of Detective Benson's passing. Of course I will arrange for a memorial service, but I understand that he took you under his wing here."

He glanced at the sergeant as if to seek

confirmation.

Lily straightened her back defiantly. "We were friends," she corrected him. "And partners."

She left out the fact that this partnership had officially barely aged by twenty-four hours. The captain likely didn't know that anyway, and the sergeant wouldn't bring it up right now.

The captain nodded, somewhat absentmindedly. He took some papers with shaking hands and began straightening them.

"I, uh," he cleared his throat, "I hear Sergeant Whitman has put you on the case of finding out who's behind this atrocity."

Lily nodded.

"So, it goes without saying that you will have any and all assets at your disposal in the pursuit of the truth. Within reason, that is. This case has absolutely priority to your other tasks," he continued. "Dismissed."

"Thank you, sir." Lily left the office, closely followed by the sergeant.

"I recommend being discreet about anything you do in this case," he muttered to her, before brushing past her.

His warning wasn't lost on Lily. If she followed the tracks and attracted too much attention getting the truth, there was no telling if the culprit wouldn't decide to take her out as well to keep her quiet. The dead didn't tell tales, after all.

Making her way to the forensics lab, she began to wonder if that was the real reason why she, instead of the other detectives, had been put on this particular case. Because the sergeant wouldn't consider her too big a loss.

Well, whether that was the case or not, she was grateful for it. She wouldn't know what to do with all that anger boiling in her stomach if she couldn't throw herself into this investigation.

"Morning," she announced as she pushed the door to the forensics lab open with her free hand. "I bring the blood of the gods."

"My exhausted titan-self thanks you," Bailee sighed, crossing the room over to her and gratefully accepting two of the three cups. Her bloodshot eyes had deep, dark rings shadowing them, and her hair was messy. Lily hadn't looked into the mirror before leaving her flat this morning, but she dared to venture that she didn't look much different. As she'd left Benson's apartment quite late, she'd had little more time than to head home, get changed, and pace about her living room half a million times before coming back here. The only reason why she hadn't come in earlier had been because she hadn't been certain she could speak without screaming.

"Chuck?" Bailee offered them the other cup and they took it gratefully, looking as overworked as Bailee, but not quite as tired, since they'd been assigned to the night shift and had slept more recently.

Lily waited for both of them to take a sip of their coffees before asking her burning question. "So whatcha got for me?"

"The bullet was fired from pretty close range," Chuck began. "A handgun, 38 caliber bullets. Whoever it was must've been pretty athletic."

"What makes you say that?" Lily asked.

Bailee raised one eyebrow. "We know the culprit must've come in through the window, because otherwise Benson would've seen 'em, and did you take a look at the ledge? Pretty difficult to get up there, even using the fire escapes."

Lily nodded. Bailee was right. The fire escape went to the bedroom window, which had been firmly locked, and had been very difficult to pry open when she'd tried, proving that it hadn't been used very often, at the very least not recently. Bits of rust had trickled down when she'd moved it. So either the killer had come in through the living room window, or they'd already been there, waiting for Benson. But even then, they'd had to have left through the window, since the front door had been locked from the inside, the key still in the lock. And leaving out that window would require a climb up the wall about seven or eight feet above the window to a narrow ledge barely spanning two inches which they'd had to have followed until reaching the fire escape, which also hadn't been fully functional, as Lily had found out. The ladder, which ought to have been moveable to get closer to ground, had been rusted through as well. Moving it even an inch had required considerable force and noise, which implied that the culprit must have jumped. Or gone through one of the other apartments.

The reports regarding door duty were waiting for her on her desk. She'd briefly glanced at them in passing. Perhaps they could tell her more about who she should be talking to.

**8 April,
8:21 a.m.
Saoirse**

When Saoirse finally made it back to her flat, she was greeted by the sight of Natalia and Mike nervously pacing.

Both of them were so preoccupied by their fretting, that they didn't even notice her arrival. Saoirse decided to wait a moment, watching with interest how Mike, taking sharp turns on the spot, appeared to be walking a trail into her carpet while Natalia commuted between the living room window and the bar, either looking outside with worry, or into one of the golden and clear liquids in the row of bottles.

Eventually, Saoirse cleared her throat to draw their attention. This was clearly beyond worrying about a detective's death. She was fairly certain that she cared about it an awful lot more than either one of them did.

"What's going on?" she asked.

"Saoirse, you're back!" Natalia exclaimed, rushing toward her and wrapping her slender arms around Saoirse.

Saoirse gave her a short squeeze. "Sure am.

Needed to take care of something." She looked to Mike who remained a respectful distance away from them. "So, what's happening?"

"Someone's going around town saying it was you," Mike said, hesitantly.

Saoirse shrugged. "So? It's a reasonable assumption to make if you don't know me. I'm expecting our friends from the precinct to come knocking within a day or two either way."

Natalia peeled herself from Saoirse, glancing at Mike uncomfortably. "That's not all."

"No?" Saoirse's eyebrows shot up curiously. "What else?"

"There are whispers of ghosts," Natalia said, almost echoing the words Lysander had said to Saoirse not even twenty-four hours earlier.

"Ghosts," Saoirse repeated.

Natalia nodded. "Apparently, an older gentleman with an Irish accent is going around town, talking about taking back the 'Vixen's' operations."

Saoirse dropped into one of the couches. "Let me guess, the description matches the picture you saw of O'Shea?"

Mike and Natalia nodded simultaneously. Saoirse closed her eyes for a moment.

What kind of fool did Carlton take her for? He seriously hired someone to impersonate her mentor just to get under her skin? No. Not just that.

Her eyes snapped open. Carlton wanted to

push her out. He was trying to claim her enterprise by way of proxy. Had that been the reason for the hit on Benson as well? If she'd taken his bait, he could've tried to ensure she'd be captured in the act. Now he opted for pinning the blame on her to get her out of the picture so he could swoop in with his make-believe Silver Fox.

Carlton was pressing her buttons, trying to get her to react. Regardless of her awareness of the provocation and what he was likely hoping to achieve with it, none of what she'd learned deterred her from keeping up her prior plan of crashing his luncheon. If anything, her plan solidified like cement around a man's feet before he was thrown in the ocean.

Carlton wanted her to react? Fine. She'd react alright.

Natalia and Mike were still looking at her with concern. She'd almost forgotten about them.

"You can ignore him. O'Shea is dead; this is nothing but an impostor, set up by Carlton I'd wager. If you hear someone spreading the rumors, set them straight, but no need to follow up on them. They'll come to a rest on their own soon enough."

Mike nodded uncertainly.

"What about the dead detective?" Natalia asked. "Won't they come for you?"

Saoirse finally smirked and gently cupped her

lover's cheek in one hand. "Are you worried for my safety?" she purred.

"A little, yes."

"Aww. Well don't you worry. They will come for me sooner or later, but it'll be just like it always is and I'll be out within twenty-four hours." Revising that calculation mentally after taking into consideration the anger some of those law enforcers might be feeling, Saoirse added, "Or perhaps forty-eight."

She softly kissed Natalia on hungry lips. When they parted, Saoirse leaned forward, resting her weight on Natalia's shoulders. "But for now, I need some sleep so I can think straight when meeting the city's newest wrongdoer."

"Saoirse," Natalia chided, her voice full of warmth and concern. "You need to look after yourself more." She began stroking the back of Saoirse's head as she spoke, her voice a little susurrus, lulling Saoirse into relaxation. "You can't continue on like this, catching no more than a few hours of sleep here and there. You need some form of a real schedule in your life, or you'll be folding up before you know it."

"I agree," Mike chimed in, stepping closer.

Saoirse could almost smell his aftershave.

As her two most trusted companions and confidants, Saoirse knew that they wouldn't be saying any of this if they weren't truly concerned. They both understood the nature of her work, of all their work, really, and they knew that hers wasn't a life that allowed for a nine-to-five mindset.

"You guys worry too much," she nevertheless said, straightening her back with a cocky smile. "I'm doing peachy!"

Mike only raised an eyebrow at her, while Natalia cocked her head to the side and asked, "When was the last time you ate anything?"

Saoirse stared into the air for a moment, attempting to find a truthful answer to the question. She hadn't eaten anything this morning yet, of course, and she wasn't exactly feeling hungry, so she'd be skipping this meal in favor of the lunch date she would be crashing, where she was hoping to steal some prawns from a certain someone's salad, and she hadn't eaten anything at *Gonzalo's Place* when talking to Talitha. Before that, she'd been busy playing with Detective Rose, and before that...

Natalia sighed. "Don't tell me it was our breakfast yesterday."

Saoirse's gaze brightened and she pointed at Natalia. "Yes! That was it! I *knew* I ate something yesterday."

She gave them both a winning smile, but they didn't appear to share her enthusiasm.

Holding her wide grin for a moment longer, Saoirse finally relented when Natalia's stern expression didn't fade, and she pulled her lover into an embrace.

"I'll do better just as soon as this is all sorted

out," she whispered. "I promise."

Natalia nodded, but Saoirse knew her well enough to know that she wasn't reassured. If she was being truthful to herself, Saoirse didn't even know if she believed her promise herself.

**8 April,
8:48 a.m.
Lily**

After talking through the details of Benson's death with Bailee and Chuck—a conversation during which Lily forced herself to detach herself from her own emotions completely, a trick she'd learned when one of her colleagues back on the West Coast had been shot—Lily headed back to her desk. One of the younger detectives was waiting for her there. Clifford, if she remembered right.

"The sergeant assigned your current cases to me," he said, by way of explanation.

"Right." She sat down and reached for the pile of notes she'd taken that hadn't made it into the official reports. Then she hesitated. Yes, she had other things on her mind right now, and yes, she really did want to put all her energy into finding Benson's killer, but... it felt wrong just passing up her cases like this. People were relying on her to solve their issues, or at the very least, do her best to try.

She'd seen how these kinds of cases had been handled before she'd arrived. And most of them barely made it into a report, never mind actual action. Thinking of that happening again to the people she'd spoken to, made her stomach churn.

But it was true that she couldn't do both. Not if she really wanted to solve this. Then again, this detective was still fresh on the job, compared to her. He'd only been doing it a few months, while she had several years back on the West Coast under her belt. Perhaps he'd just been strung along by the other, more experienced detectives in this precinct, and, if that was the case, perhaps she could set him straight.

Slowly, severely, she handed him her notes.

"I'll send you an email about what you should investigate first and about what's going on. Everything else is in here." She tapped on the notebook. "Also, I will be checking in on you, so you better make sure to do things right."

She watched him sternly, hoping her glare wasn't too menacing, but firm enough to scare him into complying. He was a pale young man, and his hands were almost shaking when he took the notebook off her. If Lily's guess was right, learning of another detective's death had hit him hard, even though she didn't think that he'd been all that close to Benson. Still, he nodded.

Lily sighed. "Look," she said uncomfortably. "This sort of thing... It's not common, but it does happen. It's why we work in teams. Just… don't overthink it. Okay?"

Clifford nodded again. "Thanks," he mumbled. "Um… Can I…" He looked over his shoulder to the other detectives and leaned in closer to Lily. "Can I get back to you if I have any follow-up questions?"

Blinking at him in baffled surprise, Lily took a beat to understand the hidden question. Then she granted him a smile. "You have any trouble, you've got my number."

He nodded gratefully and turned away, leaving her to finally look at the reports left for her by the beat cops on door duty in Benson's building.

Even a meticulously thorough reading and re-reading of the files didn't throw up any useful information, however. None of the neighbors had heard, or seen, anything. That in itself was already quite informative because, from what Lily could tell, the building's fire escape wasn't exactly silent. Meaning that the chances of the culprit having taken that way were pretty low. At least, on the way in. After hearing the shot in their building, none of the tenants would have paid attention to a few sounds outside. This led her to believe that her hunch about the culprit having waited for Benson in the apartment might be right. And it didn't seem impossible that they may have even used the front door to get in. None of the neighbors had keys to his apartment, and Lily hadn't been close enough with him to know if he'd had friends, or a housekeeper, he may have given spares to, but she had a feeling she knew who might have some more insight. Men got talkative when they drank, after all.

Taking one last glance over the reports, Lily got to her feet and pulled on her jacket while she mentally prepared herself to give Mindy some bad news.

Samson's Crib was still closed when Lily arrived. No surprise there. It was barely ten a.m., but somehow, that hadn't factored into Lily's decision to come here. Probably because it hadn't registered. The lack of sleep made her wired, and she knew she was running on fumes. Time had lost meaning, and the only things allowing her to function were strong coffee and the need to keep busy. Though considering how her plans would have to wait, perhaps she could add something to eat into the mix of energy suppliers.

She wasn't hungry, but she'd been on the job for long enough to know that it didn't matter. Sooner or later she would need the energy, and it was best she prepared for that. She'd seen enough newbies run themselves dizzy after witnessing something unsavory; she knew better than to follow their example. If you couldn't eat, you couldn't work effectively, so you ate, even if you had to force the food down.

Keeping that in mind, Lily turned away from *Samson's Crib*, and headed to one of the cafés nearby, ordering black coffee and a pretzel to take away. For a moment, she considered the cream cheese bagel sitting in the display, but she was going to have a hard enough time eating anything, never mind something that reminded her of Benson.

She pulled her wallet from the pocket of her jacket to pay, but before she could open it, a folded piece of paper that had been stuck to the wallet's outside fell to the ground. Confused, Lily leaned down to pick it up and flipped it open. It was a list of names.

The list Bailee had given her of the people whose handwriting matched the very note warning her to look out for Benson. Truthfully, with everything that had happened, she'd forgotten she even had that. More than that, she'd forgotten that she hadn't actually looked at it yet.

Staring at the names now, one of them jumped out at her.

Saoirse Kennedy.

The barista meaningfully cleared their throat, raising a pierced eyebrow at Lily.

"Oh, sorry!" Lily jumped up, stuffing the list of names back into her pocket and paid, before heading out of the café and back into the street. Despite this city's severe lack of nice park arrangements in this part of town, Lily found a place to sit in peace not far away, on a currently dead construction site, amidst concrete pipes.

Setting her breakfast aside, she pulled out the paper again.

Saoirse Kennedy.

Lily didn't believe in coincidences. Coincidences were just useful excuses for perps who tried to talk their way out of a crime by being cute. However, in her experience, there was no such thing as coincidence. At least not in this kind of thing.

But she'd been following Kennedy around town not even an hour before Benson had been found dead. And, to add the cherry on top, it hadn't been that far from his apartment. Barely a ten-minute walk at a leisurely pace.

Lily had suggested to Benson that Kennedy might want to take revenge on him, yet he had waved her suggestion away, even laughing at it. He hadn't believed Kennedy was the kind of person who'd go about her business this way. And, after studying her files and seeing the way she strutted around town like she owned it, Lily was inclined to agree. Or would have been, if these two very impressive *coincidences* weren't staring her in the face.

Kennedy liked to play games. That much she had made clear. So had this been a game? With Kennedy and Lily as the players, and Benson's life the prize?

Anger surged in Lily's chest, filling her lungs with enough fire she felt she might turn into a dragon. If this had been Kennedy's game, that woman was going to pay dearly.

Lily's hands clenched into fists, crumpling the paper, but she wasn't far enough gone in her anger to dismiss the other names. Erratically, she pushed the paper back into her pocket and grabbed her coffee and pretzel.

She was a cop. And she'd do her job properly, even if every instinct she had was screaming at her that Kennedy was involved in this in one way or another. She needed to properly investigate, instead of jumping to conclusions.

Walking fast, she passed a homeless woman on the way back to the precinct. Lily glanced down at the pathetic cup with a few coins of change and the cardboard asking in large letters for money for food. Lily pushed the untouched pretzel into the woman's hands and chucked some coins into the cup. She contemplated for a moment as the woman bowed her head several times in thanks.

"Say, do you know Saoirse Kennedy?" Lily asked.

After a moment's hesitation, the woman shook her head hurriedly, but Lily had seen the startled look in her eyes.

"I see," she said. "In that case, have a good day. I hope you'll find a warm place to sleep tonight."

The woman bowed her head, and Lily moved on. Street folk were incredibly useful informants and it always paid to give them some small tokens like pretzels, even when there was no immediate gain. Besides, with the rage burning in her chest, food could wait a little while. Yet no sooner had she finished the thought, that she changed her mind, pulling back her earlier rationalization.

Sighing, Lily gave in and decided to step into the stereotype of cops with donuts.

Catnapping for two hours was all Saoirse managed to do before her inner clock forced her awake again. Time to prepare.

Since she didn't exactly have a fully formalized plan for her lunch-bust yet, she needed to be ready for anything. And that included being there early so she could have the best vantagepoint over the situation without being seen.

No doubt Carlton knew what she looked like. The chances of Jean hanging around in the shadows for protection were also quite high, if Saoirse pegged Carlton right. More than anything, she needed to blend in, without losing any of her mobility. In the end, she settled for what she liked to call the "spoiled-heiress-look". It involved a lot more colorful make-up than she usually wore, an elaborate-looking hairdo involving a large—and more importantly sharp—hairpin, a heavy, but small purse, just big enough to hold something like a gun, though she wasn't planning on taking one, and a knee-length, lilac dress with a skirt that fanned out easily and no sleeves. For shoes, she picked a black pair of stiletto heels she knew she could run in, if necessary—a requirement for all of her footwear, really.

"Are you sure this will work?" Natalia asked, concerned as she helped Saoirse put the pin into place in her hair.

Saoirse nodded with a smirk. "You'd be surprised how little most people focus on what you actually look like. It's the general appearance they notice, not the details. If he does spot me, he'll likely just have the feeling that I look familiar but shouldn't be able to immediately place me."

Saoirse thought of her usual work attire of pants, her hair loose, a T-shirt, and a black leather jacket, along with thin black eyeliner and red lipstick, and looked into the mirror. She quite appreciated this look. It suited her. The fancy flourishes accentuated her natural beauty quite well and gave her charisma of a different kind. The kind she was going for. Powerful, yet spoiled. The kind of person who could send people reeling with empty threats. One that would almost be expected to make a scene. It was perfect.

She smiled at her lover. "Time to go."

"Be careful."

"Always am."

Natalia was about to reply but was

interrupted by Mike coming in the door. He stopped dead at the sight of Saoirse. "Holy fuck!"

Saoirse smirked. "Yes?"

"You look," his gaze wandered down to her bare legs and back up to her face, "incredible."

"She always does," Natalia agreed, smiling softly, if, Saoirse found, a little sadly.

"Nat." Saoirse took Natalia's face in her hands, peering into it with concern. "It'll be alright. I promise."

Natalia cast her eyes to the floor, a conflicted expression on her face. Saoirse knew that look. It pained her heart, but she knew what was going to happen soon. And there was nothing she could do to change it, except completely give up the life she was leading, which would have meant changing who she was.

"I'm sorry," Natalia whispered, tears coming to her eyes.

Saoirse shook her head and pulled Natalia close, holding her tightly. "No. No. It's all right. I understand."

"Um," Mike interrupted, puzzled. "Don't we ... need to go?"

Natalia nodded and pushed herself away from Saoirse, smiling. "Yes, you do. Be safe."

Saoirse took a moment to study her face, then nodded. "I'll see you later."

Finding out which table was reserved for

Carlton's meeting was easy as pie. Mike disguised himself as a waiter, pulling the maître's attention away from his book of reservations just long enough for Saoirse to glance at it. She then used her disguise to the fullest extent to gain a seat in the perfect spot to oversee their meeting without being easily seen by throwing a tantrum. Meanwhile, Mike placed a bug in the bouquet of flowers sitting in the table reserved for Carlton. Saoirse's pearl earrings were the receiving end, sending the sound via vibrations through her ear's cartilage to her eardrum without making an audible noise to anyone else.

While waiting for Carlton to show up, Saoirse kept an eye on the shadows in the room, and took note of all the waiters' faces, lest Jean should have the same disguise as Mike. She also scanned the other patrons and found that she recognized a lot of them as the city's elite. Mostly, it was rich businesspeople, but there were a few exceptions here and there, too. Some from the underworld, others from the entertainment industry.

It was around the time that her shrimp salad arrived that the table she was observing was filled. There was Dirk Dunst, the CEO of Verse, a well-known figure in this town, and then, there was Carlton, looking much like the photo Talitha had shown her, though perhaps a little rounder in the middle.

They arrived simultaneously, which didn't sit right with Saoirse. Coincidence? Unlikely.

Saoirse listened to their conversation, at first mundane as could be, covering the weather, fires on the West Coast, and discussions of European politics, but finally, they moved onto the core of the matter.

"Let me just say it straight, Dirk." Carlton said, his voice a pleasant baritone. He was undeniably American, but Saoirse found it difficult to place his accent. It wasn't distinct enough for any specific place, which matched what Talitha had told her about the man moving around a lot. "I want to invest in your company."

Dunst hesitated. "So you mentioned. But what exactly did you have in mind?"

Carlton sighed amiably. "Do you want to jump straight to numbers, or would you like to hear the general idea first?"

"Let's cut to the chase. Time is money, and I don't like it being wasted."

"Indeed. Well, my suggestion is simple. It essentially translates to me buying thirty percent of your company's shares in exchange for three hundred million dollars."

Dunst audibly sucked in his breath. Even Saoirse was startled by the number. Sure, the company was up and coming, ever-growing, in fact, but three hundred million was still a very high investment. Outrageous, even. Then again, with thirty percent of shares it wasn't going to be that difficult for Carlton to, over time, acquire the remainder of the shares to reach a majority shareholder status. And with that, he'd be essentially owning the company. It was risky, but it could pay off for both of them. Especially for Carlton.

While it was interesting to witness this potential business transaction, it wasn't what Saoirse had come here for. She wanted to find out if Carlton was indeed the culprit behind Benny's murder. But she knew better than to come for him here and now. No. She needed to lay low, until he was leaving, and follow. Find out where he stayed, perhaps catch him unaware along the way, so she could temporarily spirit him away to ask some questions. And take appropriate measures, of course.

Just as she finished making her decision, Saoirse caught wind of a familiar smell. Cedarwood and cigars.

Establishments such as this were often frequented by men who enjoyed the occasional smoke, but the scent was more intense than if it simply clung onto a person's clothing. No, this was a fragrance that had become part of the essence of a person. And Saoirse had only ever known one person with this specific intoxicating intensity of the mix. The last time she'd smelled it, she had put it down to memories surfacing and fooling her senses, but now, with everything that was going on, she just knew it had to be the imposter. If he was as convincing as the whole city claimed, he'd have O'Shea's token smell. He'd have to.

Saoirse whipped her head around to scan the faces of the people moving nearby, waiters and guests alike. No trace, but the scent was still lingering, though it was beginning to disperse.

Leaving her half-eaten prawn salad behind, along with a bank note that covered more than her expenses and a generous tip, Saoirse sauntered over to Mike, who was standing by the wall, a clean, white towel across his arm.

"Excuse me, sir," she trilled. "Where may I find the powder room?"

If Mike was confused by her unplanned contact, he didn't show it, instead playing the perfect waiter, and pointing her into the direction of the restrooms in a lowered voice.

"Why thank you, aren't you a dear!" Saoirse patted Mike's cheek with one hand while handing him her earpiece with the other and added in a lower voice, "Stay on Carlton."

Mike gave her a bow, and she pranced away, in the direction of the bathrooms, consistently following the scent of cigar and cedarwood. It led her past the bathrooms and to the service doors, and with one final glance back toward Carlton, Saoirse pushed open the doors to follow the ghost of O'Shea.

Knowing that she had at most a few seconds before some of the waiters or cooks in the kitchen registered that she wasn't meant to be here, Saoirse strode on, confident like someone who didn't expect to be questioned, whisking past the rows of cooks and waiters, steering toward the door in the back she had just seen swing shut.

The scent was gone, overpowered by the many notes of spices, oils, and fish that was so typical for any restaurant kitchen. But even though Saoirse had no more trail to follow, she was pulled forward by instinct. Fake O'Shea had passed through here. She knew it. And he wanted her to follow. Why else would he have made his presence so obvious and moved past her table? She knew by now that Carlton didn't work with amateurs. Fake O'Shea wouldn't be an exception to that rule.

"Hey!" one of the cooks finally shouted, striding toward her. "What are you doing? You can't—"

Saoirse cut off his words by passing through the far door without so much as glancing at him, and into a service hallway. There was no sight of fake O'Shea on either side, and her nostrils were still too much filled with the scent from the kitchen to determine if he had left more of a trail here. Time to follow her gut.

She turned left. Most people had a tendency to turn right when they came to a forking, but

O'Shea wasn't most people. And if this was a good imitation, then he wasn't either.

There was no more need to keep up appearances here, so she hurried down the corridor, just short of a sprint, to reach the bend and see what lay beyond.

She reached it in time to see yet another door shut and sprinted to it, pushing it open with much more force than was strictly necessary. She was looking out into a parking lot and saw a person who matched O'Shea's shape wearing the same kind of hat as he used to wear as they put a black car into gear and whisked out of the car park.

Watching it go, Saoirse cursed under her breath. She should have been faster.

But why had he led her here?

She allowed the door to fall back into its lock behind her and studied her surroundings. There was nothing special about it. Some employee cars were scattered on the parking lot, keeping as far away from the foul-smelling bins as possible, but there was nothing else of note here.

Which meant that if it wasn't a matter of where to go, it had been a matter of where to leave. Saoirse cursed herself this time and hurried around the outside of the building to the valet parking and back inside the hotel's restaurant.

Carlton was gone.

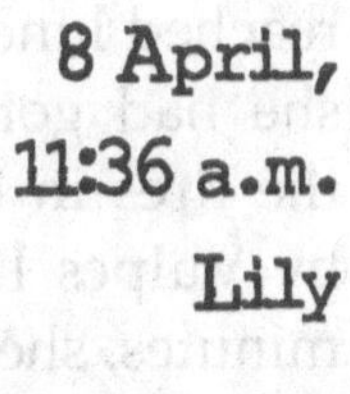

Back at the precinct, Lily decided to take a step away from her suspicions about Kennedy and look into the other names on the list. She was nothing if not thorough, after all. Or tried to be, at the very least.

Including Kennedy, there were eleven names on the list, which didn't exactly fill Lily with a lot of hope. She still entered all of them into the system one by one. She soon found that three of the names were currently incarcerated, and four were dead. Which left three more potential writers aside from Kennedy. None of them were criminals Lily had ever encountered, so the chances of them seeking her out and breaking into her apartment to leave her the warning were pretty slim. Which brought her back to Kennedy. Kennedy had seen Lily and Benson together, had spoken to them both. It had to have been her. Nothing else made any sense. Nevertheless, Lily dutifully put out a call on the other three, so she could question them if they were encountered.

By the time she was done, it had barely reached lunch time, so she pulled up the records she had gone through with Benson before, on the fires in Kennedy's properties after the sales by Vulpes Ltd. After staring at them for a few minutes, she pulled up the company's website in her browser. Even though there was a whole page dedicated to the company's history and mission, spread out across multiple paragraphs, timelines, and photographs, there was actually very little information on it. It read as though it had been written by a politician.

There were no pictures of the CEO, Sinead Norsekey, of course. And there was no mention of who had set up the company originally. However, it did say that the company had been founded about twenty years ago, which meant that it couldn't have been done by Kennedy. She would have still been a child then.

Lily glanced at the addresses she'd shown Benson. The ones that had been in Vulpes' hands for significant amounts of time without being listed. She was certain that she'd be able to find Kennedy under one of those addresses. Perhaps that should be her first step—bring Kennedy in for questioning. It didn't seem likely that the criminal would skip town, considering her history. Still the sergeant's warning rang in her head to keep things about Kennedy on the down low if she wanted to avoid a hit.

Lily sighed and pushed the papers away,

burying her face in her arms on the desk for a moment. After counting to thirty-seven in her head, she straightened her back and took a deep breath. She was thinking herself into boxes.

She'd make a few more calls to try to find out anything, and then she'd head over to *Samson's Crib* and see what Mindy might be able to tell her.

Only a few minutes had passed, but Lily felt reenergized.

Her calls hadn't brought her any steps closer to finding Benson's killer, but they had uncovered something else: She now knew the name of Vulpes Ltd's founder. A certain person by the name of Graham O'Shea. A quick search in the database had brought up references to a large number of cases, all dated back ten years or more. The timing had seemed a little too coincidental to Lily, and the references — numerous yet ambiguous — reminding her a little too much of Kennedy. So now Lily was rummaging through old case files, and her first suspicions were confirmed. Not only had O'Shea disappeared right around the time Saoirse Kennedy had shown up on the scene in this city, based on other case files and photographs therein, he bore a remarkable resemblance to the third man in the photo of the city official she believed Kennedy had killed ten years ago.

Lily siphoned through papers and files,

completely losing all sense of time. Who was O'Shea? And, more importantly, who was he in relation to Kennedy? He was old enough to be her father, perhaps even grandfather, and they both appeared to have Irish roots. The way this whole situation looked... Lily dared to wager that Kennedy had stepped in as some form of successor to O'Shea.

Which made his disappearance only more suspicious.

If Kennedy had been his protégée, he shouldn't have vanished entirely. Not as instantly as this. Which left Lily with the notion that he may have died. And that, perhaps, Saoirse Kennedy knew more about it than someone with a clear conscience might.

Lily had begun to reason with herself to talk herself out of the idea that Kennedy had been the one responsible for Benson's death, if only because he hadn't believed it, but now, looking at a picture showing her with two other men who had both vanished or died, all of that reluctance was washed away.

Kennedy was involved.

And Lily knew just where to look for her.

Determined, Lily got to her feet, and a wave of dizziness washed over her, painfully reminding her that she had given away her pretzel and hadn't thought to ingest anything more nutritious than some coffee and a power drink since. Right.

Perhaps she could allow herself a moment of reprieve which included food before potentially walking into a den of wolves. And she could combine it with her planned visit to *Samson's Crib*. A quick glance at her watch reassured her that the bar ought to be open by now for the early drinkers.

Lily paused by her desk, glancing at the other detectives, briefly considering if she ought to request backup for her visit at Kennedy's door, but decided against it. It was risky, yes, but what she'd seen of Kennedy wasn't as openly hostile as that. Shooting a police officer in the light of day just wasn't her style. It was too easy to track. The back of the head in her own home might be more like it.

**8 April
12:53 p.m.
Saoirse**

Trusting that Mike was still on Carlton's track, Saoirse headed home. She couldn't follow while they were on the move, and she was confident that Mike would inform her the moment he had anything worth reporting.

Mike had taken his own car, so Saoirse was free to use hers to return to the compound housing herself and most of her people. She received a number of appreciative looks on her way through the buildings to her loft, which she soaked in confidently. It almost made her pity that these clothes, while beautiful, weren't exactly the most useful in her line of work. Too flashy, for one thing. Too likely to get in the way, too. But also too likely to catch somewhere and tear, leaving proof of her presence. And that was something she preferred to avoid whenever possible. Sadly, the shoes left prints too easily, since Saoirse had always loved using them as weapons. They were wonderfully lethal on the right pair of feet, used in a nefariously precise manner. She'd only had the chance to prove just how deadly they could be once, with a pair of her deep-red heels. The color had been a good choice, as it turned out.

Still, Saoirse pulled the black heels she wore off her feet and dropped the dress to the ground, changing back into her usual outfit: stretchy, dark trousers with well-gripping boots and a grey T-shirt.

She half regretted that Natalia wasn't around, if only to pull her in for a short embrace and a kiss before she donned her apparel. While Saoirse didn't take a gun, she grabbed a taser and pepper spray—things that if she were to be caught with might warrant some questions, but no more.

Once she had returned to her normal look, Saoirse glanced at her phone. No messages yet. Nevertheless, she headed out and grabbed her bike, leaving the compound. If Carlton kept up appearances, he'd have a residence on the south side of town. She could cut her traveling time by heading that direction instead of waiting for Mike's notification.

She'd only been driving for a few minutes when she felt the expected buzz at her hip. After pulling in at the side of the road, she removed her phone to check the address Mike had sent her. As expected, the south side of town. Pretty far out, too. Evidently, Carlton liked his space.

Saoirse typed back: **On my way.**

Saoirse met up with Mike down an overgrown path cutting through the woods surrounding Carlton's estate. They were close enough to glimpse the large walls from here, but far enough away that the chances of being spotted by any of his personnel or the watching cameras were slim to non-existent.

In order not to be heard arriving, Saoirse had gotten off the bike a mile or so back and had been pushing it through the forest to the agreed meeting spot Mike had sent her. She had considered leaving it back somewhere farther away, but she didn't yet know how fast she might need to make her getaway, and she wasn't going to take any chances with that. Not when she wasn't sure what might be waiting for her.

"Well?" she asked. "What've you got?"

Mike shrugged, his gaze never leaving the gate ahead of them. "The gate's operated by remote, but I managed to catch and copy the signal when he drove in. There's two guards at the front, and at least one more inside. I think there might be dogs, too." He turned to her, concern spread across his face. "You sure you wanna do this?"

Saoirse smirked at him. "You're not gonna tell me you lost your faith in me, are you?"

"Of course not, it's just… This feels off." He rubbed the back of his head.

Saoirse knew what he meant. Since Carlton had undoubtedly sent his fake O'Shea to distract her, it seemed odd that he might not have suspected that Saoirse had back up. Which, in turn, meant that there was a decent chance that he was just waiting for her to make her move, perhaps only hoping to gain some time for *something*.

"Why did you run off at the restaurant?"

Saoirse returned his questioning gaze evenly.

"Chasing old ghosts," she said lightly.

"Ghosts, huh?"

They both turned back to the gate, and Saoirse watched it critically, inspecting how it was fastened to the walls and where the guards were standing. For security personnel, they weren't exactly very alert. Carlton probably didn't get many visitors, invited or otherwise.

"How long does it take for the gate to open?"

Mike sighed. "You're really just going to take the front door approach, aren't you?"

Saoirse flashed him a wide grin. "Have you ever known me to do anything else?" she asked.

"About three seconds all the way."

Which meant that she'd barely need half a second before she'd be able to drive straight through on her bike.

"Can you stop the signal and reverse it at any point during those three seconds?" she asked, her gaze remaining on the gate and the guards. One of them yawned, and the other took an e-reader from his pocket.

"Not sure. Maybe. I can try."

"That's all I ask."

If he could close the gate again before the brutes could follow her, it'd give her an advantage, even though they both carried guns at their hips.

Carlton being still new to town and *mostly* dealing above ground, chances of his mansion being as tech-defensed up as Garrison's were low. Although not impossible.

"Seen the front door?" Saoirse asked. From where they were, they had no eyes on the ground level of the building. One of the upper story windows was opened, however. Useful to know in a pinch.

"Looks like pretty heavy-duty wood. If it's not locked, I reckon you could bust it open though. But it might be reinforced."

Windows were unlikely to work either. So either the door or that upstairs window. Saoirse's gaze flicked back up to it. Announcing her presence at the door could ruin the advantage of surprise if she then still needed to climb up there. But on the other hand, Saoirse had always been a fan of using the front door.

"Let's go for it," she decided.

She pushed her bike onward on the trail, moving as silently as she was able, ducking low, so that her movement wasn't immediately visible, Mike following closely behind her. She determined a path she could bust through without causing damage to her bike or giving the guards enough time to react to her approach and nodded to Mike. He crouched down, moving back into better cover, and she swung herself onto her bike.

"Go!" Mike whisper-shouted, but Saoirse had already seen the first movement of the opening gates. The guards temporarily distracted by the unexpected opening, Saoirse brought the engine roaring to live and shot forward in a straight line toward the gate. Keeping a close eye on how wide the gate was opening, she sped up as quickly as she could and raced through the gap the instant it allowed for it. Going at break-neck speeds up a graveled driveway, Saoirse didn't have the luxury of looking back to see whether Mike had been able to close the gate again. She had to focus much more on keeping balanced, the pebbles shooting up behind her, pelting her back.

Her nerves bare, Saoirse directed the bike onto the grass instead, where she left ugly tire trails on the British lawn, a style of gardening she'd never approved of anyway.

A figure ran out from behind the house, presumably the third guard, and the barking of dogs barely made it above the engine's roar as Saoirse sped up to the mansion's door. She shifted her weight back slightly to bring up the front wheel to get up the few steps and braced for impact...

Which never came. The door swung open in

front of her, forcing her to break hard and spin in circles on the marble floor in the hallway just inside.

After a few moments, she stopped and looked toward the unimpressed man in a butler's uniform, waiting patiently for her to finish.

"You may leave your motorcycle parked here," he said, a heavy British accent marking his words, instantly rendering him Saoirse's least favorite person in the room. "Mr. Carlton will see you now."

**8 April
3:32 p.m.
Lily**

"Hey, Mindy," Lily said awkwardly as she walked into *Samson's Crib*.

Her stomach was doing somersaults as she looked around the almost empty bar, remembering too much of the evening spent there with Benson. She should have been nicer to him. She also should have insisted on working instead of letting him talk her into coming here to play darts. She'd wanted to. She'd been so set on protecting him.

And she'd failed. Because she hadn't taken the threat as seriously as she ought to have. The warning had literally arrived in her apartment, how much clearer could it have been? But she hadn't been there when it had counted.

She knew better than to blame herself for what had happened. She wasn't at fault here. But she still felt guilty, if only because she could have done *more*. *Should* have done more.

"Oh hey, Detective." Mindy had been wiping down the service area, but she stopped now, smirking at Lily. "You missed our first training sesh, y'know. You gonna be there for the next one? The team's dying to meet ya. Or did you change your mind?"

Lily walked up, awkwardly, glancing at the stool Benson had stood behind the other day, and chose a different one. "No... Well, uh... Something's come up," she said, trying to figure out how to break the news of Benson's passing to Mindy. How close had they been, anyway? "And that's why I'm here, actually," she continued, carefully.

Mindy put the wipe away and tilted her head, one of her hoop earrings sitting on her shoulder. "Oh yeah? Need a drink?"

Lily shook her head. "Technically I'm still on the clock," she said.

"Oh? Does that mean this is not a social visit then? And here I was thinking we were gonna be friends."

Lily chuckled at the cheeky smirk on Mindy's face, but the reality of what she had to say brought her back to the moment rather quickly. She met Mindy's eye, even though she only wanted to stare to the ground. She hated this part of the job. Always had. "There's something I've got to tell you." Best to rip off the band-aid quickly and not beat around the bush. "Detective Benson is dead."

Mindy froze. After a few seconds, she began moving again, picking up the cloth and wiping down the clean surfaces in front of her. Her movements were a little jerky, as though they felt foreign to her. They were no longer the same, practiced motions Lily had seen her make when she'd entered. No, these had a lot more conscious effort behind them. That and the fact that Mindy was now suddenly avoiding eye contact led Lily to believe that her hunch had been right, and they had known each other better than just as a barkeep and a regular.

Lily didn't speak, letting Mindy take a moment to process the information, to make sense of it.

"What happened?" Mindy asked eventually. "I know he wasn't sick, and since you're a cop, and you're here, I'm guessing it wasn't a normal accident, either."

Lily nodded slowly. She'd always known that barkeeps were perceptive—as good as any detective when it came to reading and understanding people. In certain cases, maybe even better.

"He was killed. Someone came after him." Lily watched Mindy, even though she wanted to leave right this second and be alone instead. But she forced her emotions down, pushed herself to remain cool and rational.

"Yeah, that seems about right," Mindy mumbled, still wiping the spotless counter. After a moment, she looked up, glancing around the room at large with a frown on her face, her gaze lingering on the two people sitting in their corners. She dropped her cloth and stalked around the bar and headed for the door in comfortable, blue sneakers that didn't really match the rest of her stylish goth outfit. Lily remained where she was, simply watching Mindy turn the lock on the door so it could only be opened from the inside and changing the sign in the small window beside it. Then, Mindy turned around and called to the other patrons.

"Bets, Lloyd, I'm closing up for the day. Just see yourselves out whenever you're finished your drinks, would ya?"

She received some grumbled affirmative responses before she returned to Lily, slumping onto one of the stools nearby.

"Got any clue who did it?" Mindy asked after a moment of silence. "Or is that classified or somethin'?"

Lily sighed. "I've got some leads," she said. "But they're loose, to say the least. I was kinda hoping you'd be able to tell me if Benson had made any other enemies aside from Kennedy."

Finally, Mindy looked her in the eye, watching her closely for a moment. "Kennedy, huh?"

Shrugging, Lily put on a smile. "Hey, gotta start somewhere, right?"

"I guess. I can tell you're not sure about that idea though. Trust your gut."

Lily gave a mirthless chuckle. "You're almost starting to sound like an aged, jaded detective now."

"I guess my former lives sometimes shine through." Mindy flashed her a grin. "But to answer your question, not really. Benny's one of those universally liked people. I once saw him empty out a drink over some guy's head, but an hour later they were doing karaoke together. Pretty sure he did some gambling, but as far as I know, he always settles his debts. Settled, I mean."

The frown crept back onto Mindy's forehead when she corrected herself. Lily didn't blame her. She was having the same problems. And what she said about Benson was not surprising, either. He was like that around the precinct as well. Or, had been, rather.

The two patrons had finished their drinks and now strolled toward the exit, giving Mindy a quick wave as they went.

They were surprisingly civil and calm about being told to leave, Lily thought.

"So you've got no clue either, huh? What about friends? Did he have ties to the," Lily hated to use the word in serious context, but she couldn't think of a better term that befit this city's ecosystem, "underworld?"

Bemused, Mindy looked at her, raising an eyebrow. "Good ole Benny? No chance. Aside from his tattletales, he didn't even talk to anyone with a criminal background unless it was to arrest or question them. Pretty sure he's the only cop in that precinct of yours who doesn't have a deal with a criminal going."

Lily shot a sharp glance at her, but Mindy only shrugged. Unfortunately, Lily wouldn't put it past the other detectives, so she couldn't defend them with clear conscience, but she also wouldn't besmirch the name of the police department.

"Sorry, I got nothing for you, Detective."

"Lily. Call me Lily. If I'm going to be on your darts team, we should be on a first name basis."

"Lily Rose? Wow, your parents really liked flowers, didn't they? Doesn't this already border on child abuse?"

Lily sighed. How often would she hear the same sentiment? "Yup," she said.

On to the next order of business.

"Have you ever heard of a man called O'Shea? Graham O'Shea?"

"Way to change the subject. Very smooth. Ten points," Mindy joked. "And yeah, I've heard the name. Think back in the day he was some big shot. Did a lot of shady deals, I think. But I'm guessing you're asking because of the rumors."

Lily perked up. "What rumors?"

"They say his ghost's come back to haunt the city."

"Who does?"

"Oh, you know. Those people with their ears to the streets." Mindy did a general wave with her left hand. "Homeless people, crooks, thieves.

You know the lot."

"And in what way exactly is his ghost haunting the place?" Lily asked, unimpressed.

Mindy shrugged. "Some of the older people say they've seen him. Said he looks just like in the olden days. But if you ask me, it's probably just some guy who reminds people of him and he's playing along with it because it gets him places. And free drinks, I'm guessing."

Lily nodded absentmindedly. She had to agree with Mindy. Though this was certainly interesting, she hadn't abandoned the idea that O'Shea had been killed. And especially the notion of him reappearing out of nowhere after ten years without having visibly aged seemed… unlikely, to say the least.

But even so, there might be a relation. It could be a younger brother, or even a son, who had come to take over for Graham O'Shea. Either way, it was something worth looking into. A random criminal reappearing right around the time Benson was killed seemed too coincidental not to be connected. And Lily still didn't believe in coincidences.

The carpet sported a deep wine-red pattern, but the curtains were a bright creamy tone that let in a lot of light to brighten up the large lounge. The antique mahogany furniture was elegant and obviously chosen to impress, yet it remained on the edge of tasteful.

Time and time again, Saoirse realized that a lot of the mob leaders really enjoyed antique furniture and all the royal pomp it insinuated. She had to admit that she hadn't expected this from Carlton.

He was sitting in an armchair, reading a book with a green-cloth cover. The title was embossed in golden letters on the spine, but from her angle it wasn't possible for Saoirse to read it. He closed it and set it down when Saoirse was led inside by the butler... without using a bookmark, she noticed.

"Saoirse Kennedy. How wonderful to finally meet you in person." He gave her a phony smile, though it didn't do much for his pasty complexion.

Saoirse surveyed the room using her peripheral vision as she cocked her hip and crossed her arms. "Funny that. It didn't sound like you had any interest in it," she said coolly.

There. There'd been the slightest movement by the curtains, in the crook between bookshelf and wall she couldn't see that well from her position. It had to be Jean.

At her back, the butler left, closing the door behind him.

"I didn't see any particular need for us to meet," Carlton admitted, though his false smile never disappeared. He gestured at one of the other armchairs. "Please, take a seat."

"Thanks, but I think I'll stay where I am."

He shrugged. "Suit yourself." He leaned back in his seat and folded his hands together. "So, tell me, what made you pay me this visit?"

Saoirse didn't like how forthcoming he played. Jean wouldn't get a surprise shot at her, not since she knew he was there, but she doubted that was the only thing up Carlton's sleeve. And she still didn't know for certain just what he was after, and how he intended to get it.

"I'd like to talk to you about Detective Benson," she eventually settled. "Why did you kill him?"

The phony smile on Carlton's face gave way for a real smirk of bemusement as it finally crinkled the skin around his eyes. "What makes you think I killed your detective?"

"Because you're the only one who wanted him dead." Saoirse looked him dead in the eye. She refused to play his game.

"Actually," he said, pursing his lips, "I couldn't give a rat's ass about that cop, dead or alive."

"Liar," Saoirse pressed through clenched teeth. No good. She normally managed to stay so cool, what was wrong with her? It felt like lava had replaced the blood coursing through her veins, burning every part of her flesh, consuming it with anger. Her breathing rate had increased, and she was glaring at Carlton hard enough that seeing him turn to ashes would not have come as a surprise.

She needed to calm down.

"He's right, you know," a familiar voice said from behind her.

The scent of cedarwood and cigars crept into her nostrils, freezing everything that had been on fire before in an instant. That voice. That presence that commanded the entire room instantly. It was *his*.

She slowly turned to look into that confident, mocking smile she'd once so admired.

"I wanted him dead," O'Shea said, "because he was making trouble for you."

If Saoirse had been the kind of person to faint from shock, she might have done so now. But she wasn't, and so she glared at O'Shea. "You should be dead," she hissed. "Why aren't you?"

O'Shea sighed dramatically. "Because you, my dear, made a rookie mistake."

"I shot you in the *head*."

"Yes, you did," O'Shea agreed pensively. "But you didn't make sure I was dead."

Saoirse's chest was heaving with mixed feelings. She'd never regretted killing—or trying to kill—O'Shea. He'd been a manipulative bastard. Probably still was. Almost definitely still was. He'd been her mentor. He'd also been her kidnapper and blackmailer. The bad definitely outweighed the good, but nevertheless he'd turned her into the person she was today.

The grey suit he wore was the same he'd worn in the restaurant when she'd chased him. It was impeccable and perfectly tailored for his build.

"So *you're* pulling the strings then. He's just your puppet." Saoirse glanced back at Carlton for a moment, who looked like he wanted to argue, but didn't say a word. "What is it you want?"

O'Shea looked honestly taken aback. "Can't a man just come by and see how his legacy is doing?"

"I'm not your legacy," Saoirse hissed, narrowing her eyes at him.

His stance was casual, not like he intended to attack, either by grappling, or by shooting, but Saoirse knew all too well that it meant nothing. She'd learned that from him, after all.

She scanned his forehead for any mark of the bullet she put in there a decade earlier, but all she found was a small scar. He must have had surgery to remove any larger traces. It was surprising he hadn't erased all of it. Unless, of course, it served as a reminder.

Despite all her training, Saoirse's muscles tensed.

O'Shea watched her sadly. "Aren't you?" he asked. "I made you. We both know that. Everything you are, everything you do... It's all because of me."

Saoirse scoffed. "If I were, I'd have killed Benson like you wanted. But I chose not to. And that's got nothing to do with you."

"Doesn't it?" O'Shea began pacing around her slowly, an almost curious expression in his eyes. She turned with him to keep him in front of her at all times. "Doesn't it... remind you of another time?"

Saoirse didn't answer.

Flashes of that evening rushed through her head. No real memories, just colors, impressions, and sensations. Her breathing increased once more, but she forced herself to calm down. She couldn't show him weakness. She mustn't show him that he'd gotten to her. He'd only use it to further manipulate her.

"I've come home," O'Shea said, smiling, his arms gently raised as if offering her an embrace.

"No," Saoirse spat. "You're going straight

back to hell."

She shot forward, taser in hand, for once wishing she'd brought a gun, but before she reached her mentor, she was struck in the temple by a sharp blow that knocked her to the ground. She just about noticed Jean with a baseball bat before everything went blurry and then black.

8 April
5:37 p.m.
<u>Lily</u>

Feeling somewhat nauseated by her conversation with Mindy, Lily finally left *Samson's Crib* and headed for the building she'd singled out as being the most likely of Vulpes Ltd's properties to serve as a sort of headquarters for Saoirse Kennedy's operations.

More than once on the way to the supposedly abandoned factory grounds, Lily wondered if she'd gone insane. She had neither a warrant, nor back-up. No one even knew where she was headed. It would be an easy matter for someone like Kennedy to make her disappear under the circumstances.

And yet, more than anything, she wanted to just speak with Kennedy, knocking on the front door. After being in this city for this long, it was unlikely Kennedy would get spooked and vanish from underneath Lily's hands. Not as long as she believed she could get away with everything.

Parking just outside of the large concrete walls, Lily doubtfully watched the heavy metal gates. There was no way to even peek inside without announcing her presence first. No way to check if it was abandoned without trespassing.

Thank god for modern technology.

Lily didn't have a drone, but what she did have was a phone. One that could connect to a website that provided satellite images of most of the globe. Almost as soon as she finished typing in the address, a blurry aerial image of the area filled the screen. Lily zoomed in as much as she could, but she didn't get a clear image. Still, she could make out some colored dots inside of the compound. They could be things like traffic cones and oddly shaped machinery, even simply trashcans, but they might also be people. A lot more people than should be milling about outside of an abandoned factory. Before she put her phone away, Lily checked the date the last photograph of the area had been taken—last year.

Kennedy might have moved on since then. But she also might have stayed.

Determined to find out, Lily got out of her car and marched up to the front gate. She reckoned Kennedy was someone who liked to play with fire, so getting an audience might be within the realm of possibilities.

Next to the gate, a surprisingly modern buzzer had been installed, including a speaker system, camera, and even a fingerprint scanner.

Lily pressed the buzzer, glaring at it. A metallic-sounding voice answered almost immediately.

"Not for sale."

Lily almost smirked. They kept up the charade even now. "I'm here to speak with Saoirse Kennedy," she said.

There was a pause.

"Who?" the person on the other end said.

Lily glared at the camera. "Your boss. I want to speak to your boss."

"An' who're you?"

"Marigold Daisy. I'm a recent acquaintance."

"Right. I'll let my boss know you stopped by. Good day to ya."

The comms crackle stopped, and Lily knew the conversation was over. She waited for a moment longer in the faint hope that Kennedy might just happen to come out. But her hope was disappointed. Nothing at all happened, which could mean one of three things. First, she might have been wrong, and this spectacularly unhelpful doorman did not, in fact, work for Kennedy. Second, Kennedy might not be there at this moment in time. Third, Kennedy had no intention of speaking to Lily.

The only thing Lily was certain of, was that Kennedy would know that it had been her who'd called. For the most part, Lily just wanted to avoid the goons not passing on her request for a chat on principle. However, hiding her name behind two other flowers was not enough trickery to fool Kennedy, of that much Lily was certain. She'd have never made it this far if it were.

She was still standing there, when she became aware of some form of commotion on the other side of the wall. People, mostly men, were running around, shouting. Lily slowly paced along the wall, away from the gate so as not to be right in front of the camera anymore and listened carefully.

"Where's the boss?"

"Anyone heard from her?"

"No, why?"

"She was meant to crash that luncheon, I think?"

"But that was hours ago!"

"Anyone seen Mike?"

"I can't find Natalia, either!"

"Dillan, take Yao and check the hotel, I'll try to get in touch with the others."

"You're not my boss, Talitha!"

"No, but you're the one freaking out. I'm calm. This is probably nothing. It's not even been half a day yet."

"Hey, what's going on out here?"

"Dillan's freaking out, 'cause he can't get a hold of the boss."

The voices were getting quieter, significantly less shouty, and it sounded like they were headed back inside.

"Tried the cops yet?"

"Not there. You *know* I'd know if she was."

Then they were gone. There'd been three or four distinct voices with a few more mixed in randomly.

Lily remained in her spot for a few minutes to see if they were going to come out again, but they were gone. If nothing else, this had told her one important fact: Kennedy's people didn't know where she was. And her hunch about Kennedy having a mole in the precinct had been right. Suddenly she was glad she hadn't requested backup for this visit. She'd have never been able to play it like this if she had.

But what now? Kennedy's location was unknown.

They'd mentioned a luncheon at a hotel. Even off the top of her head, Lily could think of seven hotels fancy enough to hold restaurants open to the public. There were probably more. Too many to quickly check out and have a ghost of a hope for Kennedy to still be there, anyway. Besides, it was long past lunchtime.

Perhaps it was time to abandon the Kennedy route for the moment and do some research on O'Shea instead.

After getting back into her car, Lily pulled up the address of the bar Benson had told her Kennedy liked to frequent. If it was shady enough for one of the big Five to visit, it might be shady enough for a "ghost" to reappear. Especially considering his connection to

Kennedy.

The bar was called *Gonzalo's Place*, and it was a corner bar with very few windows located at an extremely quiet intersection not too far from Benson's apartment. No wonder he'd found out Kennedy liked to frequent it. He'd probably seen her on her way at some point.

Tentatively, Lily stepped into the bar and scanned the room. A few murky windows and dim lights stood in crass contrast to the décor, which reminded Lily of a 1920's flapper club. It was better frequented than *Samson's Crib* had been, though it was by no means packed. The dress code was definitely of a higher level than Lily would have expected in a place like this. It looked like the people here had actually made an effort to dress up, and they covered a large range of ages, starting at college kids, going all the way up to pensioners.

Lily didn't realize she'd been looking for Kennedy until she noticed that the criminal wasn't there. Slowly, she advanced toward the bar in the center of the establishment, where a column of shelved liquors was lit up by LEDs, which were in turn reflected by the mirrors behind the liquor bottles. It looked fancy and expensive. Not to mention precarious.

"Hi," she said to the barman nearest to her. He only had help from one other barkeep, a young woman who appeared to be in her mid-twenties, but it looked like the two of them had a good handle on the orders. "Could I get a G & T?"

The barkeep looked her up and down once and raised an amused eyebrow. "You sure you want that? Looks to me like you'd be better off with a port."

Before she could respond, he had poured one for her and slid it across to her.

"*Cortesía de la casa*," he said with a wink.

Somewhat suspiciously, Lily accepted the drink and sniffed at it. It certainly smelled like port. She took a sip, the ethanol burning the back of her throat, but the sweet flavor still brought relief to her shoulders. As it turned out, the barkeep had it right—the port was exactly what she needed to loosen up some of the stress she was feeling. "*Gracias.*"

"No problem, Detective," he replied.

Alarmed, Lily's head shot up. "What did you say?"

"Please, Detective, no need to make a scene." He smiled at her disarmingly. "Saoirse said you'd be coming by sooner or later to ask questions, of course I made sure I'd know you if I saw you. And, let me just say, my sincerest condolences about Jeremy Benson." He poured another glass which he raised to Lily, looking honestly regretful. "We were schoolmates as kids, you know. I hear you've been working together."

Lily gulped, startled by the level of information he'd just volunteered, but raised her glass to him nonetheless. "To Benson," she muttered, before they both took a drink. "So you know who I am. And I'm guessing that you're Gonzalo?"

The barkeep chuckled. "Technically, yes. That is what people call me. But my given name's Alejandro, or Alex. It's nice to officially make your acquaintance, Detective."

Lily suppressed the urge to react aloud and simply nodded.

Of course, Kennedy had expected her to come by here sooner or later. The more surprising part was that she'd taken the barkeep into her confidence and that he was so open about it. Several mental notes had been shoved into parts of Lily's mind she intended to revisit at a later point. For now, there were other things to deal with.

"Any chance you can get me in touch with her?" Lily asked, eyeing Alejandro. "There are some things I'd like to ask her."

"Interesting strategy you're pursuing," he said, one eyebrow raised amused. "But I can't. I'm no part of her world; I just run this place and sometimes she shows up. You're welcome to wait here for her. Sooner or later, she always comes by. I'd prefer if you didn't make a scene though. Not good for business, you understand."

He winked at her.

Lily sighed deeply and took a sip of her drink. Then, after a long moment of contemplation, she looked up at Alejandro again.

"I have one more question," she said. "What do you know about Graham O'Shea?"

**8 April
7:26 p.m.
Saoirse**

Pounding hangover headaches were nothing compared to what Saoirse experienced when she regained consciousness. She barely managed to open her bleary eyes and lift her head slightly before pain exploded in her mind and she was overcome by an immense sick feeling which resulted in her expulsing the contents of her stomach.

Lifting a hand to her forehead proved that, despite her feeling hot and almost feverish, her skin was in fact cold and clammy. She had a concussion. Perhaps she'd had some drugs administered to her as well.

She gave herself time to breathe and collect herself, though wisps of thought kept meandering and dissipating. Her hand on her forehead wandered to her temple, where the worst pain reaffirmed its presence with every beat of her heart. She found a form of bandage, which, she now realized, was wrapped around her head. Other than that, she appeared to be unharmed, ignoring the sluggishness of her mind and body, naturally.

Finally, Saoirse found it in her to take in her surroundings.

She was on a foam camping mat in a small, stone-walled room with no more than a single, tiny window near the ceiling on one side. The acidic, acrid smell of her puke drowned out any other fragrance that could have indicated a location to her, but based on the placement of the tiny window — the only light source — Saoirse assumed she was locked in a cellar room. The only thing in the place aside from her barebones bedstead were a glass of water and two small white pills whose plastic wrapping identified them as painkillers from a francophone country.

Supporting herself against the wall, Saoirse got to her feet, wobbly, but under no danger of falling over. She took a deep breath and allowed her mind to catch up with everything.

O'Shea was alive.

Not only was he alive, but he was the one who'd killed Benny. The one who was behind everything. And, like a fool, she'd let herself be taken off guard and knocked out cold. She didn't need to check her pockets to know that her phone and other belongings were gone.

Anger rose alongside confusion.

O'Shea was alive.

But after ten years of pretending to be dead, why come back now? And more importantly, why hadn't he killed her when he'd had the chance?

She should be dead. By any rights, she'd tried to kill him, and he was trying to take her operations from her, so why not do the only sensible thing and kill her so she couldn't interfere? It didn't make any sense.

Saoirse hated when things didn't make sense.

In a bout of frustration, she banged her fists against the metal door, which, unexpectantly, gave way and swung outward, making her stumble forward. Startled, Saoirse looked back at the door swinging in its hinges. It hadn't been locked. Why hadn't it been locked?

What the *hell*?

Puzzled though she was, Saoirse wasn't one to look a gift horse in the mouth. Taking quick stock of her surroundings, she grabbed a wrench sitting on a workbench on the opposite side of the cellar room and ducked behind several rows of stacked wine toward the wooden stairs leading up to the ground floor. Whoever had lived here before Carlton had arrived clearly had a strange array of interests and interior design ideas, assuming she was still on the same premises.

Saoirse slowly and carefully pushed the door at the top of the stairs open, holding out for any shadows or sounds from the other side. But the night seemed to be mostly still. She slipped through the crack, stepping in behind an old suit of armor before she took a new look around. No one moving or breathing in the shadows—check. Cameras around the large hall—check. The front door—check.

Since there was no way to avoid the cameras without taking them out one by one—and Saoirse wasn't exactly equipped for that, never mind that she was fairly certain one of them had already caught her anyway—she stepped out of her hiding spot and walked slowly and confidently straight across the hall toward the front door. From experience, she knew that someone walking with calm purpose was less likely to be noticed as a problem than someone rushing or attempting to stay in cover. Additionally, it gave her the chance to see her belongings that had been taken from her set out on a table. Glancing at them for only half a second, Saoirse left them where they were, untouched, and headed for the door, pushing it open while half expecting it to be locked. It swung open silently with neither complaint nor resistance.

Instead of hurrying toward the front gate, Saoirse slipped out to the side, heading straight for one of the large brick walls. One of the trees at the edge of the grounds was quite high. Glad that she'd exchanged her high heels from the luncheon for more practical shoes before coming here, Saoirse climbed the tree quickly, going up as high as she could before turning to the wall and gauging the distance.

It wasn't an impossible jump to make. Under normal circumstances, she'd have no concerns, but as she was still feeling nauseous and a little disoriented from her concussion, she wasn't entirely certain that she could reach the wall's ledge. She was still contemplating the jump when a voice from below her called up.

"So you're leaving without even saying goodbye? How rude. I thought I taught you better than that."

Looking down, Saoirse found O'Shea smiling up at her, his white teeth gleaming even brighter in the moonlight. She didn't respond.

Waving her bike keys, he continued, "Don't you need these? I left them for you by the door and everything."

Yeah, Saoirse had done well to leave her things where they were. All of them could be replaced, and the chances of them having been tampered with—whether it be a tracker, bug, contact poison, or even some form of small explosive—had just been too high. O'Shea's renewed mention of them solidified her certainty in her choice.

Then again, he clearly didn't want her dead, for whatever reason. He didn't even want her imprisoned. She probably *could* have simply walked out the front gate without issues. Even the thought of it infuriated her.

"What do you *want*?" she asked.

He contemplated her for a moment, perched

in the tree as she was. "Why don't you come down and we can discuss this in a civilized fashion?"

"As civilized as beating me unconscious with a baseball bat, you mean?" Saoirse countered.

A real smile crept onto O'Shea's lips. "I see you haven't lost your quick wit," he said. "I'm glad to see it. But fine. Let's talk like this, as childish as it may be."

While giving O'Shea the main focus of her attention, Saoirse didn't forget to keep a look on the area as well, in particular the windows of the mansion, which made for excellent sniper positions right now, but also out over the other side of the wall, in case Mike was still waiting in the forest somewhere. The quicker she could find him and return to headquarters using his car, abandoning her bike, the quicker she could begin to sort all of this out.

"I intend to turn back time, metaphorically speaking," O'Shea continued, his cunning vulpine gaze fixed on Saoirse. He hadn't earned the name Silver Fox for nothing. "You and me, leading the city to glory. Ridding it of the scum, of the hollow promises, of opposition."

Saoirse didn't react, despite the many emotions rising up in her chest at his words. Mostly different flames and strands of anger, mixing in a vortex of rage.

"Or perhaps," O'Shea said, potentially misreading her lack of reaction, "we could return to Ireland, reconquer their underworld. What do you say?"

Saoirse tensed her muscles, getting ready to jump and readying her wrench.

"I say: leave my city before I kill you again."

She leapt, chucking her wrench at him as she flew, just about caught the wall's ledge, and scrambled over, dropping and rolling on the ground on the other side before sprinting to the forest's edge.

8 April
7:55 p.m.
<u>Lily</u>

"O'Shea? Surprised you've heard of him." Alejandro was watching Lily closely.

"Why is that?" she asked.

He snorted. "You haven't been in this city for very long and he's been gone something like a decade. Cropped up in one of your backlog cases, huh?"

Lily took care to guard her expression and slowly swished her drink around the glass. After a long moment, she raised her gaze to Alejandro again. "Have you seen him recently?"

"No." He met her look without concern. "I've only heard rumors. Which, I'm assuming, you've also heard."

"A ghost returned to take back the city?"

He nodded. "That's the one."

"How's Kennedy taking it?" It was a bold move to bring Kennedy back into the conversation like this, but Lily just couldn't stop herself.

Alejandro only shrugged. "Who knows? 'Scuse me."

He moved down the bar to take the orders of two greying men wearing hats.

Lily took them in dispassionately. They looked like they were heading out to some ranch any moment now, except their shoes were definitely not made for ranch work with their shiny new leather and soles without grip.

Tacky.

Against her expectations, Alejandro returned to speak with her after he'd finished with the two men. Lily had thought he'd take the chance to put some distance between them, but he didn't appear bothered by her questions at all. If anything, he seemed *interested.* Which immediately made her inner alarm bells ring out like crazy. No one was *interested* in a cop's questions, unless they were hoping to get something out of it, and so far, she had no clue what that might be in Alejandro's case. It was also possible that he was trying to cover something up, being nice and forthright to stop her from snooping around on her own, maybe hiding something like money laundering or an illegal gambling ring.

"That's a mean glare you've got, Detective," Alejandro noted, amused.

Startled, Lily jerked back, fighting to get her expression back under control. Normally interrogations were done differently, and she was *supposed* to glare at the other person. She wasn't used to this... jolly demeanor Kennedy and anyone who associated with her seemed to put out there.

"So what else do you want to ask me? Jeremy once stood up for me, back in school, so I'd like to help. Go ahead. If you think it'll help your investigation, I'm an open book."

"Right." Lily straightened her shirt while she tried to regain her stance in the situation. "Having known Detective Benson as long as you have, can you think of anyone who might have had it in for him? Aside from Saoirse Kennedy, of course."

"No," Alejandro said, raising his eyebrows meaningfully. "Aside from people he put away, I can't think of a single person. Including Saoirse Kennedy."

"What do you mean?"

"Saoirse loved the guy. Killing him is the last thing she'd want to do. She always said that she had so much fun playing their little game." Alejandro waved his hand in the air vaguely.

Lily didn't let it show, but she was inclined to agree with him. It matched what she'd seen anyhow. Which made it all the more likely that Kennedy was the one who'd slipped Lily the warning.

"Look, I really need to talk to her," Lily said, getting up from her stool. "Are you sure you can't get me in touch with her?"

Alejandro shook his head while shrugging. "Sorry. But I'll let her know you're looking for her when she comes by. Got a number I can pass her?"

Lily took the pen and notepad he held out to her and jotted down her personal phone number. Giving her number out to a criminal might not be the wisest decision she'd ever made, but Kennedy already knew where she lived and worked, so what difference did it make?

For all the questions and searching she'd done today, Lily hadn't expected to run into Kennedy on her way home. She just about saw the criminal duck around a corner into a dark alley, and, if she was being honest with herself, Lily even wondered for a moment whether she'd even really seen her, of if it had merely been wishful thinking. Still, she dropped into police mode and ran after Kennedy.

Lily caught up without issues. She didn't even bother to shout.

"Kennedy," she said, stepping into her way. "I've got some questions."

The rest of what she'd planned on saying was stuck in her throat, when she looked at Kennedy. Even in the dim light of the streetlamp, Kennedy looked like hell. She was pale, with deep, dark rings under her eyes, her hair was messy, and her temple bloody. No wonder it had been so easy to catch up. Kennedy was clearly on the edge. Exhausted and hurt.

It took everything Lily had not to ask about *what in the ever-living hell* had happened.

"Hi, Detective." Kennedy smiled crookedly. "Does it have to be right now, or is there time?"

Well. If she hadn't lost her glib, it couldn't be that bad.

"Now," Lily said sternly. "Come on, let's go somewhere more private."

Kennedy giggled, but she allowed herself to be led along by the elbow without resisting. "Oh my!"

8 April

9:18 p.m.

Saoirse

After running into the forest, finding no sign of Mike, and somehow making it to town on foot, Saoirse was even more exhausted than she had been earlier. The concussion was certainly not making things better, even after she'd torn away the bandages pressing on her temples, and flashes of weakness painfully reminded her that the only thing she'd eaten in about forty-eight hours had been a salad... which she hadn't even finished.

She felt dizzy, her head was pounding, and the only thing keeping her moving was the knowledge that Carlton and O'Shea could rock up in a car at any second, so she clenched her teeth and told her body to pull it together and suck it up.

She could have slowed down; she could have taken a break somewhere, waited until morning, or ducked into one of the open bars or take-away fast-food places and asked to use their phone to call Mike or Natalia or any of her people, but she didn't dare lose any time. Any moment she stood still could be all O'Shea needed to find her again. There was a decent chance he was already waiting near her home, but that was a risk she was willing to take, because her own people would be there, too. It was *her* turf, not his.

He'd talked as if he wanted to go back to how things used to be—back in the days when she'd looked up to him and followed his lead. He'd even been a sort of father figure for a while. But after coming to several realizations ten years ago, Saoirse knew she couldn't return to that. O'Shea was not the kind of person she wanted to have close by. And she knew that despite what he'd said, there was still a very real chance that he would try and kill her now, since she hadn't exactly been very receptive to his ideas.

The thought spurred her on as long as she focused on it, and she held onto it, clung to it like a lifeline. So much, in fact, that she didn't even notice Detective Rose until she was blocking her path.

As soon as Saoirse stopped moving, the pain in her head returned more ferociously than before and her head began spinning, so she was rather grateful that the detective wanted to talk, if only because it meant she wouldn't be a solitary target for O'Shea.

Part of her wanted to accept the detective's help and lean on her to walk, but a much larger part refused to show weakness in front of Rose. They didn't speak while the detective led her to a taxi rank, though Saoirse did perk up when the address given was not that of the police precinct. Instead, it was Rose's apartment.

The detective led her inside of her home while keeping a very close eye on her. Saoirse looked around with interest. The apartment looked much the same as the last time she'd been here, though it was surprising to note that a cop like Lily Rose had not deemed it necessary to add more locks to the door or take any form of extra precautions after an obvious break-in. The windows still had no alarms or bars, the door sported no more than the same flimsy lock and a weak chain which the detective didn't bother sliding in even now, and the windows weren't—

Oh, no. Upon closer inspection, Saoirse could see that the windows had, in fact, all been locked this time. She wondered if the way Benny had been killed was the reason.

She dropped gracefully into one of the living room couch chairs, her back retaining its poise, though she wanted nothing more than to lean back and curl up in a ball to sleep.

"Nice place you've got," she said, appreciatively looking around.

Detective Rose scoffed. "Yeah right, as if you haven't already seen it."

Saoirse smirked, though in her most innocent of voices she said, "Whatever do you mean, Detective? I don't believe you've ever invited me to your home before."

Rose just glared at her, before pulling a note from her jacket pocket and slamming it on the table.

Saoirse's rounded handwriting stared back at her. "My note." Under normal circumstances, Saoirse would have kept up her usual games, but she had no energy left for that. Rose wanted answers, and Saoirse wasn't in a position to argue. She could get up and leave, but that would put her in an even worse situation. Besides, getting the detective on her side in this should be useful. Especially now that she had a better understanding of what had actually happened. Or rather, *why* it had happened. Still, she needed to tread carefully. If Rose got wind that Saoirse had been the reason Benny had died, even if she'd not been involved, things could get bad real fast.

Saoirse looked up at the detective to find her staring at her in puzzled wonderment.

"What?" she asked.

"I..." Rose cleared her throat. "I wasn't expecting you to be so forthright about admitting the note is from you."

Saoirse shrugged and then looked toward the kitchen as her head swirled in another dizzy spell. "Any chance you have some snacks around? Energy bars or fruit? Cereal? And some... water."

Rose watched her for a moment, contemplating her in silence, before she got up and headed out of the room. Saoirse allowed herself the luxury of closing her eyes, while still paying close attention to the sounds around her, lest the detective was going to make a call. But Rose was only gone for a moment, and the noises reaching Saoirse's ears were only her steps and some cupboards as well as a fridge opening. A running tap, too.

"Here." Rose was holding out a bowl of chocolate cereal floating in milk when she opened her eyes again.

"Thanks, Rosie."

"That's Detective Rose to you," Rose said stiffly.

The sternness in her voice almost made Saoirse giggle with delight. She was going to be *so much fun* to tease. Knowing that right now was not the right moment to make the detective angry, Saoirse dug into the cereal instead of responding.

Rose watched her take a few bites before she asked, "So, what happened to you? Why are you in such rough shape?"

"Allow me to ask a counter question," Saoirse said, looking up from her bowl of chocolatey goodness. "Why are you asking me here, in your own home, instead of the police station?"

Rose raised an eyebrow, and her upper lip tensed. "Would you prefer we go there right now?"

Saoirse tilted her head to one side, eyes fixed

on Rose's. The detective was annoyed, possibly erratic, but she wasn't a fool. She had deliberately chosen to come to this place, and she wouldn't change her mind only because Saoirse got on her nerves.

"I don't put much stock into empty threats, Rose," she said seriously. "And they don't suit you. You're better than that."

The way Rose choked back her snide response and swallowed her words was practically visible.

This time, Saoirse couldn't stop a grin from spreading on her face. "So why *did* you bring me here, of all places?"

"I wanted to ask you some questions without anyone else knowing. I imagine your goons already told you I'd stopped by."

"Stopped by where?" Saoirse perked up, gaining even more interest, when Rose recited the address of the compound where she lived. Despite herself, Saoirse was impressed. Rose had figured that out within a week. Benny hadn't managed that within ten years. The downside was, that it meant that Rose had probably also drawn the connection between Saoirse and Sinead and Vulpes Ltd by now. She'd have to drop the company and create new lanes for herself. It was a good thing that she'd already set up the groundwork a few years ago when it looked like Benny was getting closer.

To be fair, with O'Shea's return, she needed to

do that anyway. The less of their past connection remained, the better. Especially once she'd dealt with him.

"I expect you won't be living there for much longer now," Rose said, contemplating Saoirse.

Saoirse responded with a smirk. "Probably not. So go on then, ask your questions. I'm guessing number one is why I sent you that note."

Rose nodded.

"It's simple, really. I became aware of a threat, and I figured someone who was already around Benny was a better bet for keeping him safe than a criminal. Especially since I didn't know how serious the threat was, exactly. I..." A shadow crossed Saoirse's face as she realized how badly she'd underestimated the situation until only twenty-four hours ago. "I wasn't expecting it to be quite this severe."

She'd messed up.

But it wasn't going to happen again.

**8 April
10:10 p.m.
<u>Lily</u>**

Even though Lily was still deeply suspicious of Kennedy and her motives, the look on her face convinced Lily at least a little that Kennedy was telling the truth. She read confliction on it, a mixture of guilt and anger. It was only for a short moment that Kennedy allowed her feelings to shine through before the mask came back, but it was enough for Lily to see a reflection of her own feelings, confirming her hypothesis that Kennedy really had wanted to prevent Benson's death.

"How'd you find out about this 'threat'?" she asked, leaning against the armrest of one of the other chairs in her living room.

Kennedy hesitated and her piercing gaze inspected Lily closely. "Are you worried about moles?" she asked, tilting her head with a slight smile. "That's smart."

Lily's back went rigid. Based on what she'd overheard at Kennedy's headquarters, she'd already assumed that her hunch about moles had been correct, but this confirmed it. More than ever, she was glad that she'd decided not to do this at the station.

"Are you going to answer all of my questions with another question?" Lily snarled, nevertheless.

Kennedy's grin grew wider. "Isn't that what you're doing now, too?"

Lily glared at her, much to Kennedy's amusement, it seemed.

"Fine." Lily grunted after a moment and flopped into the other seat. "I want to make a deal. Unofficially. You interested?"

"What's in it for me?" Kennedy's response had come like a shot out of a pistol and her eyes were glittering with curiosity. Lily almost regretted the suggestion.

"That will depend on your answer to my next question," she said, careful about her phrasing. "Did you incite the attack on Detective Benson?"

Silence followed her words. Anticipatory on her part, contemplative on Kennedy's. The ticking of the clock Lily had received as a gift from her grandfather felt awfully loud.

Ticktockticktockticktock.

Time seemed to stretch. Kennedy's next words would determine the outcome of this conversation.

Kennedy straightened in her seat, for the first time tonight truly reclaiming the same charismatic authority she'd carried the last time they'd met as she looked back at Lily, unphased and serious.

"No," she said, her words sounding oddly loud and clear in the approximate silence of the city flat. "I neither killed Detective Benson, nor did I order his elimination. I did not want him dead. If I had, I would not have sent you that warning."

"But it does involve you, doesn't it?" Lily pushed, frowning. "How else would you have known?"

Kennedy didn't respond. Not even a muscle twitched in her face.

Lily had no choice. She had to make a deal if she wanted to progress. Kennedy was the only real lead she had, and one that she knew would go somewhere. Nevertheless, she hesitated. On the one hand, this could be her key to solving Benson's murder. On the other hand, Kennedy was a criminal mastermind, responsible for thousands of crimes over the past few years. She probably had half the city on her payroll in one way or another.

But the sergeant had made it clear that it would be best if Lily didn't ask for back up from the squad. That fact didn't exactly inspire her with much hope for the future, but that was an issue to be dealt with at a later point. Right now, all she wanted to do was put Benson's murderer behind bars. And she was going to do it, one way or the other.

"I will not compromise my integrity more

than I absolutely have to," she began. "But I am prepared to overlook any connection you might have had to this if you help me find the person responsible for Detective Benson's death and bring them to justice. Provided that you are not said person."

If Kennedy was as innocent as she claimed to be, this probably wasn't a great deal. At least for someone as capable of talking herself out of trouble as Kennedy was. But it would mean leaving the note out of evidence, which might save her some trouble. And if Lily's hunch was right, Kennedy was more involved than she cared to admit.

Making under-the-table deals like this was common enough with low-level thugs to get them to talk, but it was not usually a tactic employed to get the big fish on board with investigations except in extreme cases. There was too much at stake. At best, an offer might be made with the district attorney's approval. And yet, despite Lily's insides basically churning with distaste for this move, she knew she had to do it. The time was now.

She jerked her hand toward Kennedy, waiting for her to take it, and, after a moment, they shook hands.

"I'll gladly help find the person responsible, as long as you keep my involvement out of any papers. This includes records about helping you. That kind of thing could really hurt my reputation, you know." Kennedy smirked, and Lily almost found herself responding to it with a grin of her own. Almost.

She deepened her frown, more to keep herself from smiling than anything else, and leaned forward in her seat.

"Deal. So tell me what you know."

"You'll have to be more specific," Kennedy chided. "I can tell you who ordered the hit right now, but I don't have proof to give you. At least nothing that wouldn't implicate me more."

"What do you mean? Why would it implicate you?" Lily's eyes narrowed. Had she just made a mistake in offering Kennedy that deal?

"Because someone tried to hire me to kill Benson. I have a flash-drive with the order and Benny's details. I refused and warned you instead while I tried to find out why this person wanted Benny dead. I wasn't expecting him to find someone else so capable."

Lily was stumped by Kennedy's forthrightness. Everything she'd seen of the woman so far had indicated that she'd simply continue saying cryptic things, talking circles around what Lily wanted to know. She hadn't expected Kennedy to be so... frank.

"Who?" she asked when she'd reminded herself how words worked. "Do you know who it was?"

Kennedy tilted her head to the side. "Who gave the order or who did the deed?"

"Both?"

"The order came from a businessman named Timothy Carlton. In fact, I happened to just come from his mansion when we met today. There's a good chance someone's in the streets looking for me right now. I have a suspicion about who pulled the trigger, but I don't know for certain."

Lily got the feeling that there was much more to the story than Kennedy was sharing, but even so, she was struggling to absorb all the information just provided.

"Why… were you at his house?" Lily asked.

Finally, the little smirk returned to Kennedy's lips. "I'm a rather… direct person, in case you hadn't noticed. I decided to pay Mr. Carlton a little visit in his mansion out west of the city so we could have a *chat*."

"You killed him?" Lily shrieked and jumped from her seat in disbelief. She'd been right—she never should have made that deal.

"No, of course not, I'm not an animal!" Kennedy looked offended as she beckoned Lily to calm down again. "I went there to talk, not for a massacre. And, by the way, your morals don't exactly overlap with mine. Sure, I liked Benny, but I'm not going on a murder rampage over him. No. I went there to talk. I wanted to find out *why* Carlton wanted him dead. For all I knew, Benny had it coming."

As disturbing as Kennedy's words were to

hear, Lily sort of understood where she was coming from. "Did he?" she asked instead of going into any of the other millions of questions screaming to be asked in her mind. "Did he have it coming?"

She was afraid of the answer. What if Kennedy said that Benson had been running with a bad crowd in secret, maybe been a dirty cop himself?

Kennedy watched her for a moment, something like sympathy appearing in her eyes. "No."

8 April
10:17 p.m.
Saoirse

In a way, it was heart-warming to see how much Rose cared about Benny, and how much she wanted to solve his murder. Despite her honest surprise at the offer of cooperation, Saoirse wasn't going to pass up this opportunity. After all, this way she could get the police to deal with Carlton, while she dealt with O'Shea herself. His death certificate from a decade ago was still valid so long as it wasn't disproven. If he quietly disappeared again, no one would be the wiser.

Rose swallowed hard, obviously trying to stay in control of the visible mix of relief and anguish in her face. "Okay. I need to take a look at that flash drive, in case there are any clues on it. Did anyone except you and Carlton have access to it?"

"It's at home. And I promise you, there's not much more that you'll get from it. I've already had one of my techs check it out. If they couldn't find anything, I guarantee that you won't either."

Rose jutted her chin forward and furrowed her brows. "I'll be the judge of that."

"Suit yourself."

Pacing up and down the room, Rose crossed her arms, possibly trying to determine what other questions to ask. Saoirse applauded her foresight. Even if they had just struck a deal, there likely weren't going to be many opportunities for either of them to approach the other without creating suspicion. Rose clearly wanted to keep a large part of this investigation secret from her squad, and Saoirse had no desire to make Rose appear like a dirty cop who was in her hand. Saoirse already had her moles, and they were wonderfully undetected in positions that had a lot of access to information but were unlikely to ever be directly involved with her as a suspect.

Saoirse used this short reprieve to take another glance around Rose's apartment. The detective really hadn't found it necessary to install *any* other security measures. Saoirse wasn't sure if she ought to be flattered or hurt by the lack of reaction to her breaking in.

Her eyes fell on a TV guide on the living room table with a few evening programs circled. The pen still sat beside it. With a glance at the still-pacing detective, Saoirse leaned forward and jotted down her personal number at the top of the next day's page.

She hadn't given this number to many people,

not even within her own group, but she got the impression that Rose was going to need it. Better this than have her show up at her headquarters again as she appeared to have done. That would only invite trouble.

"Why me?" Rose finally asked as she came to a halt in front of Saoirse, her arms crossed. "Why did you leave this note for me? You could have just told Benson directly, or the sergeant, or *anyone*. Why me?"

Why me? One of Saoirse's most hated questions. Everyone asked it, all the time. It didn't even matter whether it was a good thing or a bad one, the question remained the same. *Why me? What's special about me? Why did this happen to me?*

Rarely was there an easy answer. Except this time, there was.

"I considered warning him directly," Saoirse admitted, meaningfully leaning forward in her seat. "But do you honestly think that he would have believed me?" She waited for a moment for her words to sink in before continuing. "I had reason to believe you would take a warning like that seriously, and I've seen you together. Plus, I reckon you know as well as I do that a large number of *your* colleagues are under the thumbs of *my* colleagues. I didn't want them to get a whiff of this."

What she didn't say was that she simply *liked* Rose. Well, she didn't say it in words. But she hoped that her smirk still conveyed the message.

The red of anger flushed to the detective's face, but she struggled to put her feelings into words. Her movements were sharp, as if she had to force herself to not do anything more than turn away and begin pacing anew.

Saoirse's mind began to get foggy. She didn't have an awful lot of energy left, not even after that cereal. Fainting from blunt force trauma wasn't exactly the same as restful sleep, and she couldn't remember when she'd last had a full eight hours. Or six, for that matter. Hell, when had she last had even four hours?

Rose stopped short again as if she'd suddenly thought of something. Her head whipped around to Saoirse. "Who's O'Shea to you? What's your connection?"

"O'Shea?" Saoirse echoed, less because she didn't understand, and more because she wanted to find out what Rose already knew.

"Yes, O'Shea. Graham O'Shea. He disappeared ten years ago in this city. I have a photo of the two of you together. What's your connection?"

Saoirse yawned. "We're both from Ireland. Well, were. He's dead, you know."

One of Rose's eyebrows twitched up. "Is he? How can you be so certain?"

She was trying to be sneaky, getting Saoirse to slip up, but she was so godawfully *clumsy* about it. Saoirse had no doubts about the detective's deduction skills, but her interrogation needed some serious work.

"Why wouldn't I be? There's a death certificate, isn't there?"

Rose hesitated. Clearly, she'd already known as much, but likely didn't have any further information. She might not even know about his link to Vulpes Ltd, like the fact that it had been his company, originally.

"There've been rumors," Rose said.

"Yeah, I've heard. But I don't believe in dead men walking." And she didn't have to. She'd seen him. Spoken to him. She *knew* he was alive, relieving her of the believing part. Walking or not, he'd thoroughly proven his state of not being dead.

Saoirse yawned again, and Rose sighed.

"Fine, that's enough for tonight, I guess." Rose looked her up and down with a frown. "You're in no state to go out and about if someone willing to kill is after you. Spend the night and we can talk some more in the morning."

Saoirse batted her eyelashes at the detective with a mischievous grin. "Normally women buy me dinner first, you know."

Detective Rose turned pale, then blushed heavily. "I wasn't— I'm not—" She whirled away and practically ran out. Her reaction gave Saoirse no end of delight. Rose was even more fun to tease than Benny had been! It was just too easy. What a pity that she was a cop because she was so damn *adorable*.

Rose stormed in again, carrying a blanket and a pillow, and dumped them on Saoirse's lap without looking her in the eye. "Here. See you in the morning," she growled and stomped away again.

Saoirse waited for a moment and listened for the sounds of Detective Rose getting ready for bed, before allowing herself to close her eyes for a few moments. While she wasn't exactly in a safe place, no one would expect her to be here, which made it as safe as she could be. Exhausted as she was, Rose was right, she wouldn't make it far. A few hours of sleep wouldn't hurt.

9 April
6:01 a.m.
__Lily__

She should have known. Looking at the empty couch in the early morning light, Lily chided herself for not having considered that letting a criminal sleep on her couch and still expecting her to be there the next morning might not have been such a good plan. At least nothing appeared to be missing. Even the blanket had been folded again neatly.

She'd originally planned to call in sick so she could grill Kennedy more with a fresher mind, but since that had fallen through, she decided to head into work after all. If nothing else, she'd be able to do a little research on that Mr. Timothy Carlton Kennedy had mentioned and check if he'd ever committed a known felony. And what connection he had to Benson, though she doubted she'd find much on that front.

The part of her conscience that was worried Kennedy might have played her like a fiddle, kept announcing its opinion with sudden churnings of her stomach every now and then as she got ready. Chances were high that Kennedy had just played along for the sake of getting information out of Lily, finding out how close she was to solving Benson's murder. Perhaps hearing about how much intel Lily had on Kennedy herself. Everything she'd said might have been a lie. Maybe she was trying to frame an innocent man. Or perhaps there was no Timothy Carlton. The name didn't ring any bells, anyhow.

No matter what, Lily was going to have to do some good, old-fashioned police work. Even if Kennedy had been telling the truth, knowing who the culprit was didn't give Lily enough to warrant an arrest. She needed evidence. Conclusive evidence. And as she stood in the shower, she got the hollow feeling that finding such clues might be harder to come by than in an ordinary murder case.

Determined to not let her judgement be swayed, Lily threw on her police jacket and headed out to the precinct. On the way she stopped by a bakery to get some bagels—intentionally not of the cream cheese variety—and coffee. As she left again, the smell of freshly baked bread still in her nostrils, she noticed a familiar-looking person sitting on some cardboard on the opposite side of the street. Realizing after a moment that it was the same beggar she'd given her pretzels to before, Lily crossed the street and went down on her haunches in front of the woman.

"Hey, what's your name?" she asked gently.

The beggar woman, her dirty blonde curly hair covered mostly by a scarf, lifted her blue eyes to Lily.

"Tatjana," she said, her voice stronger than Lily would have supposed, considering how frail and thin she appeared.

"Hi, Tatjana, I'm Detective Lily Rose. We met the other day. Do you remember?"

Tatjana nodded slowly and uncertainly. Her eyes were darting between Lily's hip and behind her, as though she were expecting to find a threat. "Thank you for the pretzel," she said eventually with a Slavic drawl.

"No bother. Can I get you something else to eat?"

Lowering her eyes to the ground, Tatjana shook her head quickly. "It's okay."

Lily almost gave a mirthless smile. How often had she seen this? Even some beggars had too much pride for charity—if it came with a face and personal contact.

"How about a trade, then?" she offered.

Tatjana warily looked back up at her. "What kind of trade?"

"You come to this address and ask for me whenever you really need anything—clothes, a sleeping bag, food, whatever—and in return, you'll be my ear to the streets. What do you say?"

"I don't know any criminals!" Tatjana hissed,

panicked. Her eyes had once more turned to darting around.

Lily smiled, still holding out the card with the address of *Samson's Crib* out to her. While she hadn't exactly discussed this with Mindy, she had a feeling that once she helped the bar's darts team win a few games, the barkeep wouldn't mind so much if Tatjana came by every now and then. "But you might know others who do. I don't need you to go around and ask questions, only keep an ear out and tell me whatever you happen to hear. Sound good?"

Tatjana still hesitated, frowning, glancing from the card up at Lily and back again.

"Here. Just think about it." Lily placed the card, along with a ten-dollar bill, into the cup Tatjana used to collect her coins and dollar bills and got up to leave. "I hope to see you there!" she called back over her shoulder.

Lily made a mental note to pop by Samson's as soon as it opened. She wanted to head over and take another look around Benson's apartment again anyway and stopping by the bar only required a minor detour.

Without further delays, she headed for the precinct. The young detective who'd been assigned to her cases, Clifford, was hovering by her desk already, clearly just waiting for her to arrive. She ignored him and sat down in her chair, silently counting the seconds until he was going to step up to her.

One.
Two.
Three.
"Um, good morning, Detective Rose!"
Good lord. Just under four seconds.
"Morning," she responded simply, glancing down at the stack of papers he was carrying, if only so she didn't have to look at the troubled, yet hopeful expression on his face.
"I was hoping," he began and stopped himself, glancing around at the other detectives present. Most of them hadn't arrived yet, which was typical behavior here, Lily had found. It was nice to see that this way of treating the job hadn't infected this young man yet. He continued in a lowered voice. "I was hoping you could help me out with a few of these… I'm kind of stuck."
Now, Lily curiously peered into his baby-face, so cleanly shaven that she was beginning to doubt he was even growing a beard yet. How had someone so young managed to become a detective? He must have some serious props, even if they weren't in the confidence department.
"What kind of help do you need?" she asked.
His face lit up. "Some pointers would be great! Like, if you could tell me which angles you would have covered, that would be very helpful!"
Lily's shoulders relaxed a little. He wasn't

lazy. He wasn't hoping to dump the work back to her. His only flaw was his inexperience. She didn't even bother to question why he'd waited for her instead of asking one of the other detectives. They likely would have only laughed at him or given him the absolute worst advice. The few who were present were already shooting amused glances over at them, and Lily was fairly certain that she was about to overhear some sexist comment or another.

"Let's go to one of the meeting rooms for this," she suggested, pushing herself up again and taking her coffee and the little baggy with the bagel with her.

The next half hour was spent looking at the three cases Clifford had brought with him and checking the things he'd done already before trying to coax him into the right direction so he could think of what needed and could be done next on his own. By the time they were finished, there was no uncertainty left in the young man's face. He beamed at Lily.

"Thanks so much! I'll get on these right away. Oh, and uh, if you ever need any help in one of your cases... I mean, not that I think you can't deal with them yourself, I just mean that you know, if you needed help. Not because you're a woman or because of anything, I think you're a great detective, I just..." He trailed off, and Lily chuckled.

"Relax," she said, smirking. "I understand.

And I appreciate the offer. If I ever need a hand with anything, I'll keep you in mind."

His shoulders loosened, and he smiled in relief. "Great!"

Finally, Lily was able to focus on her own work again.

First, she scoured the database for any information on Timothy Carlton. There wasn't much. A private citizen who built up a large business empire with money he had likely inherited and then leveraged through investments. He had a few parking and speeding tickets and only one inspection for tax evasion which had been dropped fairly quickly. Once, as a teenager, he'd broken into a school and vandalized the drama department. Apparently, he'd been found wearing a multitude of costumes at the same time, after jumping into the school's pool, ruining them. It had been a private school, of course, so the charges had been dropped after a generous anonymous donation had come into the school's hands.

In other words, Carlton's record was too normal to tell anything. He hadn't been connected to any larger crimes, and whether that was because he genuinely had no connection, or whether he was just good at hiding his tracks, Lily didn't know.

One phone call was all she needed to verify that he was in town, renting a mansion to the city's west, just as Kennedy had suggested. An email from the sergeant, asking her to come to one of the meeting rooms, diverted Lily from her research.

When she got there, he had the blinds shut so no one could peek in and sat at one of the tables with his hands folded.

"Detective," he said darkly. "How is the investigation coming along?"

Not having expected to provide an update just yet, Lily's mind raced. Saoirse Kennedy's involvement certainly needed to be kept out of this conversation. The way she was handling this was very much against protocol and could get her in serious trouble. And since she didn't have any evidence that Timothy Carlton had been involved yet, she couldn't really bring that up, either.

"I've been looking into Detective Benson's list of acquaintances and enemies. Past arrests who got out of prison and such, as well as his open cases to see if someone might have been spooked by how close he was getting to them," Lily settled after a moment.

"And?"

"I'm about to head out to the crime scene once more to see if I can find any identifying clues around the area. The tapes I viewed from the security cameras came up empty, but there might be something we've missed. I'll also be speaking to one of his acquaintances on the way."

She had nothing. They both knew that, even without her outlining it like this.

The sergeant grunted misgivingly and rose from his chair. "I need you to solve this case, Rose. Quickly. Detective Benson's funeral is tomorrow at four o'clock. If you do not have any arrests by then, or even conclusive leads, there will be consequences." He spoke while walking past her, not even bothering to look her in the eye, but upon reaching the door, he turned back over his shoulder. "One more thing... the squad was concerned about a woman taking the lead on this case, which is why I've told them that I am personally handling it. My reputation is on the line here, Rose. Don't fuck it up."

Lily had nothing to respond to that, and she simply stared at the door as it fell closed again behind the sergeant.

9 April
4:41 a.m.
Saoirse

Normal sleeping and activity schedules had never applied to Saoirse, and they certainly wouldn't start while she was staying in a cop's apartment.

She awoke just long before the first rays of the morning sun peeked over the ocean, and sneaked out, taking a bag of trash sitting in the kitchen with her to bring outside. The detective had helped her out last night. The least she could do was return the favor. Plus, their agreement should come in handy. Saoirse only wondered how long it would take Rose to find her number and connect the dots. She hadn't left her name, but she reckoned there shouldn't be a need for it. Rose was a detective. She'd figure it out.

In these early hours, there weren't many people on the streets. There were bakers and garbagemen, newspaper deliveries and journalists. It was the time when stores received their stock, especially those that needed fresh ingredients every morning. It was quiet enough that Saoirse would notice anyone tracking her, and yet also busy enough that she wouldn't stand out too much.

A smile granted her a lift with one of the garbage trucks, passing through almost half the city unnoticed, because no one spent much time looking at the people who dealt with a city's dirt, though, surprisingly, the sewers were a different story. A very busy system of tunnels indeed—one of the lesser reasons why Saoirse didn't like using them. The stench and general dirt did the rest. And they were rarely as useful in getting to the place she wanted to go quickly as one might suppose. Taking her bike down back alleys was significantly more effective.

Once she ditched the truck, home was close enough to walk. It was busy. She could tell even from a distance. Despite the time, there were lights everywhere, but no yelling, at least. Taking a last glance around to double check no one was around, she walked up to the door and pressed the buzzer.

"Morning!" she said cheerfully, when she heard the sound of someone enabling the speaker.

"Oh shit, you're back!" Yao was managing the door today, it seemed.

Already, he'd activated the mechanism to open it and Saoirse slipped in, quickly. Mike was running toward her across the courtyard. She noticed her bike standing beside the door with equal measures of satisfaction and relief. It would have been an acceptable loss, but she would have still been sorry to lose it. Especially to Carlton or O'Shea.

Mike didn't bother with meaningless questions about her wellbeing. One glance at her head told him everything he needed to know and, wordlessly, he turned and walked back into the building alongside her. As they were crossing through the door, he took out a walkie-talkie. "Call off the search. She's back."

"Roger that." Unsurprisingly, Talitha was on the other end. That woman was a wizard when it came to quick and effective communication across their entire organization. Saoirse hated to think about what would happen if Talitha ever decided to retire.

Saoirse headed straight for her quarters, despite Mike's suggestion that she should stop by the infirmary to get checked out. Instead, seeing she was determined, he called up their resident doctor to her apartment.

Bursting through the doors to their shared living space, Saoirse had somewhat expected Natalia to be pacing with concern or sitting on the couch in worry. She'd thought she would be greeted by a wild embrace, full of love and relief. But instead, there was nothing. The couch was empty, the room abandoned. Natalia wasn't there. In fact, by the looks of it, Natalia hadn't been here since Saoirse had gotten changed the day before.

She turned to Mike. "Where's..."

Instead of responding, he pulled a folded note out of his pocket and handed it to her.

Saoirse's chest grew heavier as she took it from him. So it had finally happened. She'd known it was coming; she just hadn't expected it so soon. She'd hoped there still might have been time to rectify things. To change. To be a better match for Natalia.

She sat down on the couch, barely even noticing the doctor arriving, and read the note while he worked to patch her up.

I can't do this anymore. I tried. I really did. But I cannot keep watching the woman I love constantly run herself down while throwing herself into danger. And so... I won't. I know that this is who you are, and I wouldn't change it for the world. But I can't be a part of it.

This is goodbye.

Love, Natalia

PS: This was really difficult, but I have come to a point where I am certain and determined that this is the right decision. But if you need to talk, I'll be at Gonzalo's Place this afternoon between two and three.

Saoirse lowered the note and closed her eyes.

The time to fight had passed, and she'd missed the battle. She'd been vaguely aware of the problems, of what was gnawing at Natalia, but clearly, she hadn't been paying enough attention. The reason was clear: Running something akin to an empire stretched her attention and presence thin. She could delegate more, and pass responsibility to other people, taking herself out of the equation, like all the other bosses seemed to like doing, but that would mean giving up a part of herself.

Natalia had never asked for that.

Sometimes, things like this just happened. Sometimes people drifted apart because neither of them could change for the other, but they couldn't stay as they were either.

And yet, rationalizing it to herself, didn't make the deep crater in Saoirse's chest feel any lighter. She'd lost something precious. And she'd let it go with her eyes wide open.

Guilt and regret created a whirlwind cocktail of negativity in her entire being. A question formed in her mind.

If she didn't have Natalia with her, why was she even doing all of this?

The fog in her head only remained for a moment, a distinct shape growing as it faded.

Saoirse's eyes snapped open with anger and new determination.

For the city.

For *her* city.

So she loved Natalia. So she'd lost her. It didn't change the fact that she couldn't let O'Shea destroy her city, poison it with his decrepit ideals. Yes, this was a blow to her personally, but this was for the best. Now, Natalia could find someone who she could be happy with without compromise. Someone who could devote themselves to her the way she deserved.

And Saoirse could turn her full attention back to the city, starting with dealing with O'Shea while Detective Rose handled Carlton.

While her regrets hadn't vanished entirely, or at all, they had been put into perspective by her burning desire to protect her city from a man she knew would destroy it without so much as blinking.

"What have I missed?" she asked Mike who was still standing in front of her, waiting awkwardly and watching her with concern, once the doctor had left.

"Not much. We've mostly just been trying to get a hold of you. When you didn't come back out, I knew something was wrong, and apparently Yamaguchi tried to get in touch with you in the meantime, as did someone called Marigold Dandelion. At one point, we noticed that a search party left the mansion, with dogs and flashlights, so we reckoned you'd made it out, but we couldn't find you. What happened?"

Saoirse shrugged. "I got careless and was knocked out. Then I escaped, but they took my stuff. I could've taken it back, but I didn't wanna touch it anymore." She made a face. "Gross.

Anyway. Ran into a friend in town and held out there for a few hours to check the coast was clear."

"I have... *so many* questions!" Mike gestured wildly. "What friend? We checked with everyone! And how is it possible that *you* of all people got knocked out? What *happened* in there? Did you talk to Carlton?"

"I did." Saoirse hesitated. But this was Mike. Her right-hand man. The person she trusted most. "The rumors are true."

"What? What rumors?"

"The ones about O'Shea. He really is back."

He stared at her, the frown on his forehead deepening. "But that's impossible, isn't it? You said you killed him."

"I did," Saoirse admitted. "And I thought a shot to the head would do the trick, but evidently not. He must have gotten insanely lucky. But the point is, he really is back. And he's the one pulling the strings, using Carlton. He's also the one who instigated the whole Garrison business, I guarantee it. And it wouldn't surprise me at all, if he annoyed or approached Yamaguchi in some shape or form as well."

"Shit." There wasn't much more to say, and Saoirse wholeheartedly agreed. "So what's the plan, boss?" Mike asked.

With a sigh, Saoirse got to her feet again. No rest for the wicked. "For now, I'm going to stop by Lysander's shop. I asked them to keep an ear out for any info. Maybe they heard something. After that, I might stop by Gonzalo's. I'm expecting a call from someone who shares our current interests at some point today. Chances are decent that we'll move out either later today or tomorrow." After a second's reflection, she corrected herself. "More likely tomorrow or the day after, actually."

"Might that new associate be that Marigold person?" Mike asked, raising one eyebrow.

Saoirse flashed him a smirk. "I don't think she would appreciate being 'associated' with us. And she usually goes by the names of two other flowers."

Mike's mouth changed into an O shape as he connected the dots.

9 April
1:45 p.m.
Lily

It was frustrating to look for clues where there were none.

Before long, Lily gave up on finding any traces of Carlton in old files and decided to head out to warn Mindy about the possibility of a homeless woman occasionally appearing.

Samson's Crib was just opening when she arrived. Mindy was unlocking the door, her face pale, eyes red, and rings under her eyes so dark, they couldn't even be covered by make-up and concealer.

"You're making a habit of showing up here early, aren't you, Detective?" Mindy said, looking up the steps.

"Lily," Lily reminded her. "We're on a team now, remember?"

Mindy laughed. "Right. Well, come on in. I'm guessing you're here on business again. You don't strike me as a day drinker."

"I'm not," Lily agreed as she followed the woman inside.

Mindy wordlessly poured Lily a water and

leaned across the bar. "So, what is it this time?"

She sounded tired, though she was attempting to cover it up with wry humor.

"I was wondering if you'd be willing to play liaison for me," Lily said, her finger tracing the rim of the glass.

"You'll have to be a bit more specific than that."

Lily sighed. There was no way around this. "I may have made a contact in the streets — one that didn't seem to like talking openly to cops, so I was hoping that she could come here to deliver messages and tell you if she needs something so I can get it for her."

"Let me guess," Mindy said, "she'll get to pick up those things she wants here as well?"

Lily did finger guns at the barkeep. "Got it in one. So? What do you say?"

Tilting her head, Mindy looked Lily up and down with enough intensity that Lily began feeling guilty for ever having even considered the option, never mind already putting it into place. They didn't know each other well. Lily was just some customer who'd been here twice and was friends with a regular who was now dead.

"If you're gonna actually bring us a victory, I'll let you get away with almost anything. So for now, okay. As long as you don't skip game days unless there's something like a bomb threat to the city or something," Mindy sighed.

Lily thrust her hand forward for Mindy to shake and broke into a grin. "You won't regret this!"

"I already am."

Looking up at the large, unassuming building Benson had inhabited, Lily wondered once again if she could have prevented his death. She could have dragged his ass to a safe house, gotten the squad to follow the lead of the note which would have led to Kennedy and then... And then nothing. Kennedy wouldn't have told them. Not the way she'd told Lily.

So by the time Lily would have deemed things to be safe—possibly after a few days, maybe a few weeks or even months—Benson would have gone back to his normal life and presented just as much of a target. If only Lily had remembered to circle back to the question of *why* Carlton wanted Benson dead... Though, in her defense, she'd intended to talk more with Kennedy in the morning, except that *someone* had vanished.

Of course, she could go by Kennedy's headquarters again, but Lily really wasn't sure how well that would work. Or how wise it would be. The only thing left for her now was to do her job and solve Benson's murder the old-fashioned way: by finding evidence at the crime scene.

Instead of entering the building, Lily veered

off to the left and around the building to the back. As she'd told the sergeant, she'd already looked into footage of the security camera she'd noticed before, but it had given her nothing. There'd been no one, not even any moving shadows from cats or rats. But that didn't mean that the culprit couldn't have come the way she'd suspected.

The ladder was out, as she'd determined before, but it would have been possible to leap across from the roof of the opposite building. It wasn't quite as high as Benson's building, but they could have jumped to the fire escape. Granted, it would have made some noise, but depending on the time of day, it could have been drowned out by the usual sounds of the city. Even though she was standing in a back alley, Lily could hear the traffic loud and clear. Benson's apartment must have fantastic insulation in its windows to keep the noise out. When she'd been in there before, she'd barely heard anything. Granted, her mind had been more than just a little occupied, but nevertheless, it had been extremely quiet.

Glaring at the fire escape, she made up her mind and went inside, back through the front entrance. She climbed up the three flights of stairs to Benson's flat and opened the door, ducking under the police tape to enter.

The place had been cleaned of Benson's blood, but Lily still thought she could see it. It was like it was still there, at the edge of her vision, the crimson splatter across wall and floor.

She shook her head to clear her thoughts.

There was no time for this. She couldn't allow herself to indulge in returning emotions. Not now, anyway.

She crossed the room with energetic steps and went over to the windows, remembering only after opening it that it was easier to get to the fire escape through his bedroom window.

His stuff was still all there. It had been searched for any sign of the threat, like a letter or anything else that would indicate a warning, but nothing had been removed, except for Benson's work-related items such as his laptop, gun, and badge.

After pushing the furniture out of the way, Lily pried open the window over Benson's bed, an endeavor that required significantly more effort than it had any right to, and climbed out onto the fire escape.

Reassured by the distinct lack of wobbling on the metal structure's part, Lily stood up straight and looked to the building across. If someone had jumped, they likely would have hit the fire escape about two levels above, she estimated. Keeping an eye on the other building, she climbed up the steps, noticing from the corner of her eyes that not a single person of the apartments she passed so much as glanced at her. Whether that was because they didn't notice her, or because they didn't care, she couldn't tell.

When Lily reached the approximate height she'd expect someone to land, she inspected the metal railings of the stairs more carefully. Every discoloration and every chip was examined. She even climbed up another whole level just in case, taking pictures of the notches she came across.

One marking was particularly interesting, and not only because it was on the same part of the metal railing that also had bent outward. There were two notches right beside each other, and they looked fresher than the other nicks—they were brighter in color, as if they hadn't been touched by the weather much.

Lily glanced back over to the other building. Time to extend her search.

She hastened back across the fire escape to Benson's apartment, climbed back in, closed the window, and then headed out the door. In less than five minutes she was at the door of the other building, which yielded without Lily expending any effort. A small, concerned frown appeared on her face. This was terribly unsafe... no sign of a lock on the front door? Anyone could just walk in and get to the roof. Like she did.

Without interceptions, Lily went to the stairs, as the elevator was marked as being out of use, and climbed up all the way to the top, where she only needed to push the door open. Conscious of the one-way locks these rooftop-doors often had, she wedged a brick in the way of the door's path so it couldn't shut and trap her up here. The brick's handy location beside the door and the markings along the bottom inches of the door itself proved that this was a common enough trick employed here. Lily didn't even want to think about all the things that might be taking place on a roof like this—drugs, teenage sexcapades, underage drinking.

She forced her mind away from such things and back to the task at hand.

The first sweep of the flat rooftop didn't provide any distinct clues, except proof for the kinds of things she had feared took place on top of this building and didn't want to think about any more than she had to right now. Although she should look into getting a lock on that door, if only for the sake of safety.

A second, more thorough sweep across the roof illuminated little more. The only thing worth noting was another set of notches similar in size and depth in the rock on the façade facing Benson's building. Like before, Lily took detailed photographs, hoping that Bailee or Chuck might be able to shed some light on it. She had her suspicions about what had been done, but they were the forensic experts.

A third sweep brought nothing else to light, so, after watching the roof in contemplation for a moment, Lily decided to head back to the precinct. Perhaps there was something in

Carlton's affairs she'd missed. Something she could follow up on.

She'd barely rounded the corner from Benson's building, when she spotted a familiar blonde head of hair a little farther on, walking briskly in her black trousers and leather jacket. A car was stopping and going at small intervals to keep pace with her. From her vantage point, Lily couldn't make out the driver, but it was clear that whoever they were, Kennedy wasn't enjoying their conversation. Her gait was brisk and energetic, her gaze set straight forward with her jaw jutted out.

Lily could only stare. Even though Kennedy had been near unconscious last night, showing a more vulnerable side of herself than Lily would have suspected possible, it had been nothing compared to how much emotion was shining through Kennedy's body language now.

Then, suddenly, Kennedy stopped and turned to the car, anger blazing in her eyes. A moment later, she'd gotten into the passenger's seat, slamming the door. The car picked up speed and drove past Lily, allowing her to catch a glimpse of the driver. The air almost froze in her lungs from the shock.

She recognized the face instantly. It was the same handsome gentleman she'd seen in a picture with Kennedy before. Graham O'Shea. A man who was meant to be dead.

**9 April
3:10 p.m.
Saoirse**

Stopping by Lysander's shop had done little for Saoirse in terms of information gathering, other than the fact that O'Shea had apparently done some stirring in pots that should be left alone. This much Saoirse had expected. It appeared that not only had he made some appearances as his own ghost in a few places, he had also created several more set ups involving Saoirse like the one with Garrison. At least, she had to assume it had been him orchestrating it, because she could think of no one else who was dumb enough to dare, yet cunning enough to pull it off. Normally, she'd go and deal with the ruffled feathers right away, but she didn't have the luxury of time right now.

Deciding that there was one person she did in fact still need to make time for, she headed for *Gonzalo's Place*.

Natalia would be waiting for her, and Saoirse knew that she owed it to them both to go. To have that conversation, no matter how ultimately pointless it would be.

Seeing Natalia's face in front of her mind's eye, Saoirse played through what she imagined might be awaiting her. Pragmatic as she was, she didn't believe for one moment that this conversation might end up with them getting back together, with Natalia changing her mind and remaining by her side, and Saoirse knew herself too well to make any promises about changing. If these were calmer times, break-up sex might have been on the table, and so Saoirse found herself indulging in thinking how that might come about.

She was so caught up in her thoughts, she didn't notice the car approach her until it had slowed down beside her, vaguely keeping pace with her.

The window rolled down.

"Get in, kiddo," O'Shea said.

Saoirse glanced at him. He was smiling slightly, as though he were amused by the actions of an irrational child. She walked a little faster; the car kept pace.

"We have things to discuss," he continued, "and we would both prefer to do it at a secure location."

He was talking calmly, and unlike the previous night, Saoirse knew she had nothing to fear from him. It was the way he spoke. Last night, after she had chucked a wrench at him, he could have done anything. She didn't think he'd have killed her, but there were other things a man like him knew how to do. Enjoyed doing, even.

But right now, she knew this tone of voice. He was thinking rationally—or at least as rational as this megalomaniac ever had been—and he wanted to speak with her.

Too bad she didn't have anything to say to him. Not now. Not while Natalia was waiting for her.

"I can tell by your expression that you're angry," O'Shea said, speaking as though they were having a pleasant chat over tea about the weather. "And I'd like to understand why that is. You're the one who tried to kill me, after all. And, by the way, why was that? Not that I hold it against you, mind you… getting rid of me and taking all the power for yourself? That was masterfully done, and I applaud you. I taught you well, certainly. But what have you done with it?"

Though he kept talking, Saoirse didn't waver in her stride, her eyes straight ahead.

"You're stagnant, kiddo. You've reached a point where you don't know how to move forward. Well, I do. So let's talk about this."

"There is nothing to talk about," Saoirse finally snapped. "I knew what I was doing when I killed you, and I'll do it again!"

A satisfied smirk crossed O'Shea's lips. "Now that's the killer instinct I raised. I was worried you'd lost it after your feeble attack last night."

Saoirse shut her mouth, regretting her outburst. She should have known better than to engage, but here, along this stretch of the city, there were no back alleys she could take and lose the car. She'd been looking out for an alternate route, but she couldn't find what wasn't there.

As long as he was on her tail, there was no way she'd go to *Gonzalo's Place*. He knew the bar, of course, he'd gone there a fair amount himself, and she was certain that he'd been there recently, when she'd smelled him, putting it down to a sensory illusion. But she didn't want him to encounter Natalia.

On the other hand, she also wasn't equipped to deal with him right now. Not in the middle of the day, out in the open, while she only wanted to speak to her ex-girlfriend.

Exasperated, her gaze brushed through the street, along store windows and past people. It lingered on the car's reflection in a storefront for just a moment.

Jackpot.

The car windows were reflecting distinct movement somewhere behind her. A familiar gait following her discreetly. Saoirse's hand in her jacket pocket closed around the flash drive she'd brought. She needed to figure out a way to get it to Rose, so the detective could deal with Carlton. That would leave this situation wide open to take O'Shea up on his offer and use his pride against him. For some inexplicable reason, he seemed to think he still had a hold on her.

"You know you're not a leader. You don't have what it takes to delegate. You like being out in the field, being active, part of the action. You're like a rogue crossbow, ready to fire, but you lack the steady hand to give you direction." O'Shea spoke quietly, but his blue eyes remained fixed on Saoirse. "There's too much for you to handle right now. Too many fires to put out. You *need* someone else on the reins."

Saoirse scoffed, though she had less conviction than she pretended. "Ridiculous. Ramblings of an old man who should have stayed dead."

In response, O'Shea chuckled.

"What?" Saoirse asked. "Realizing how stupid you sound?"

"I *know* you, kid. It'll take more than that flimsy façade you put up to trick me. I'm probably the only person in this world who can ever truly know you." He smiled at her. "And you know why?"

He paused, allowed Saoirse to respond, but she didn't have the words. Her chest was clenching with every word, drawing parallels between his words and her reality despite herself.

"It's because I made you."

He was right.

Saoirse stopped in her tracks. *He was right*. He had created her. And he did know things about her past she had never shared with anyone. He understood parts of her that no one else could, *because* he had shaped them.

But he was also wrong.

"What do you want?" she asked, finally facing him head on, her hand in her pocket closing around the flash drive.

His grin widened. "I want you to get into this car and have a real conversation with me. I have some plans, and I think they will interest you."

"Fine."

She pulled open the passenger door and sat inside, dropping the flash drive in the gutter when she reached out with her hand to close the door. She didn't turn her head when they sped past Detective Rose, only hoping that the detective had been watching them closely enough to realize that Saoirse had dropped the key for her to find.

O'Shea was wrong.

Knowing her past only gave him part of the picture. He was missing everything that had shaped Saoirse since then. He had no idea how much she cared for this city, and about the bonds she had created within it. He couldn't possibly know about Lily Rose, a detective Saoirse herself had only met less than a week ago. He couldn't understand the unspoken connection between them, so different to the connection Saoirse had had with Benson.

She could be wrong. She could be very

wrong. But Saoirse had always been good at reading people, at judging them. And she was certain that Rose was like her. Or at least, like what Saoirse might have been, if it hadn't been for O'Shea. Saoirse also believed that Rose understood. That she understood not only who Saoirse was, but also how she thought and operated. Not fully, of course—after all, the detective had been worried that Saoirse had just gone ahead and killed Carlton, which, admittedly, wasn't entirely out of Saoirse's ballgame—but considering the small amount of time they'd spent together, that seemed permissible.

She'd listen to what O'Shea had to say. And perhaps, in the meantime, Rose would deal with Carlton, taking away O'Shea's cash cow. And once Saoirse had determined what O'Shea's ultimate goal was, she could decide whether it was worth keeping him around, or if perhaps, she should exorcise the ghost haunting her city for good.

**9 April
3:21 p.m.
<u>Lily</u>**

Lily stared after the car even after it had disappeared around a corner, trying to put her thoughts in order. Graham O'Shea was alive—unless he had an identical twin—and Saoirse Kennedy had known and lied about it to her face.

The confirmed lie surprised and hurt Lily more than she'd been prepared for. Sure, consciously she'd been aware that Kennedy was still a criminal and couldn't be trusted, but there'd been a part of her that had felt like there'd been a connection. An understanding. They'd made a *deal*.

Lily didn't believe that Kennedy would have lied just for the sake of it, however. There had to be a reason. But what?

Almost subconsciously, Lily walked over to where Kennedy had gotten into the car. Where had she been heading? The bar she frequented, *Gonzalo's Place*, was a distinct possibility. It was the right direction. But then why had she gotten into O'Shea's car? *And why had she lied about him being alive?*

Lily wracked her brain for answers—O'Shea had to lie low for a few years, faking his own death to escape justice or the revenge of another criminal; the man in the car hadn't been Graham O'Shea but someone who struck a remarkable resemblance; O'Shea was the real boss and Kennedy only his figure-head—but none of them felt right. The only thought that lingered, was the suspicion that perhaps the reason why Kennedy was silent about O'Shea was because he had something he was holding over her head. Something she couldn't fight against... yet.

Lily hadn't gotten to where she was by ignoring her gut, and her gut was telling her that this was all connected somehow.

Without realizing, Lily had been scanning the ground, but now she caught herself doing it. Why? What was she expecting to find? Her instincts had drawn her here, which meant that some part of her consciousness must have noticed something she wasn't aware of yet. What was it?

Her eyes passed over a dark-grey rectangle the length of her thumb. A flash drive.

Had she seen Kennedy drop this? Was that why she still wanted to trust her, why she'd come over here?

Without hesitation, Lily leaned down and picked up the drive.

Kennedy had told her that there was proof of

the assigned hit on a flash drive given to her. It wasn't outside of the realm of possibilities to assume that this might be that very drive.

As much as Lily wanted to check the contents right this moment, she also wanted to know what Kennedy was going to do in *Gonzalo's Place*, if she was going there at all. Perhaps she'd just been heading there for a drink and changed her mind when O'Shea showed up, but perhaps there was more to it.

It was worth a shot. It wasn't like she could track Kennedy right now without putting out a call on O'Shea's car and that would be difficult to justify at the moment.

Slipping the flash drive into her pocket, Lily put herself in gear and headed for the bar.

Mid-afternoon was usually the time bars started to get busier with people catching an early dinner or late lunch. And indeed, Lily saw several individuals already scattered at various tables, all of which were visible from the bar. A woman was sitting on a stool by the counter, but Lily steered clear of her, heading to the opposite side, where she saw Alejandro working.

"Good afternoon, Detective," he said, an eyebrow raised in amusement. "Here to see Saoirse again?"

Lily shook her head, contemplating how to deal with his straightforwardness. "No, not this time. I actually just saw her."

"Let me guess... arrested her and she isn't

talking?"

Lily was well aware of the few glances she was suddenly receiving from other people in the bar, including the woman on the other side. She reckoned they must be involved with Kennedy somehow. Best to tread lightly. She didn't want them to get the wrong idea and act impulsively. After all, she had no idea how much—if anything—Kennedy had shared with them about this deal they'd made.

"No. I haven't arrested her. I actually just saw her get into a car with a dead man."

Her words had come out a little more sternly than she'd intended, but she paid no mind to it. Instead, she scanned the reactions around her with interest.

Most of the silent listeners hadn't budged. A few were whispering, though too quietly for Lily to hear. The woman at the bar had cast her eyes down, her delicate fingers tightening around her glass until the knuckles whitened. Lily was almost surprised the glass didn't shatter under such a tight grip.

Alejandro's brows were furrowed. "She got into a hearse?" he clarified.

Either he was an excellent actor, or he had no idea about O'Shea. Unlike that woman.

"No." Lily sighed and glanced at the colorful bottles behind him. Could she allow herself a drink? She definitely wanted one. She felt like she deserved one with all the stress eating away at her. But she was also still on duty. And even if she weren't, she had a feeling her day wasn't over yet. *Something* was going to happen. "Can I have a glass of OJ?"

She wasn't even sure why she'd come here; what she'd hoped to find. She'd simply been following her instincts. Realistically, she should be going home, or to the precinct to check the contents of the flash drive and try to find some shred of evidence that could help her arrest Carlton. But something urged her to stay. She wasn't sure what it was until she lifted the orange juice to her lips and her eyes happened to meet those of the young woman across the bar when she set the glass back down and the fruity citrus taste washed over her tongue.

She recognized that woman.

She'd seen a picture of her when she'd scoured the files in which Benson had suspected Kennedy's involvement. She'd been younger in the picture, and dressed more lavishly, but it was the same woman, undoubtedly.

The woman looked away immediately, pretending she hadn't been watching Lily, but she made no attempt to leave. Lily decided to take a leap. It couldn't hurt, not at this point.

She pulled out a little notepad she normally reserved for investigations and wrote a brief note to the woman.

I know who you are, Ms. Piarelli, and I expect that through your involvement with Saoirse Kennedy you also know who I am.

I would like to speak with you privately. Please come to see me at the following address tonight at six p.m. You may bring someone with you if you wish.

Detective Lily Rose

Lily jotted down the details of her apartment building down below and folded up the note. Once this was all over, she'd have to move, but right now, her apartment seemed like the safest place to meet undetected.

She waved Alejandro over and gave him the note, along with money for the juice and a cocktail.

"Get that young lady over there a Cosmopolitan on my account, would you?" Lily smiled at him. "And give her that note, too."

Bewildered, he did as she asked. "The women in this city…" he muttered, leaving Lily with the mystery of what he meant.

She remained in her seat just long enough to reassure herself that the note and drink received their intended target, before she slipped away, leaving the bar. She still had work to do before receiving any sort of visitors.

**9 April
3:43 p.m.
Saoirse**

Saoirse didn't face O'Shea as they drove through the city. Her gaze was directed out into the streets, watching the grey concrete blow past them, only stopping occasionally at a red light, proving that O'Shea didn't know this city the way she did. If she'd been the one driving, she could have avoided almost any and all traffic lights, using backstreets and secret, unofficial paths that weren't even marked in any of the city maps or satnav. It was probably the biggest proof Saoirse had seen that this was not O'Shea's city. He didn't know it like she did. He didn't know what it meant when a person had a Dalia sitting in their window, nor did he know which beggars were real, and which were the eyes and ears of a crime group. He might venture guesses—and he was smart enough that a lot of them would be correct—but he didn't *know*. He didn't have a connection to the city, and he never had.

A long time ago, he'd been one of the Five. But even back then, the city had held little interest to him. It'd been a means to an end. Still was, it seemed.

They didn't speak at all until he left the city lights behind them and they traveled south along the suburbs. At this point, Saoirse already knew where they were going. It was the only property she hadn't burned down after taking over Vulpes. She wasn't sure why she'd left the house as it was. But the melancholy came flooding back when O'Shea parked in the driveway. This was where they'd lived together when they'd first come to this city. She hadn't been back here since she'd turned on O'Shea, but she hadn't let it go to ruin, either. She'd had Oliver come by every now and then to make sure the house was still intact, and the garden wasn't getting too overgrown. He'd told the neighbors he was the owner's nephew and that his uncle lived overseas.

Unlike the other properties, Saoirse hadn't had the heart to destroy this place. Why? She wondered now, watching O'Shea walk up the few steps to the front door. Was it because of him? Her last tie to him and the memories they shared?

She followed him inside, the layout as familiar to her as if she'd only been gone a week. Gently, almost as if she were worried it might crumble to dust, Saoirse touched the wooden railing of the stairs near the front door.

She'd had dreams about coming back here.

Nightmares, too.

Her gaze grazing across everything in the hallway, her stomach began to churn and twist. It was all too much like she had left it. Memories came alive at the sight of every inch of the place. When she glanced toward the kitchen, the memories of having pancakes with O'Shea were so vivid, she could almost smell them.

Back then, she'd actually thought of him as a father, having repressed the memories of how they'd met, of the horrors he'd put her through before she'd become his tool.

She shuddered.

"What are you waiting out there for?" O'Shea called from the living room. "Get in here so we can have a chat!"

Feeling like Alice going down the rabbit hole, Saoirse followed his order.

He'd taken his usual place in the armchair, leaving the couch to Saoirse. Despite the uproar of emotions she was feeling, she covered up her uncertainties, and, adopting her usual air of superiority, she planted herself into the most comfortable part of the couch and crossed her booted feet on the living room table in front. "Whatcha got, old man?"

He grinned at her. "Ah," he sighed. "It's like old times. How I've missed this."

It was a real effort on Saoirse's part not to agree.

"You said you wanted to talk," she said

instead. "So talk." Her gaze was directed at the ceiling, the same egg-shell color she remembered. She noticed him shift in his seat from the corner of her eye. He was watching her.

"Saoirse." His tone was thoughtful, and yet there was a clear air of urgency in it that involuntarily made Saoirse's abdomen tense. "Do you remember why we came here? Our goal?"

"*Your* goal," Saoirse corrected him without missing a beat.

O'Shea sighed. "I was afraid you might say something like that. So you did get lost along the way. You used to believe in our goal, you know. You were willing to do anything to make it happen."

Saoirse didn't respond this time, instead stubbornly staring at the ceiling. She had been carried along by him in the past. Back before she'd started to think for herself. She'd been a doll and he'd been pulling the strings. He'd forced those strings on her, attached them by knotting them into holes he'd created himself, needles in hand. Over time, she'd forgotten they were there. Until that day when her eyes had been pried open again.

"Money is power. And power means being able to do *anything*. Humanity doesn't know what's good for it. People are stupid. You know that. They need someone to nudge them in the right direction. To show them the way toward a future." O'Shea believed in those words. He always had, and Saoirse figured that he always would. They made up his essence. He believed himself to be a sort of savior. Benevolent, but forced to take drastic measures.

Most crime bosses tended to have the goal of a certain level of power and wealth and then only fought to retain that level. O'Shea was different. For him, crime was only a means to an end. He thought bigger. If he'd been less powerful, less intelligent and cunning, people might have called him a fanatic. It had taken Saoirse a while to figure that out.

"You know what needs to be done, Saoirse," he continued, his low, calm voice creeping its way into Saoirse's mind. "All I'm doing is giving you a little push in the right direction, that's all. You remember, back then? Back in Dundalk? You were uncertain back then, too. And I gave you that push you needed."

The thought of their first encounter in Saoirse's hometown sent shocks of chills through her body.

"You wouldn't be here, if it weren't for me." He was still monologuing as Saoirse did everything she could to force herself to retain her calm, aloof outward appearance. She couldn't let him see that he was getting to her. Not while she wasn't entirely sure how to discern the separate ingredients of the turbulent emotional cocktail stirring in her heart.

"What do you want?" she finally asked, looking at him.

A small smile played on his lips. "I want you."

"Gross."

"Saoirse," he reprimanded her gently. "You're like a daughter to me. You're a part of this, whether you like it or not. Besides, this is just a phase. You'll come to your senses soon enough."

Saoirse scoffed. He talked as if she were a fourteen-year-old teenager who'd told her unsupportive dad for the first time that she liked girls. "You don't need me for your master plan. So why did you come here? What's in this city that's of so much interest to you?"

He watched her evenly, not even the twitch of a muscle betraying his thoughts. "I told you. I'm here for you. Why else do you think I had that pig killed? He was getting too close. And you were getting too soft. I tried to give you a push, to give yourself the chance to get rid of your shackles with your own two hands but... I realized I was being optimistic. So I had him removed for you."

Saoirse flung her feet from the table to lean forward and glare at him. "You didn't do this for me. You've been impersonating me, setting me up and riling up the other bosses so they'll come at me. You're trying to destroy me."

He still only smiled.

"Is this your revenge?" Saoirse got to her feet,

beginning to pace the room while speaking, almost as if to herself. "It's been ten years since I shot you, so why come back now? Is this some sort of pivotal moment in your life?" She stopped dead, a thought suddenly occurring to her. A thought that carried more dread than a hospital waiting room when the red light above the door turned off. She whipped around to him. "Are you dying?"

She wasn't sure why the mere thought of Graham O'Shea, her kidnapper, blackmailer, and puppet master dying of natural causes was so terrifying to her. But as she saw him sitting relaxed in his chair, his navy suit as pristine as it had always been, not a hair out of place, his jawline strong, his blue gaze fierce and sharp, she only saw her mentor, father figure, and role model. And she imagined the life fading from his eyes slowly, the face hollowing rapidly and his frame thinning until the suit seemed three sizes too large for him.

Killing him had been one thing. Watching him die slowly was another matter entirely.

"That's ridiculous, Saoirse."

The words were simple, even reprimanding, but they did wonders to reassure Saoirse. She still hadn't fully decided if she wasn't going to kill him again herself, but at least he wasn't going to be taken by illness.

9 April

4:47 p.m.

Lily

Stopping by the precinct, Lily judiciously avoided the bullpen, along with any of the detective's desks and the elevator, instead choosing to take one of the lesser used staircases behind the evidence lockers to head up to the forensics lab.

Only Bailee was there at the moment, typing away at her desk, Chuck's computer already off for the day.

"Detective," she said, smiling at Lily when she came through the door. "Watcha got for us this time?"

Lily arched an eyebrow. "What? I can't come by just to chat?"

Bailee chuckled, leaning her elbows on the table and weaving her fingers together. "You could, but somehow I don't think that's your style. Besides, you might just be the detective who's been keeping us busiest. You and that new kid, Jonah. You *always* have something new up your sleeve."

Lily wished she could disagree. If only to not

feel quite so guilty. Nevertheless, she stepped forward and placed the flash drive on the table. "How are you with electronics?"

Bailee made a face. "I mean, I can check it for prints, but if you're looking for more technical intel, you should probably check with the IT team. They probably also have someone in cybercrimes who can take the thing apart and look for hidden clues."

Lily nodded; she had been somewhat afraid of that. "I'd appreciate the prints," she said, looking around the room, her gaze stopping on some contraption that included various wires and thin metal rods. "What's that?"

"Oh that?" Bailee looked over. "Chuck's hobby. They like tinkering with that electro stuff. Actually, now that I think about it, there's a chance they could look at this. Save you talking to those asses from cybercrime."

"So… tomorrow then?"

"Oh, well, Chuck should be coming in within the next half hour or so. Graveyard shift again, y'know."

Lily shifted her weight uncomfortably as she nodded, wondering how much extra info she should be providing at this time, particularly since she hadn't seen the contents herself yet. She considered waiting for Chuck, but she doubted they'd be done with this by the time she had to leave to potentially receive Natalia Piarelli in her home.

Bailee cocked her head to one side, observing Lily closely. She almost seemed like a cat. "Anything in particular you want us to look out for?"

"Something hidden," Lily said. "I was told there aren't any obvious signs."

She refrained from mentioning Carlton, refusing to color the techs' opinion before they'd taken a look themselves, lest they should conjecture to find something *because* she'd told them, sort of like a self-fulfilling prophecy. She could always bring up the name later.

Bailee looked down at the stick with a mild frown, and Lily could see the question in her head clear as day. If she'd been given this by a trustworthy person, why hadn't she checked the contents?

Bailee slipped on some gloves and took the stick over to another table, her back to Lily. She rummaged around a little and then turned back around to her. "No obvious prints," she announced.

Lily wasn't overly surprised by that. "Can we... look at it?" she asked.

"Sure." Bailee rolled out a desktop from a corner that was standing on a wheeled projector-table along with a monitor, a mouse, and a keyboard. She plugged them in and turned the computer on. "This is the computer we use to check items of unknown content. It's unconnected to the network and gets wiped completely after every time we use it. It's to avoid any security leaks."

"Of course." While Lily wasn't exactly a stranger to technology, she was still a little overwhelmed. She reckoned that clinging a little to the old ways might be part of the territory when one grew up with their grandparents.

While Bailee got the computer ready, Lily took a glance out into the hallway, but at this time of day, most of the detectives had already gone home. Only those few assigned to work the night shift were still around, and, unless something dramatic happened in the city, they wouldn't be coming here, she figured.

Still good to check.

Satisfied that they wouldn't be interrupted — or caught — Lily joined Bailee to look at the flash drive's contents. There weren't many files, and no folders. The filenames were random jumbles of numbers, whether just by happenstance or intentionally, Lily couldn't say. There was a single image file, which Bailee opened first, instantly sucking in her breath. Lily received the view of Benson's face on the screen much more calmly, though she couldn't keep from clenching her fists a little more tightly. If nothing else, it proved that this really was the flash drive Kennedy had told her about. Which also meant that Kennedy must have seen her standing at the corner. It inspired Lily with new hope about their covert plans of working together.

"What is this?" Bailee asked, disturbed, turning her head to Lily.

"Open one of the other files," Lily said by ways of explanation, her eyes not flitting from the screen for even an instant.

Hesitantly, Bailee obeyed and opened one of the text files. It was a simple file, including not much more than Benson's personal info, such as address, workplace, birthday, height, weight, profession... The longer Lily looked at it, the more it looked like either some sort of confused resume, or some even worse dating profile.

Bailee went on to the next text file, which revealed detailed information about the layout of Benson's apartment, his route to work, the addresses of any close family members and friends, the exact position of his desk inside of the precinct, his favorite bar, and his weekly Zumba as well as his cooking classes, along with his running route on days off. It even included his work schedule for the month.

Whoever had set this up had really done their homework. Lily's heart sank. When her enemy had this much intel on their target, how in the world could she have kept him safe? The thought of a safehouse came to mind again, but based on how comprehensive this list was, she wasn't sure that it would have done much. Considering how loose the warning she'd been given was, she'd never stood a chance.

And she still didn't know *why* he'd been

wanted dead. These files didn't shed light on that either.

"What is this?" Bailee breathed. "It kinda looks like…"

"A very detailed report on everything connected to Benson to figure out the perfect time and place to kill him?" Lily asked. "Yeah. That's exactly what it is."

"Where did you *get* that?"

Lily shook her head. "It doesn't matter. And please make sure neither one of you tells anyone that I've got this—it might compromise the investigation. But basically, I need you to find any sort of trace with an indication to the author. I need to know where it originated."

Bailee nodded slowly, as if she were still trying to wrap her head around all of this. "I'll get Chuck on that as soon as they get in," she promised. "I'm assuming you'll be lying awake at home waiting for any info, so we'll call you."

"Aren't you finishing your shift soon?"

Bailee scoffed and shook her hand at the screen. "Are you kidding me? This is way beyond anything I've got at home. Nah, I wanna be a part of this."

Lily watched the other woman for a moment, thinking of the other several times this week when she'd worked overtime. "You're a bit of a workaholic, aren't you?"

Bailee laughed. "As if you're one to talk!"

"Touché."

**9 April
5:37 p.m.
Saoirse**

Saoirse watched with hawk eyes as O'Shea made pancake batter. After the mention of a potential illness driving him to his forceful return, he'd suggested taking a break for food, remarking on how spent Saoirse looked… in not exactly the most tactful of manners. Saoirse hadn't said anything against the matter, and so they'd moved to the kitchen, which—to her surprise—was actually stocked with food. Evidently, O'Shea must have taken to living here again, without her knowledge. Since Oliver hadn't told her, it couldn't have been for very long yet.

They didn't speak while he cooked, particularly once the butter greasing the pan began to sizzle. The stack of pancakes beside the pan got higher and higher, the first and last pancakes resembling horrible abominations, as was the most universal rule of nature of pancake-making.

Satisfied that O'Shea hadn't tampered with any of the typical ingredients, Saoirse dug into the stack of pancakes he placed in front of her with gusto just a moment after he started his own.

She might mistrust him to her core, but she wasn't going to miss out on his signature pancakes. Since it had been a decade since she had last tasted them, Saoirse had expected to be underwhelmed by the reality—after all, one did tend to hype up fond memories without realizing. She was sure she was no exception to that. But the pancakes lived up to her recollection. They were soft and fluffy, neither greasy nor burnt, and the taste of the egg and melted butter perfectly blended with the sticky sweetness of syrup.

"Saoirse," O'Shea purred after letting her devour about three-quarters of her stack undisturbed. "I want you to work for me again. Let's create a new world together. You know I'm the only one who you can see eye to eye with. The only one who could ever truly understand how you tick."

Slowing down her chewing, Saoirse set the fork down, with a slightly regretful thought to the pancakes that would be left uneaten. "I see now." Answers were written for questions that had been bothering her and fell into place. "That's why you've been sabotaging me. You wanted me to think less of the other bosses, and hoped to make my own people lose faith in me, didn't you?"

She cocked her head to the side, watching him closely. He'd been smiling before, but now his grin grew wider. "See?" he said. "You and me. We understand each other. In a way that no one else could comprehend. We're *family*, Saoirse. You're so talented. You're a prodigy at what you do. But you know as well as I do that the *field* is where your strengths lie. Your passion, too. You're not one to manipulate the strings from behind the scenes. But that's where *my* strengths lie. Together, we used to be an unstoppable team. And we can be that again. I forgive you for killing me. So, what do you say?"

Something about his words and the way he said them held sway over Saoirse on a nostalgic level. Working with him had always allowed her to focus on being part of the action in the past. No one had ever told her she couldn't go out, and he'd been the only one waiting for her at home. But he'd always been there. He'd never expected her to be anything different. He'd never worried that she might not make it back one day because he *knew* what she was capable of and trusted her to keep herself safe.

It had been an easier time. A less complicated and convoluted time.

But it had also been a hollower time. Her world had expanded since then. She'd found her own goals. Her own reasons for fighting. She didn't need O'Shea anymore.

But based on how intent he was on getting

her on his team again, it seemed that he needed her.

"No." Saoirse stood up, leaving the last few remnants of pancake untouched on her plate. "This is *my* city. I know I'm good at what I do, and I certainly don't need you to tell me. But I do things my way. So, out of respect for old times, I'm going to give you a choice." She paused, her fingertips resting on the table as she looked straight into his ice-blue eyes, unwavering and determined. "You can either leave now, or you can die a second time." She raised an eyebrow meaningfully. "What'll it be?"

O'Shea held her gaze for a moment. "Alright." He sighed and pulled a phone from an inside pocket of his suit jacket. He typed a few things and then put it away again, a nasty glint in his eyes above a self-satisfied smirk. "We'll do things the hard way."

9 April

6:15 p.m.

Lily

Lily was pacing up and down in her apartment, waiting for Natalia Piarelli's arrival. Of course, she didn't know if she was going to hear from the woman at all—her hunch might have been completely incorrect, or she might have freaked her out with her direct approach, but she held out hope until fifteen minutes past the time she'd written on the note.

Now she was contemplating whether she ought to wait any longer or check in with Bailee and Chuck to see if they'd found anything on the drive yet. And, failing that, there was a bar with a friendly bartender where she was welcomed.

Just as she was making up her mind to stop by the precinct on her way to *Samson's Crib*, there was a knock on the door.

Seconds later, Natalia and a tall Afro-American man were standing in her living room.

"You wanted to speak with me, Detective Rose?" Natalia looked straight at her, without the usual hesitation of someone who was dealing with law enforcement for the first time.

Lily nodded. "Please, sit down, Miss Piarelli and Mr. ..." She looked at the man questioningly.

"It's Mike," he said gruffly, and took a seat on the couch, though there was a tension in his shoulders and elbows that didn't fade. The bulge in his clothing where he carried a concealed handgun didn't escape Lily either.

"Natalia," Natalia said and sat down beside him.

"Then we might as well make this even. Call me Lily." Lily took a seat as well. "This is not on police records. Anything that is said here tonight will remain confidential and under the radar."

She didn't like bending the rules, but she had good reasons. Besides, this probably extended to the same agreement that she'd made with Kennedy.

Natalia nodded hesitantly. "Well?"

Lily had planned what to say. She'd run over practiced lines a million times, playing out the entire conversation through multiple variants, but now that it was real, she was having trouble finding the red thread connecting all the different parts of her mind.

"I have an old case file about your disappearance from a few years back," she began. "We're relatively certain that Saoirse Kennedy was responsible, and it was your fiancé who reported you missing. Considering who your father is, it struck us as strange."

When Lily mentioned Kennedy, Natalia's shoulders squared up, and there was a miniscule twitch in her lips before her gaze grew steelier.

"I wasn't kidnapped," she corrected. "I was saved. My fiancé was not a kind man."

Natalia had skillfully avoided bringing Kennedy into her answer at all, and Lily wasn't about to push for it. She knew it had been Kennedy. But that case was not why she was here. All the mention of it served was to cement her gut feelings about how Natalia connected to Kennedy. Clearly there was a level of gratitude, at least. Possibly Natalia had chosen to continue working for Kennedy in some manner after whatever incident had provoked her disappearance.

Judging by Mike's presence, Lily had to assume he was also involved with Kennedy, unless, of course, he was just Natalia's new boyfriend.

Subtlety had never been Lily's strong point, so perhaps it was best to just come straight out with what was on her mind. "Graham O'Shea, does his name ring a bell for you?"

"Isn't he dead?"

Lily had to admit Natalia was a good actress. She put on a very convincing performance of confused surprise—only a slight twitching of a vein in her neck implied that she wasn't entirely truthful. Meanwhile, Mike remained completely and utterly stone-faced.

"So I've been told," Lily admitted. "But it strikes me as a little odd that Saoirse Kennedy would get into a car with a ghost."

Natalia's face fell as she paled. She glanced at Mike, and he put a reassuring hand on her shoulder, before turning to Lily. "If you're trying to sniff out your partner's killer, you're barking up the wrong tree with Saoirse."

"I know she didn't do it." Her words had exactly the effect of surprise on them she had expected. Kennedy hadn't shared their little deal with her people any more than Lily had done with the precinct, it seemed. "But she told me who did. Thing is, I know there is a connection to her, and I need to know what that is, if I'm to prove that Timothy Carlton ordered the murder of Detective Jeremy Benson. So how do I get in touch with her... or this ghost who randomly appeared in the city after haunting elsewhere for ten years?"

Perhaps she was pushing a little too far, hoping for too much, but she was grasping at straws no matter where she looked.

Natalia dropped her eyes, biting on her lower lip. Then, her mouth parted, and she pointed at the TV guide as she nudged Mike in the side. His gaze followed hers, and his eyes also widened in surprise.

His attention flicked back to Lily. "She left you her number," he muttered. "Why? How? I mean..." He frowned, apparently trying to make sense of it.

Lily, confused about what either of them were talking about, took the TV guide. Unexpectedly, there was a phone number scribbled on the top of the page, something Lily herself would have never done.

Kennedy hadn't just up and left, then. She'd intentionally left a line of communication here. Once again, Lily felt frustrated by just how many corners she seemed to have to turn in this investigation.

Before she had the chance to continue asking any questions however, Mike's phone rang out, and he answered hurriedly.

"Yeah?" His face lost all color instantly. "We'll be right there. You know what to do."

He pushed the phone back into his pocket and looked at Lily. "Our headquarters were just blown up."

**9 April
6:18 p.m.
Saoirse**

"What are you talking about? You gonna set one of the other bosses on me?" Saoirse scoffed.

O'Shea got to his feet, smiling benevolently as if talking to an ignorant child. "I'm removing obstacles, that's all."

Suddenly, the blood in Saoirse's veins froze. "What do you mean?"

"I've always done that for you. Over and over and over again. Whenever something held you back, shackled you... I removed it."

Memories of the past flashed into Saoirse's mind, mostly from their joint time in Ireland. She narrowed her eyes at him. "You're planning on removing the *city*?"

Not even O'Shea could be that stupid—or powerful.

Right?

He still smiled his upsettingly cocky smirk. "I don't need to."

Saoirse loosely crossed her arms, and shifted her weight to her left leg, freeing up her right in case she needed to drop quickly without losing mobility.

"All I needed to do," O'Shea continued, "was destroy your place within this city."

"Needed?" Saoirse growled as his words got through to her. "What did you do?"

"Not much," he assured her, also getting to his feet. "Not much more than you did, at least, ten years ago."

Slowly walking around the table to stand beside her, every step was a threat, and a promise about what more he could do. Still, his words made little sense to Saoirse, though they were filling her with dread. Her neck was suddenly aware of every hair touching or brushing past it, her forehead was hot, her shoulders cold, and her stomach was a churning factory of acid.

She waited until O'Shea was within her reach, playing up the trembling in her legs, though she didn't have to add much, waiting for that cocky, self-satisfied smirk to be close enough...

The current of agitation throughout her body made her faster, though it still felt far too slow and sluggish. Saoirse ducked into a half-crouch, and stepped forward, toward O'Shea, placing one leg behind his as she rose up again, her own face inches from his, thumbs pushing into pressure points behind his collarbones.

He went down easily, allowing her to straddle him as he lay on the floor on his back, pinning his arms to the ground by pressing her knees into his muscles. For good measure, she removed his gun from the holster and pushed it into her belt.

A long time ago, back when they'd first met, he'd been able to defeat her easily. In fact, he'd trained her, teaching her assorted bits and pieces from various martial arts and street fighting. But while he had aged and removed himself from the fieldwork, she'd been honing her skills in the front lines, even after his death. Well, assumed death.

Although he had retained his looks, he'd aged. His body and muscles were no longer what they once were. And how could they be? He'd been shot in the head once—it must have incapacitated him for a long time, and his muscles would have atrophied. Building them up to the point where they'd once been might have been possible, but not at his age.

"I said," Saoirse hissed at him, "what did you do?"

Even though she had him pinned to the floor, he showed no signs of fear or lack of ease. He smiled at her, as if he couldn't imagine being in any nicer situation than this.

"I removed your distractions. I imagine you'll be more receptive to what I have to say." Even the way he spoke was just as confident and measured as before. The only sign that Saoirse's attack had had any real impact on him was the slight breathiness in his voice, almost wheezing, though he covered it up well.

Synapses in Saoirse's mind finally connected, firing ideas at her. After all, what had she done ten years ago?

She'd blown up some buildings. *His* buildings.

She'd barely finished the thought when she felt her personal phone buzz twice at her hip. There were only three people who had that number.

O'Shea was still smiling. "Better check what they have to tell you," he suggested. "I imagine it'll give you new perspective."

Without giving him an inch more of wiggling room, Saoirse slowly pulled out her phone to check the text message.

Someone blew up your home. Heading there now with N & M. Tulip.

Burning anger made way for cold, calculated fury as Saoirse returned her gaze from her phone to O'Shea.

For the first time since he'd risen from the proverbial dead, a flash of uncertainty crossed his face.

9 April

6:21 p.m.

Lily

Lily slid the phone back into her pocket. Mike and Natalia had run out of her apartment the moment after Mike had shared the news, and she'd only taken the time to tear off the part of the TV guide with Kennedy's number and grabbed her keys as she ran after them.

Mike had managed to hail a taxi by the time she caught up to them and they piled in together, Natalia and Mike anxiously whispering to one another, while Lily texted Kennedy, telling the other two that she was doing so.

The cab driver had caught on to the urgency in Mike's voice, and tore through the city's streets, only barely remaining within speed limit allowances. Like any experienced cabbie, she had a few shortcuts up her sleeve, with added suggestions from Mike here and there, which brought them to their destination much faster than Lily had thought possible. Of course, it helped that the evening rush had already passed.

"What the...?" the cabbie murmured as she brought the taxi to a screeching halt in front of the burning compound.

Mike and Natalia practically fell out of the car when they scrambled to the group gathered ahead. Lily made sure to pay their driver before she followed them.

A woman with long, straight, dark hair and an amber complexion along with almost black eyes had placed both hands on Mike's shoulders when Lily got there. "Breathe. It's fine. No one's in there. Some of the guys got hurt," she glanced back to where a few people were laying on the ground, being tended to, "but they'll be all right."

"Tally..." he pleaded, but the woman shook her head.

"Look, we gotta find Saoirse. She's not responding to her beeper. I thought she was planning to meet with you," her eyes flicked to Natalia, "but I'm guessing she was held up somewhere."

As if on cue, Lily's phone buzzed in her pocket, a glance revealing Kennedy's number calling.

"Looks like everyone's alive," Lily said by ways of answering.

There was an audible sigh of relief at the other end. "How bad is it?"

Kennedy's voice was measured, even. There was no sign of grief there, though she had just been told that she'd lost her home. She didn't even sound angry.

Lily glanced at the furnace in a ruin that had been an intact cement block only a few hours earlier. "I don't think you'll be wanting to invest into renovating it," she said. "A few of your guys are injured, but no one seriously from what I've heard. *Where are you?*"

"Thanks. Hand me to Mike, please."

Aware that everyone had stopped talking when she'd picked up the phone and was now staring at her, watching, Lily resigned herself to her fate and handed the phone to Mike. He took it readily.

"Boss. ... We don't know who did it yet. Tally's already organized a transport. ... No, the cops aren't here yet." He glanced at Lily. "Well, excluding your pet."

Lily gave him an intense glare, which he duly ignored. But he was right. The cops weren't here. By now she should have been hearing sirens, at least, but there was nothing. A blast like this one should have been noticed and reported, so why was nothing happening?

Newly deprived of her phone, Lily didn't have the option of calling for backup, whether it be Detective Clifford or Bailee, so she decided to take a closer look at the carnage. She headed toward the still flaming compound, aware of scrutinizing eyes staring at her back, and Natalia following her at a distance.

Though she was no forensic expert by any means, Lily gathered by the lay of the remains that there must have been two sets of explosives, attached to two corners of the compound, but she had no idea what type or why.

She could imagine that Saoirse Kennedy had ruffled a lot of feathers in the underworld over the years, but except for those fires a decade ago, Lily had seen no evidence of anything of this measure happening to her. She'd gotten the impression that the other criminals in the city respected or feared Kennedy too much to do anything like this. Apparently, she'd been wrong.

She glanced back at the group mostly huddled together. If that was all of Kennedy's guys, then there were significantly less of them than Lily had supposed. Even if they only made up half of the group, it was fewer than she'd ever ventured to guess. A couple of unmarked vans in muted colors came racing around the corner, stopping near the group. They moved quickly, filing into the vehicles with remarkable speed. By the time Lily returned to them, everyone bar the dark-haired woman, Natalia, and Mike had climbed or been carried in.

Mike gave her phone back and then nodded toward the van. Finally, the first wails of shrill sirens were disturbing the night.

"We gotta run. Hope you get the guy."

She nodded, and his eyes fell on Natalia.

"Coming?" he asked.

Natalia took a step closer to Lily. "No. I think it's time my kidnapping was resolved."

Mike nodded. "Take care." He and the other woman jumped into the last van, and it ran on, around a corner, moments before the first vehicles of the fire brigade and first aid appeared. With a certain level of exasperation and annoyance, Lily noted that it was another two minutes after that, while the firemen were already running around the place and working on extinguishing the fire, before her fellow police arrived at the scene.

One of the firemen came running toward her while the others were busying themselves with the hose. "What happened? Anyone injured? Was anyone inside?"

Lily shook her head. "Not as far as we know," she said, putting on her police face — the one that was matter of fact and didn't allow for disagreement. "There seems to have been some explosives, but we don't know who did it or why."

The fireman looked at the burning building with a frown. "Any idea who owns it? We need to contact them ASAP."

Lily smiled slightly and pulled out her badge to flash at the fireman who nodded in acknowledgement. "I'm on it," she promised.

It was only then the police car arrived with wailing sirens, Bailee and Detective Clifford bursting out.

"Wait here," Lily told Natalia, before she jogged over to them to explain the situation in the same terms she'd given to the fireman. After giving them her initial impressions, Clifford rushed away to talk to the lieutenant of the fire brigade to coordinate and find out what else they needed, before Bailee could go in with one of their own forensics.

"No one was inside?" Bailee repeated as if to reassure herself.

Lily shook her head, watching Clifford taking charge of the situation.

"And how did you get here so quickly? Were you in the area?"

Bailee's questions were sending bouts of uncertainty and worry though Lily's system, but she managed to keep up her calm and professional charade, though she wished Bailee would stop asking.

"I happened to be nearby," she said. "There's a bar around the corner."

She wasn't sure if that was true, but seeing as no matter where you were, there was always a bar around a corner *somewhere*, she figured it probably wasn't a stretch, provided no one asked her for the name or to take them there.

Bailee watched her for a moment longer. "Right. Well, I've got good news for you."

Immediately, Bailee had earned every ounce of Lily's attention. "Yeah?"

The other woman smiled and pulled out two folded pieces of paper. "Chuck told me to give this to you. Seems they found something worthwhile."

Lily didn't wait to check the paper, despite the large number of people nearby. None of them were paying her any attention.

There was an IP address on the sheet, along with a physical address it corresponded with. An address in the west of town, in the posher parts of the outskirts, right around the location Kennedy had mentioned Carlton living.

"How did they get this?" Lily asked, incredulous of how much luck she'd had.

Bailee shrugged. "Beats me. Something about the image of Detective Benson, apparently. It was downloaded from our website recently, from this IP address. Apparently, the only time this year."

It wasn't evidence. Really, it was barely much of anything. But it was something, and in combination with other details, it might become something akin to evidence. Now Lily just needed to find those other pieces to complete the puzzle.

9 April
6:27 p.m.
Saoirse

"Well?" O'Shea said, when Saoirse hung up after speaking with Mike. The flash of uncertainty she'd seen in his face before was gone again, exchanged for the self-satisfied, confident smirk of one who thoroughly believed he couldn't lose.

"You blew up my home," she said evenly, coldly.

He shrugged, insofar it was possible considering his pinned position on the floor. "Which means you are now free... untethered. So why don't you let go of me and we can plan out the next steps over a nice cup of tea? Well," he reflected, "whatever passes for tea here."

He'd always been a snob about tea. He really only drank one kind—Irish Breakfast Tea—and even there he was very particular about what type from which brand. Saoirse had quite literally seen him kill a man over an argument about which tea was the "correct" one. He liked it strong, steeping for several minutes until the tea was so heavy and thick, it was almost like drinking bitter mud. And then he added a splash of milk. Not more than a single drop, just enough to brighten up the liquid into an earthy color from its deep, dark blackish brown.

Saoirse had always been more adaptable. She took the tea as it came. Sure, she had her preferences, and she also enjoyed a cup of coffee now and then, but in the end, it was all just leaf or bean water.

"You miscalculated," she said, watching him unempathetically. Rose's text message had left her afraid—scared, not for her own safety, not for her future, but for her people. In their line of work, things happened, and people could die, but not like this. Not while they were home, unsuspecting, inoffensive. Not all of them at the same time.

Luckily, it seemed that it had been O'Shea himself who'd ensure their safety. Almost no one had been there, all of them busy working at the other storage hall, dealing with shipping out the illegal cosmetics that had been delayed thanks to the interference from Garrison, induced by O'Shea himself.

There'd been some injuries, Mike had told her, but no deaths. And Rose was dealing with the follow up. Saoirse didn't believe the detective would cover up that this had been Saoirse's hide-out, and truthfully, she didn't expect her to. It wasn't part of their deal. Not directly, anyhow.

It hadn't sounded like the detective had made any progress on getting Carlton off the streets yet, which was a pity. Then again, O'Shea had just taken away the last qualms Saoirse had about removing him.

Looking at O'Shea, she no longer saw her old mentor and father figure. Instead, she saw a lunatic who would stop at nothing and stoop to the lowest depths to get what he wanted. She saw the kind of person she hated most—someone without honor, without principle.

Someone who was poison.

"I don't miscalculate," O'Shea said smugly.

"Oh no?" Saoirse smiled, feeling amused and disparaged in equal measures. She pulled lipstick from a pocket of her pants and applied it with an easy, practiced movement. She didn't need a mirror to know how it looked. It was a bright, matte tone, like the color of fresh, oxygen-rich blood. It was a color that made her skin look even paler than it already was, but in a way, that only heightened the effect she was aiming for.

"You're stalling," O'Shea said. "You don't know what to do, now that you've lost everything. But that's okay. Not everything is gone, you know. It's like a new start. You and me, back together like good old times."

She glanced down at him, bemused at his continued insistence, but also by remembering just how much power he had held over her until only a few minutes ago. His hold over her had broken the moment she learned of the line he'd crossed.

There were some things that were more important than a shared past and shared connections.

"Like old times," she repeated, pensively. "Yeah." His grin widened, though her gaze regained no warmth as she contemplated him. "But this time, I won't be as sloppy."

Realization dawned on him, and his smile faded, his eyes—clear as a summer day—seeing her for who she truly was, perhaps for the first time. "You don't carry a gun anymore," he pointed out.

Saoirse tilted her head to one side, a stray strand of hair having escaped her ponytail, now cascading along her neck to her collarbone. She smiled at him, gently, because after all, he had meant something to her, once. "No. But you do."

Unbeknownst to him, she'd taken his gun off him during their little fight and wedged it into her belt from whence she now pulled it. She checked for ammunition first, then undid the safety. Like her, he'd always preferred using a beretta. Unsurprising, considering he'd been the one to teach her to shoot.

The weight familiar in her hands, she pointed the barrel at him, at his eyes. This time, she'd do it right. Back then, she hadn't had the heart to look him straight in the eyes as she'd killed him.

She'd done it in the style of an assassin—an unseen shadow in the night—but that had been her mistake. There'd been distance between them, and she hadn't gone back to check, too certain that the deed had been completed. Of course, she'd also set the building on fire, confident that it would deal with his remains in their entirety.

But this way, in this close range, there was no way he could return to haunt her once more.

She smiled at him, softly. "Goodbye, Graham."

The sudden splatter of blood gave her neither the relief, nor the grief she'd expected to feel. Then again, she hadn't felt those things before, either. Or perhaps, she was feeling both, intermingled? She really couldn't decide. Suffice it to say that body would never move again of its own accord, the blood on the kitchen tiles almost the color of her lips.

Slowly, Saoirse stood up, wondering about her next move. Mike had informed her where Talitha had decided to bring everyone, which was going to be their interim HQ, until she had the chance to organize one of the backups she'd set up a while ago. But, since she knew her people were safe, she had no real desire to go meet them right now. There'd be questions to answer and far too much to handle, and for once, Saoirse really did just want to relax for a while. Besides, her own clothes had been splattered with blood, too. It would be simply unseemly to go out into the street looking like this.

Perhaps a bath was just what she needed.

Without another glance, Saoirse stepped across the body and headed up to the second floor for the first time in ten years.

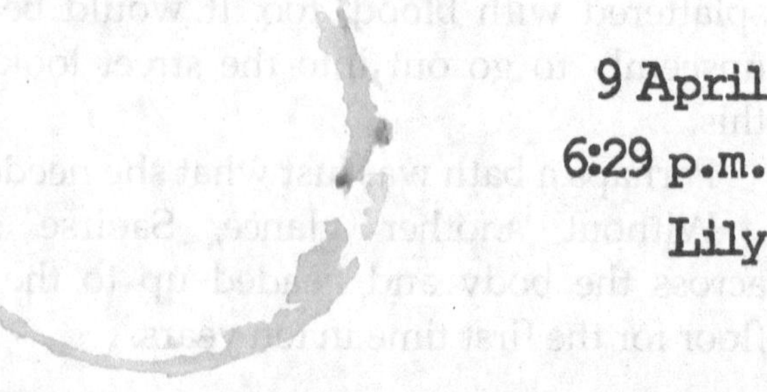

9 April
6:29 p.m.
<u>**Lily**</u>

"This is Natalia Piarelli." Lily introduced Natalia to Clifford and Bailee. "She was reported missing a few years ago by her fiancé at the time. As it turns out, she didn't want to be found by him, and there may have been a certain level of physical violence involved." Lily glanced at Natalia, who affirmed the statement with a nod. "So we will be starting work at resolving that case tomorrow and also file a restraining order against the man, just in case. I'd like you to help me out with that, if you don't mind."

She clapped Clifford jovially on the shoulder and he nodded hurriedly. "Absolutely!"

"For now, would you bring her to a hotel? You can tell them to send me the bill," Lily added, as she gestured toward his car.

Again, he hurriedly assured his help. "But couldn't we take that out of the budget?" he asked.

Lily smirked at his naivety. "Some detectives maybe could. But there is a proper way, involving a lot of paperwork and prior permission for most of us. I don't think I'd get approval since Miss Piarelli has not been kidnapped but disappeared of her own volition. I suppose you could say this is an act of kindness from one woman to another."

"Right..." Though the young man seemed perturbed by her explanation, he accepted it and led Natalia to the car, Bailee hanging back, still watching Lily with a certain amount of mischievous curiosity. It reminded Lily a little of Kennedy. And not in a bad way.

Lily's buzzing phone saved her from having to come up with something to say. Without checking the number, she lifted it to her ear.

"Yup?" she asked, expecting to hear Kennedy talk, but she was disappointed. Instead, she heard Mindy's voice.

"Hey, Lily?"

"Yeah?"

"Oh good, I did get you this time. I think I got the number wrong before and ended up talking to this woman working at a crocodile sanctuary or something in Florida. Weirdest conversation I've had all week, and that's saying something, you know."

"Mindy," Lily interrupted, trying to steer the barkeeper back to her reason for calling. "What's up? Need anything?"

"Oh right, yes. Your homeless friend came by, y'know, Tatjana?"

Immediately Lily perked up. If the homeless woman had stopped by *Samson's Crib*, chances were high that she had some intel. "What did she say?"

Lily nodded, listening careful to Mindy repeating the woman's words. Her smile widened with every sentence she heard.

As she listened, she hurriedly gestured for Bailee to give her something to write, which she was promptly provided with. She scribbled the plates she was given down and handed the paper back to Bailee, along with the number, tapping on it meaningfully. Bailee nodded, then walked a few steps away to call the precinct to run the plates, while Lily continued listening to Mindy.

Finally, they finished, Lily giving Mindy instructions to let Tatjana order whatever she wanted, which Lily would pay for later.

By the time she finished, Bailee was also done, holding up the notepad, with an address and a name now written underneath the plates. "What is this for?" she asked, waving it through the air.

"It's our connection to the flash drive," Lily answered, grinning. "See, that car was seen acting very suspiciously in front of Benson's building the night he was murdered. And now we know that it's registered to Mr. Timothy Carlton. It might not be enough to convict him, but it is certainly enough to arrest him. So, if nothing else, it's a start."

"And the witness?"

"I'm going to talk to her now. Wanna come?" In her elated state, Lily added, "I can buy you that drink I promised."

Bailee flashed her a sinful grin. "Thought you'd never ask."

Having been served a proper meal, Tatjana had acknowledged that Lily really did hold up her end of the bargain and where she'd been tight-lipped and jumpy before, she was now chattering away, giving Lily all sorts of details she remembered.

"Would you be comfortable testifying, if it comes to it?" Lily asked gently, while Tatjana was sipping at a lemonade.

The homeless woman hesitated, confliction clear in her face, but Mindy having told her about Benson's fate, and the food in front of her seemed to help her make up her mind. She nodded. "People like that are not good," she said. "They need to be stopped. It's not like stealing bread because they are hungry. It's evil, stealing a life." Then, hurriedly she added. "Not that I would steal bread... I am not a thief!"

The suddenly frightened expression on her face made Lily smile. She seemed like a bunny who'd just noticed the shadow of a falcon. "Don't worry, you're fine."

Mindy had left the bar to be tended to by one of her employees—a young, nervous-looking college student Lily hadn't met before—and had ushered them all into a back room when they'd arrived, where Tatjana had already been eating with gusto. Even now, the five women were sat together around a table, everyone with a drink of some description in front of them, though Tatjana was the only one eating.

"Want me to find you a bed for the night?" Lily asked.

Tatjana shook her head. "I have a place to sleep. I prefer the outside."

Lily accepted her response without argument. Tatjana wouldn't be the first homeless person she'd met who slept in the outdoors by choice. Back when she'd still lived with her grandparents, she got to know a friend of theirs—a man who had once been a dentist, well respected at that. But when his home had burned down along with his sleeping wife, he hadn't been able to sleep easily inside anymore. He'd tried, at first, but he'd always have one panic attack after another, so he started going camping, far away from other people. Before long, he even ditched the tent, instead sleeping under the clear night sky, and after that, he'd told her, he just didn't want to sleep in a building again. He liked having the stars sing him to sleep every night too much. And so, he'd instead become a homeless man in their community, still respected by those who had known him before, but he no longer practiced dentistry, and he slept in the parks or just outside of town in the fields or forests. Her grandparents had occasionally invited him for dinner, which he accepted, but any invitation for a bed or an overnight stay was declined, unless it had him sleeping in the garden.

Whatever Tatjana's story was, Lily didn't need to know.

The only thing that mattered was that she'd been nearby, and she'd seen a shadow climb across the fire escapes after a gun had been fired, and then, the figure had gotten into Carlton's car one street over.

The only drawback of her story was that she hadn't actually seen Carlton. From the way she described the shadowy figure, it was obvious that it hadn't been the man himself, but someone who'd been hired for the job. Just like Carlton had attempted to hire Kennedy.

Two pieces of circumstantial evidence on her side of the court, and Carlton probably didn't know that she had those pieces of information, meaning he might be feeling quite safe in his position. It wasn't out of the question that he'd been the one to blame for the explosion, hoping that the flash drive that might give him away would be caught in the fray.

But, lacking any evidence linking Carlton to this particular incident, Lily put this suspicion on ice for the moment. Kennedy probably had more than enough enemies who might decide to go on the offense if they saw an opening. No need to assume this was linked only because it happened to temporally coincide.

Like any cop worth their salt, Lily knew that crime didn't sleep. Thinking back to how exhausted Kennedy had been when she'd picked her up, perhaps that was more literally true than she had previously supposed.

Lily took a sip of her juice. She needed more. More evidence linking to Carlton. More evidence to remove any ongoing suspicions that Kennedy might be playing her, working only to get Lily to do her dirty work and get rid of someone in her way. It was still possible that Kennedy had planted any and all of the evidence. She might have even blown up her home herself. It was terribly convenient that none of her people had been killed.

Lily bit herself on the tongue the moment the thought occurred to her. It was a terrible thing to think, considering she'd seen the injuries on those people. Bad burns, one of them looked like he might have lost a leg. Lily hadn't had the time to look closely.

If she only got one more piece of evidence, she'd feel more at ease about all this. Just one more, to be certain. Because while she wanted to put Benson's killer behind bars, she didn't want to risk damning someone innocent.

9 April
7:16 p.m.
Saoirse

Baths were so nice and pleasant. The warmth seeping into every part of her body, heating her up until she was floating on air, the sensual smell of bath salts and the bubbles!

Oh, the bubbles.

Saoirse couldn't remember when she'd last taken a bath, much less one as luxurious as the one she was allowing herself now, but the bubbles were really the strawberry on top of the cake. Saoirse had never been much a fan of icing, but strawberries... now there was something good. Now that she was thinking about it—the tension leaving her muscles and the warmth soaking her—a bowl of strawberries with some fresh cream would make this just perfect. It was a pity she hadn't thought of that before getting into the steaming tub, because she knew it wouldn't be the same if she got up now and went to get it.

The bubbles had turned pink after she'd gotten into the scalding water; they'd match the inside of a strawberry so wonderfully. Perhaps that was the reason they'd come to mind in the first place.

Maybe it was wrong to enjoy herself like this when there was a dead body in the kitchen downstairs, but she needed this before clean-up. Besides, now that she knew her people were safe for the moment, and she'd already called her contact working in cremation, there really wasn't much for her to do except wash the blood off her body and give herself a moment to breathe.

It wasn't over yet. She was no longer being haunted, and this spirit was now laid to rest for good, but there were still so many things to take care of.

Carlton was still on the run, for one thing, though he didn't know that O'Shea was no more. How would he react once he found out? There must have been something that enticed him to help O'Shea. If he shared the same goal, he might try to continue O'Shea's legacy, try to *become* O'Shea. Saoirse didn't know how long they'd been working together, but it might have been long enough for Carlton to understand how these things worked. If he had, that'd be bad, because he had money, and no one really knew of him yet. Of course, it was nothing Saoirse wouldn't be able to handle, but it was bothersome. Much better to leave it to Rose.

Curious about how that side of things was going, Saoirse fished for her phone, and scripted a text to the detective.

Got him yet?

The answer was swift and to the point.

No. Need more evidence.

Saoirse sighed. *Time to get back to work.* She never liked leaving things for another day when they could be done now. Too many chances for something to go wrong. For someone to have a stupid idea. For people like O'Shea to show up.

Resigned to her fate, Saoirse sat up and climbed out of the bath, the washing machine being almost through the quick cycle she'd set it to, so her T-shirt and pants should be free of blood again momentarily. A quick spin in the dryer and she'd be all set to go.

Sitting on the edge of the bathtub, dripping onto the floor, Saoirse went through her mental list. She'd already called the crematorium, so all of that had been set in motion. She knew that the stuff she needed for her next act of arson was stored in the basement of this very building, so she didn't even need to go out, and she could use O'Shea's car for now, his keys probably being in his pocket. She'd need to check his body for any other useful items anyway. Perhaps she'd even find another piece of evidence for Rose. Talitha and Mike had the situation with her people under control for the moment, so she could deal with the next steps there at a later point.

Remembering that her bikes had also been lost in the explosion left Saoirse with a sudden flash of sadness, but at least one of them was still safely parked at Lysander's shop. She'd check in with them later and pick it up, maybe when she passed on O'Shea's car to Yamaguchi. He liked dealing with stolen cars. It was kind of his specialty. If nothing else, he might appreciate it as a gesture of peace on her part. It would help smooth over the ripples O'Shea had created.

But first things first.

While her clothes were being dried by the old machine, Saoirse went downstairs, naked, and searched O'Shea's body. There wasn't much to find. Having already taken his gun, she found only his car keys and a burner phone. Not even a wallet. Frustrated, Saoirse had to acknowledge that not much had changed there. She'd hoped for something more. But no matter.

She took the keys and the gun, placing them on the table near the front door, before going down to the cellar and getting the two cannisters of gasoline waiting there.

She began distributing it in the kitchen, moving on to the living room and then up the stairs to the bedrooms, making sure to leave space for her to move down without having to trudge through the stuff. By the time she was done, she only had a few more minutes to wait for her clothes to finish up, so she went back downstairs and grabbed a kitchen knife before using it to pry the rings off O'Shea's fingers. Some of them hadn't been removed in decades it seemed, so instead of pulling like a maniac, Saoirse settled for the easy choice in those cases.

That done, she headed back upstairs and rinsed off any splashes of blood that might have hit her and finally put her clothes back on. They weren't fully dry yet, still feeling a little damp, but they were warm, and that was good enough for the moment.

She took a set of matches from the kitchen and fired another text to Rose while she waited in front of the door.

You'll probably hear of a fire some time soon. Don't let it bother you, it's not worth investigating. I'm about to pay a visit to Timothy Carlton. <3

She pressed send and then lit a match, holding it to the tablecloth, until it caught fire. In a moment or so, some of it would drop to the floor, igniting the trail of gasoline. Time to go.

Without a single look back, Saoirse said her silent goodbyes and took the gun and keys as she walked out the front door to the car that was still waiting.

By the time she rounded the corner of the street, the house still hadn't caught. She halted the car there near an old phone booth and paid a quarter to make a call to the local fire department. Changing her voice and accent to mimic an older, southern American lady, she spoke quickly, the moment her call was picked up.

"There's a fire at 421 Ellen Street! It's the whole house just gone and gone up in flames! Please help!"

She hung up before the operator could ask a question and sauntered back to the car and drove off, heading straight for Timothy Carlton's estate.

9 April
7:42 p.m.
<u>**Lily**</u>

Lily paled reading Kennedy's latest text.

"I've gotta go," she said sharply, heading straight for the door, but Bailee held her back with a frown.

"What's going on?" she asked. "Need backup?"

Gnawing on her lip, Lily allowed herself a moment to contemplate the situation.

She certainly didn't have enough proof to arrest Carlton, but according to the text she'd just received, Kennedy was about to set his house on fire… potentially with him inside.

While a part of her, the vengeful part that wanted to see karma and cosmic justice at work, wouldn't have minded that happening, the rest of her screamed at the thought. It wasn't justice. Justice would be if he paid for his crimes, did his time while doing things that benefitted society. That was what Benson would have wanted, too. And that was the part that mattered. Saoirse Kennedy had no right to come down on Carlton like a wrathful angel of vengeance. And so Lily was left with one single option: Stop Kennedy and save Carlton, so she could put him behind bars.

She shot Clifford a text.

Call for back-up to 18 South Barrington Avenue. I'm heading straight there. Come prepared, might be multiple perps.

Lily could have put in the request herself, but she imagined that there was going to be more luck with him doing it.

Leaving him to his task, Lily jogged over to the bar. "Mindy, I need to borrow your car."

Apparently, her expression was serious enough, because Mindy didn't ask questions. Instead, she simply slid some car keys across the bar.

"It's a red Toyota. Parked at the corner of 4th."

Lily nodded her thanks and raced out. Locating the car easily, she thrust herself inside, glad to feel the weight of her gun and badge at her hip, though wishing she'd kitted up before heading out with Natalia and Mike. Bailee dropped into the passenger seat, along with a large handbag.

"Equipment," she said in response to Lily's look.

Instead of replying, Lily kicked the gas pedal. No more time to lose if she wanted to beat Kennedy to the punch.

It took no more than a few minutes for Lily to cross town, but even though she made full use of the flashing lights of Bailee's portable Cherry beacon, it felt as though the entire city had conspired to delay her.

She was gnawing on the insides of her cheek, surprised that she hadn't tasted blood yet, her eyes staring ahead, squinting to decode the city colors and lights through the heavy rain that had begun.

At least in this downpour it was unlikely that any fire Kennedy set would be able to keep up for long. But Lily was under no illusions. That woman didn't need a fire to kill Carlton. She probably didn't even need an excuse.

"What's happening?" Bailee asked for the third time. "Is he making a run for it?"

Lily's fingers wrapped tightly around the steering wheel as she stared ahead. The joints in her fingers were actually beginning to hurt from the constant pressure.

"Looks like Kennedy is about to kill him. We gotta stop her." Lily growled the response through grinding teeth, glaring at the cars in her way, taking so impossibly long to move aside to let her pass.

"How do you know?" Bailee asked, confusion and curiosity mixing in with her voice. "You got an informant? The one who gave you that note, before?"

Lily didn't respond. Partially because she was

weaving through cars trying to avoid her at the highest speed she could manage without losing control over the car on the partially flooding road, partially because she really didn't want to say anything that could get her uncomfortable questions later, or even manage to get her in trouble.

Finally, they raced up to the address Bailee had found for Lily earlier. Home of Timothy Carlton, businessman extraordinaire.

It was a large, imposing mansion, not out of place in this part of town, but nevertheless impressive, even by these standards. A large wall was surrounding its vast grounds, a metal, fenced gate occupying the driveway up to the building. Except that the gate was standing wide open, with not a soul in sight.

The building wasn't smoking, and there were no signs of any fire, but it looked deserted, and, more worrying than that, was the fact that even the front door of the building was swinging openly in its hinges.

Her stomach churning, Lily drove straight in, all the way up to the entrance steps. She didn't even pull the keys from the ignition before she tore the car door open and raced up the steps to push into the house.

**9 April
7:43 p.m.
Saoirse**

Knowing that she was significantly closer to Carlton's mansion than Rose was, Saoirse grinned to herself about her ambiguous text message. By the time Rose would make it to the front door, Saoirse figured she'd already be done with her business. She was looking forward to the frantic and probably angry expression on Rose's face though.

Now that she knew that O'Shea was dealt with and could never return to haunt her again, or put anything or anyone she loved in danger, it felt as though a glacier of weight had been lifted off Saoirse's shoulders. The bath having rid her of the last stretches of tension, she was feeling like her old self again. Mischievous, and determined.

Saoirse didn't bother breaking for the large, iron-wrought gate when she arrived at Carlton's mansion and a downpour began. Instead, she drove straight through without a care for the impact or the unhappy sounds from the car, seeing the guards jump out of the way with a bout of satisfactory glee. Racing up the driveway, she only steered to the side at the last moment, skidding over the wet grass around the building.

As she had hoped, the back entrance was opening, letting out a number of armed guards, pointing their weapons at her. Unfortunately, they hadn't kept in mind that not only was she in a car, she was in *O'Shea*'s car. And if she knew her mentor the way she thought she did, it would be bulletproof. One didn't get as far as he had by taking unnecessary chances.

Saoirse used the momentum of the car and the slickness of the ground to skid, gliding across the grass in a spinning motion. She caught several of the guards with the rear end of the vehicle, throwing them aside, the bullets hitting the windshields and windows barely creating impact. The car came to a sudden halt when it crashed into the building's wall, giving Saoirse a bout of whiplash. Before getting out, she rubbed the back of her neck and gave the world a moment's time to stop spinning while she assessed the situation. There'd only been four guys, she noticed now. Two had been hit by the car's swinging, one had run back inside, and one she had trapped between the vehicle and the building. By the looks of him, he'd live, but he might need to take some time to rehabilitate.

Time for the show to start.

Taking the safety off O'Shea's gun, Saoirse left

the car, and walked calmly toward the still open door, keeping a close eye on the guards, lest one of them should come to make a fatal decision. Fatal for him, of course.

It appeared that they'd learned that their job wasn't worth their life, because even though Saoirse was met with some hateful glares, none of them made a move toward their weapons. Carlton hadn't invested in securing their loyalty, it seemed.

And so, Saoirse headed inside, undisturbed. No one came to meet her until she was standing in front of Carlton's office door. An unwelcome memory of being knocked out the last time she'd been here flashed into her mind.

Instead of questioning it, Saoirse dropped to the floor, sweeping her leg across the ground behind her with momentum. Jean's body weight and resistance barely made a difference to her move. His legs were caught from underneath him, and he toppled over, dropping the tissue undoubtedly soaked with something like chloroform. Saoirse was on top of him before he'd even realized what had happened.

Confused and impressed, he looked up at her, his arms pinned, her knee on his throat, ready to drop her weight on it.

"Hi, Jean," Saoirse said, smiling at him cheerfully. She was feeling good. Her game was back, and her instincts had returned to something she could trust. "I just have a question real quick... what's your tie to him?" She jerked her head to the door when she said it.

Jean's eyes followed her movement. "He pays me," he said, as though that should have been obvious.

Saoirse nodded. "And O'Shea?" she continued. She was willing to believe whatever he'd tell her. Right now, he didn't know if there was a benefit in lying. And besides, assassins weren't in the habit of lying to one another. It was bad practice. And irrelevant, anyhow. Lying didn't do you any good because lies could be found out. It was always safer to tell the truth or say nothing at all.

"He told me I could be like you." Jean's eyes took on a sparkle. "Powerful. *Someone*."

Saoirse couldn't hold back the snort of laughter. The notion that anyone would want to "be like her" was ridiculous. But she could see how O'Shea had ensnared the boy. She'd thought it was odd that an unknown assassin could be found by someone like Carlton. O'Shea sniffing him out made an awful lot more sense. He'd done it before, after all. Saoirse knew better than anyone how good the silver fox's nose was when it came to these things.

"Well, let me give you some advice then," Saoirse said, holding Jean tight, though he was struggling against her grasp. "You wanna be like me, you find something you care about. And then you protect it *no matter the cost*. Got it? You don't need O'Shea for that. Or Carlton, for that matter."

She didn't bother telling him that O'Shea was dead. After all, who knew whether that would even make a difference to a boy like him? She didn't know how long he'd been trained by O'Shea, but if he was anything like Saoirse had been before she'd snapped and broken free of her mental conditioning, he wouldn't believe that O'Shea could be killed. He'd attack her for the lie and then go out and search for O'Shea.

Unable to trust he'd just let it go and leave, Saoirse dropped some weight on his airways while clocking the back of the beretta against his temple, knocking him out. Though his muscles had gone lax, Saoirse retrieved his tissue and held it against his face for a few moments, just to be safe.

Now, to the endgame.

Gun still in hand, Saoirse opened the door to the study. She found Carlton sitting in his armchair, calm and collected on the outside, the gun in his hand trained on her.

"Oh, Timothy," Saoirse said in mock-pity. "So you haven't heard yet, have you?"

Carlton narrowed his eyes at her. "Heard what?" he asked. Now that she got a closer look at him, Saoirse could see droplets of sweat forming on his temple. The first sirens reached her ears, still muffled, but approaching quickly. Her red-lipped smile widened, like that of the

devil about to take a soul.
"Let's make this quick."

11 April
5:54 p.m.
Lily

Unsatisfied, Lily dipped back and forth in her chair, gnawing at the nail of her thumb.

"That's not good for you, you know," Bailee informed her as she sat down on a chair in front of her. "And what are you so annoyed for, anyhow? You got him and he confessed, isn't that what you wanted?"

Lily glared at her friend. After all that build up with the explosion and Kennedy's cryptic message, Lily had run into Carlton's mansion, ready to wrestle Kennedy to the ground and take a lighter from her, but the woman hadn't even been there. Not only that, but Timothy Carlton had been unharmed. Well, mostly unharmed. He had been sporting a broken nose and some reddish marks that had later developed into fairly nasty bruises, but he hadn't been dead. Or even nearly dead. He had, however, been a sniveling mess, and, upon seeing Lily, he'd practically screamed his confession at her, begging her to take him with her.

Back-up had arrived moments later, though it hadn't been needed. Some hired security had been hurt behind the building. Some had fled the scene, according to their co-workers. There was also talk about an individual called "Jean" who apparently wasn't a guard, but no one knew much about him. He couldn't be found, either.

On one hand, Lily knew she ought to be happy. She'd found the man who'd ordered Benson's death and he'd confessed. She'd avenged his death in that way. But she hated having been played by Kennedy. There was something more to all of this, something that included the man who was supposedly dead but who'd looked very much alive when he'd been driving a car past Lily.

Then there was the other fire. Not only had Kennedy's headquarters exploded, Lily had later found out that there'd been a house in a calm, suburban neighborhood that had suddenly gone up in flames, seemingly out of nowhere. Surprise, surprise—a quick check into Lily's notes had confirmed to her, that, once again, one of Vulpes Ltd's buildings had mysteriously caught fire. She couldn't even follow up by accusing them of insurance fraud, because they never collected the insurance.

After only two days, things at the precinct had almost gone back to normal. Lily was still given the cases no one else wanted, but she didn't mind. They were cases that mattered to people. And, more importantly, she was allowed to keep the Saoirse Kennedy trail.

And really, more than ever before, catching Kennedy and making her spill everything and just *tell the damned full truth* was all she wanted to do.

She could have tracked the number of Kennedy's phone. She could have gone through what she'd learned of Vulpes Ltd. But Kennedy had helped her, as Lily had to begrudgingly admit. So she was going to play fair and stick to the deal they'd made, keeping everything she'd learned of Kennedy in relation to Benson's murder to herself and out of the files. But next time, she'd catch her for sure.

"Detective Rose!" Clifford stopped beside her desk.

"Lily," Lily growled and glared at him.

Immediately he looked taken aback and a little scared, and Lily felt sorry for having acted so brash.

She sighed. "Call me Lily. What's up?"

"Um. It's Jonah, then. I wanted to ask if you would join me on this case I have." He set down a number of files on the desk, but Bailee jumped from her chair and placed her hands across it, covering most of the information.

"Yes, she will," she said to Jonah Clifford. Then, she turned to Lily, grinning. "But as of thirty seconds ago, your shift is over, and you owe me a drink. And a round of darts."

Grimacing apologetically at Jonah, Lily asked, "What sort of case is it?"

"It's a B&E, but it's not urgent. All the immediate stuff has been done. It's just that it looks like it might be connected to a string of other B&Es, and I know you're good at seeing patterns, so…" He shrugged.

"Are you off now as well?" Lily asked, tilting her head to one side.

"Yeah, why?"

"You're joining us. Let's go pay Mindy a visit."

"Who's Mindy?" Jonah asked, though he showed no disinclination to the forced invitation.

Bailee jumped from her seat, laughing. "Let's go already! I'm thirsty."

Bemused, Lily watched how Bailee dragged Jonah with her to the exit, despite his protests about having to turn his computer off, and she wondered how she'd gotten to this point in a little over a week. She had Benson to thank for that. And, in a way, Saoirse Kennedy.

**12 April
03:18 a.m.
Saoirse**

Saoirse waited motionlessly in her corner, engulfed and embraced by shadows. She was watching a figure in the large, white bed with tenderness, observing the steady rise and fall of her chest.

A strand of stray hair had fallen across Natalia's face, but Saoirse restrained herself from moving it.

This was goodbye for her.

She had missed Natalia's offer at *Gonzalo's Place*, and she had messed up their relationship. She could have blamed the craziness with O'Shea for that, but she knew too well that it wouldn't have been true. No, Saoirse alone was to blame for this. She hadn't made time when she should have, and she hadn't considered Natalia's feelings enough when it came to all the worry and concern she must have been suppressing every day.

Saoirse couldn't blame her for leaving, and she didn't want to. This had been the natural ending point. There was no good in dragging things out.

But despite knowing all of this, she'd had to see her again, if only to reassure herself that Natalia was well.

The police, or rather a young, eager detective, had helped her find a nice, small house in the suburbs. Natalia even had a garden, something she had told Saoirse many times she wished were possible. A few plants in their shared flat had been all Saoirse had really been able to provide. Now Natalia could have whatever she wanted.

Giving a silent sigh, Saoirse peeled herself from the wall and left, leaving Natalia to her new, peaceful life.

Mike was waiting for her out front, handing her back her motorbike helmet. "Well?" he asked.

Saoirse put it on and swung her leg across her bike. "We've got a meeting with Yamaguchi," she told him, ignoring the implication in his question.

He sighed.

"Are you sure you don't want to—"

"No. But this is how it is."

Saoirse glanced up to the upstairs window, her eyes meeting Natalia's. Her past love was looking down at her, gaze filled with sadness, and she gave a little wave, mouthing *goodbye*. Perhaps it was *good luck*, but Saoirse preferred to believe the former. She nodded, to acknowledge having seen the gesture, and then kicked her bike into gear, traveling forward, leaving behind old homes, old loves, and old ghosts.

THE END

Author's Note

You may have noticed that the city is never named. This is not a mistake, and you won't find it on a map, either. If you must give it a name, you can always call it *Saoirse's city*.

(For those of you who may not be familiar with Irish names, Saoirse is pronounced *Sear-shah* and O'Shea should be *Oh Shay*)

Saoirse was born of a series of short stories that I wrote during a writing challenge I did with a friend. For some reason, I kept writing about her over and over, until my friend informed me that Saoirse not only deserved but *needed* to get her own book.

Ta-dah! Here we are.

Considering this, I believe thanks are first and foremost due to the friend who made this happen— Trina. Secondly to my wonderfully supportive partner who had me read the story aloud for my final run-through.

If you're curious about the short stories that created Saoirse, you can get a free copy of a compiled short story predating this novel by signing up to my newsletter: dl.bookfunnel.com/xatb2s5bsd

Crimson Fox Publishing

Crimson Fox Publishing is an independent, author-driven publisher of New Adult and Adult fiction of all genres. We were founded in 2020 by authors from Snowy Wings Publishing and its former sister imprints, Animus Ferrum Publishing and Caleo Press, using the unique co-op model developed by SWP.

Our Mission

We are an UN-traditional publisher focused on providing authors with a team that supports and boosts each other, while also enabling each author flexibility and independence. In a time when the publishing industry is in a constant state of flux, we strive to chart our own course and find a new way that unites traditional and independent publishing to bring our works to all readers, whether they be committed Kindle owners, print book hoarders, or library lovers.

More By Janina Franck

Short Stories

The Weight of Time (*A Touch of Magic, 2019*)
A Spark in Space (*A Touch of Magic, 2019*)
Override (*Brave New Girls: Girls who Tech and Tinker, 2020*)
Káto Kósmos (*Sing, Goddess!, 2021*)
The Wizard's Bride (*Space Bound, 2021*)
Midnight Train (*Beyond, 2022*)
Tribute (*Hope Riot, 2022*)
Scrapyard Witch (*Brave New Girls: Girls who Engineer and Explore, 2023*)
The Night I Died (*Into the Dark Wood, 2023*)
Runaway Renegade (*Magic Under The Big Top, 2024*)

Novels

The Chronicles of the Bat
Captain Black Shadow (*2016*)
White Devil (*2019*)
Sand and Snow (*2020*)

A Spark in Space: A Space Witch Novel (*2021*)

Devil Deal (*2022*)

After Halastaesia (*2024*)

9 781963 870251